Vivid

Lois Vincent

Contents

Chapter One: Karma's a Bitch

Chapter One: Karma's a Bitch

My name is Kagen. People call me Kae. And at the moment I'm freezing my ass off in these woods. I don't know what my brother hopes to find out here in the bang smack middle of winter but here I am in a forest wading ankle deep in sludge of dirt and sleet. The clouds overhead threatened to pour more of the damned snow any minute now in an attempt to drown us.

Shivering, I had my arms crossed and my hands deep in my armpits as I trudged deeper into the forest, looking for my older brother. It was that cold that I was puffing clouds. Urgh, I wanna go home.

"Cody," I call and only met with silence. Cupping one of my gloved hands to my mouth, I try again. This time louder, "Cody!"

As I came up a slight hill I saw some partially crumbled ruins of a small weird looking grey brick building. As I came closer, I noticed a faded blue sign of a white stick person and realised it was one of those old 'public toilets' obviously no longer operational. Who would willingly use one of these places anyway? My brother told me stories that long ago back before the Disaster, people would willingly go and use these as sex stops and stuff and were rarely cleaned or working. Rounding the side of it, I began to call again, "Co-" only to be cut off by something pulled me harshly from the side, jolting me into the wall and ending in a strangled squeak, "-dy."

Looking around I saw my brother at the end of the tight grip on my coat.

"Would you shut up!?" a hiss escaped his lips, his eyes focusing on the trees.

"Sorry," muttering I looked out to the forest. "What's going on?"

"It's them."

Frowning, I forgot he automatically assumes I know what's going on. "What?"

"Ssssh!"

"Don't shush me-"

His hand came slamming against my mouth, pausing me in my attempt to complain. Holding onto me tighter, He pressed himself over me, pushing my back further into the wall as if hoping we would merge with the flaking paint and brick rubble.

That was when I heard the shuffle of cloth and the deep tap-tap of boots marching on the road and a distinct ring from some sort of metal chain. From what I could tell, you know being fully incapacitated by this hulk pressing down on me, there is at least two people.

"You said that it was last sighted here, correct?" A male voice sounded out in the cold still air, which made me freeze.

"Yessir. The last pulse was felt thirty metres that way two minutes ago." Another male, if not a little younger, voice answered back. It felt like they were shouting even though they are speaking in no more than above a whisper.

Oh fuck. I look up at my brother who was out looking towards them, completely forgetting that I was here and his hand was making it hard to breathe. I lick it to get his attention, succeeding as his face screws up in disgust while removing his hand as if I had shocked him with electricity and wiped it on my coat with a half-hearted smack to go with it.

I pull a face back at him, wondering what was going on. Pressing a finger to his lips, he again asked me to be quiet before turning back out to look at what these intruders were up to. Seeing that he was going let me go, my headed rounded the corner to get a better look. My eyes widened in shock and probably what clutched at my heart the most, raw fear.

There were three men standing in the middle of a well-worn road that were once used by vehicles a long time ago. The black leather coats and high-quality garments underneath with the blue serpent insignia across their back, there was no mistaking them. Suppressors. What were they doing this far south of the Fence!?

My head snaps back at my brother who had gone back to ignoring my presence again. He was completely enraptured by them.

"Very well. X." a tall man who was the first voice that I had heard, called attention of a blonde haired boy who couldn't have been much older than my brother.

The blonde boy, X, stood straight like a pole, "Yessir?"

"Start scouting the northern side for about a fifteen kilometre radius. The target will not be going anywhere too far."

"Right away," X disappears into the trees like a flash of light.

"What do you require of me?" I realised that the third person is a girl with short black hair, her voice somewhat unsure about herself.

"You are to remain in my sight for the time being. Come, we will do the south perimeter."

A little deflated, she nodded, "Yessir."

The pair of them walked right passed us and our little hideout, going off into the tree skeletons.

Oh that's just perfect. We are surrounded by these people who have been known to shoot on sight, especially of our type. I shot a glare at Cody, what the hell was he wanting out here in the first place? Markus and Anne were waiting at home and if we don't show up before sundown they'll start balling their eyes out. Not to mention that there was a Miasmic Beast lurking about.

"What are we gonna do?" deciding to voice my mental frustrations out in a small whisper instead of the scream that I wanted was probably the safer option for now.

Looking down at me finally, Cody only blinks before stepping out of our hidey-hole, "Ideally, we should kill them."

"What!?" it was my turn to hiss. Was he insane? Did he finally snap? Did a screw fall lose and his brain fell out somewhere out in the woods on the way out here? "Are you nuts? There are three highly trained monster killers versus us two. I don't like our odds. And I'm not feeling particularly suicidal at the moment."

"They aren't exactly going to freely give us their weapons if we ask now are they?"

I think my brain just farted. "...What?"

"You saw them right? Those black swords? They're made out of black crystal and we need all the protection we can get."

"And you're suggesting we go against the people who are wielding them? They probably also have guns, filled with black bullets."

"Those would be helpful too, yes."

"I'm not making a grocery list!"

"And we cannot go on living out here without some sort of protect other than this flimsy knife!" yanking out said flimsy knife, he flashed it in my face.

I sigh, looking away.

"Also getting rid of them now before they discover Markus or Anne would also be in our favour. They would either kill them or take them away for their sick experiments."

"And what about you?" I snap. "You're also Cursed or maybe you forgot."

"I'll die before they take me away and drag as many of them down to hell along the way."

Giving him a deadpan look, I had no reply ready. Typical old Cody. Go down dying while taking everyone else with him. I loved and hated him for it.

"Good. Now that we're on the same page, I think we should-"

"Oh no. We are definitely not on the same page. I just wanna go back to the place Anne found for tonight. I'm cold and I think my socks are wet cos I can't feel my feet anymore."

"Then what do you suggest, Kae?"

"How about we sneak out really quietly?"

"You know that's not gonna be possible. The moment they spot us, we're dead."

"I think they be more preoccupied by the-"

A loud lung piercing animalistic screech choose to sound off from the trees not too far from us, shaking the top branches and small black birds from their branches.

"...Miasmic...beast..." I finish softly. Typical.

A large creature made a dash from the woods, too fast for me to catch more than a glimpse at before it landed on top of the public toilet building and my eyes widened as it too that moment to open its maw to let out another loud scream that hurt my ears. A demon monkey. Oh you've got to be kidding me. The large monkey was the size of a cow, its long tail twisting around in the air. Large protruding fangs which were too large for its mouth were dripping with saliva and what appeared to be black goo from its last meal. Covered in tanned yellow fur with a large black face, hands and feet with six green beady eyes on top of its head.

"Oh fuck," my brother voiced my sentiments exactly.

We both backed up just a step before those spider-like eyes made a turn to us and my brother shoved a protective hand out in front of me.

"Any bright ideas?" I mutter as we step back again. And again. Jumping off the half gone roof, the monkey began to follow us. Taking a step closer as we took a step back.

"I'm thinking..."

"Well, we're running out of room." I look back, seeing that we were heading for the trees and that was not a safe place to be with a giant jumping spider monkey.

A/N: Vote and comment if you like :3

Sorry about lateness and stuff...and no i haven't necessarily abandoned my other works...its just that I have/will be distracted for a while.

Chapter Two: Monkey's Paw

A /N: Dun dun-dun dun dun ha! I have an update!

This is for Dark_Safrina

I genuinely thank you for being a fan :3

Chapter Two: Monkey's Paw

"Cody," his name escapes as a hiss between my teeth as I took my first step into the woods, my grip on his arm tightened but he didn't seem to notice. I did not want to end up as monkey crap.

Cody then decides to stop, digging his feet into the squelching mud in order to secure himself into a grounded stance. The monkey stalks to the side, trying to get us into the woods but my brother wasn't budging. It hisses sounding more like a snake, baring its teeth as it puffs up its chest and shoulders in order to enlarge itself to frighten its newly found human-chow. I for one didn't need the extra incentive but Cody didn't show any outward fear. In fact, from the way his shoulders were squaring, he was calm. Calm and ready to fight.

Did I forget to mention that my brother is a tad suicidal?

"Get ready to move."

Sure. I'll just do an Irish jig, shall I? It'll confuse the hell outta everyone including the monkey. Come on Kae, no time for sarcasm…

There's always time for sarcasm.

"Ready?"

Nice to know he's asking for once.

"Run, Kae!" He pushes me to the side, earning two things; me, tumbling rather clumsily into a nearby shrub and the monkey, now fully enticed to rush forward at the sudden movement. Crawling my way out of there, I realised I made it just in time as the monkey seems to have made me the target as it had completely ignored my brother and landed in the bush that I had just gracefully rolled out of. Quickly turning itself around to lunge at me again, I scramble to find my feet as the mud and snow was slick and trying to pull me under. Half crawling, half falling over myself I make my way in a panic haze back towards the public toilets.

While I was making my half-assed attempt at escaping, Cody charges forward to stop the monkey. As they struggle with each other, the monkey lands a solid kick into my brother's gut, winding him as he curls up, almost collapsing. Biting my lip, I hesitated to go back in case the spider-thing decided to take my brother now that he was weakened. Before realising what my body was doing, I scamper for the nearest thing to throw and threw something like a rock at the monkey, landing squarely on its head. It shoves my brother to the ground and turns its attention back on me.

Oh.

Right.

Shit.

I scurry away, trying to get as far from Cody as possible just in case it changes its mind. Just as I was about to get my fingers to touch the slab of concrete I felt a grip around my ankles -when did I lose my shoes? Not the point.

Suddenly pulled back down, I awkwardly turn over onto my back with the monkey looming over me. Struggling to get its ugly head and creepy multiple eyes and rather big teeth out of my face, I try to kick and wriggle my way out but with it have hands for feet, it grips my arms and legs, spreading me out, exposing me completely. Leering down into my face, I turn a little to get as far from it as possible while being pinned down. My eyes shut tight, ready to be ripped apart.

I could feel it sniffing me. Oh god it's smelling me like some cheap date. I wanted to scream for help but fear had closed down on my throat. My heart was ramming against my rib cage and I was too afraid to open my eyes as its nose was almost nuzzling against the soft skin of my neck.

Letting out a loud screech, my ears are left ringing as I scrunch up my eyes.

I'm gonna die I'm gonna die I'm gonna die I'm gonna die I'm gonna die I'm gonna die I'm gonna die! Fuck it! Cody! The flight or fight response kicks into gear as my eyes flung open and I struggle against it again. My arm somehow came free. I manage to make a swipe at its face, knocking it in the eyes with my elbow and taking it completely by surprise. Taking my chance, I twist myself so that my legs got free from its grip and wrestled with the mud to escape.

Enraged, the monkey let loose a low bestial growl behind me. I felt it on me again, turning me over so that it could scream into my face as both its hands clasp around my neck and squeeze. I gasp with no air reaching my lungs, drowning in the panic that was now overtaking any rational part of my brain. Clawing at its arms, my struggles were feeble as it was using enough force to almost break my neck. Choking the last of the breath out of me, I felt the world was going black with a painful haze.

With the last of my breath I choke, "Co-..dy..." My arms failing against my sides as the last of my strength leave me...

Air snaps into my lungs as my now raw throat is exposed to the cruel icy air and I am savouring every stinging gasp I'm taking. Coughing, I realise that the monkey had somehow let go. Turning to my side, I was confused, looking for the monkey. Instead another dark figure towers over me, breathing heavily. Realising its Cody, I snap out of my daze and scramble to sit up. Battered and bleeding, my brother's focus was completely on the thing. His fists curling tightly, ready for another attack.

My eyes widen, realising what he was going to do. He can't. I reach for him, my hand shaking as I try to stop him from exposing himself. If the Suppressors saw, it'll be over. But I can't seem to be able to reach far enough, my arms have no strength left. "Co...Cody...no..."

"Sssh," his eyes never left the beast.

Again with the shushing!

Cody takes a defensive step forward waiting for the next move. As he does, the monkey shakes it's head to clear it, hissing at him as he had disturbed it. It makes its way round us, circling so that it was almost at my back before charging ahead. This time it had successfully got in behind my brother's defence as both go down, its jaws tightly over my brother's shoulder. I try to stand to go to him but someone rushes up behind me and saw that it was the boy X, aiming for both the monkey and Cody.

Paralysed by shock I watch as he swings the blade in a disgruntled screech left the monkey's throat as something thick and wet lands in the mud not too far from me. It was an arm that was sliced clean from a body. For a moment I thought it was Cody's, panic rising in my throat before I realised it was black and covered in fur underneath all the mud and black blood.

My brother watches from the side, weary about joining in but as the Monkey lashes out at X my brother quickly intervenes. As he did the monkey lands a hit to his gut, sending him skidding across the ground away from all of us. Blood was freely gushing from a new gash across his stomach. The sound of metal on metal brings my attention back to X and the monkey for a moment as I try to get up. I need to get to Cody. Looking over I saw that the boy called X was poised with his black sword, looking rather cool and collected while the monkey was wearily sizing him up, clutching at the now bloody stump gushing with blood that was its arm. The blood flow slows almost immediately, leaving only a trickle then a drop of black blood. The monkey changes posture, attacking head on, this time fury was completely overtaking it. It was far faster, far crueller and far stronger than when it was dealing with me. I realise with horror that it was playing with me.

Using his sword as a shield, X was stuck in the middle of whirlwind of a yellow blur. It was too fast for my eyes but every now and then the sound of metal against an attack of something just as strong sounded. X was fast enough to defend himself against the onslaught but not enough to turn around and attack.

Just as I thought that they were in a stalemate, X's comrades race in to help. The older man, probably their captain, raises a gun to shoot. A bullet flies passed X only to land in a tree as the monkey successfully dodges. With irritation, the monkey flips over towards the captain, faster than before.

Just as it was on him, the girl manages to flick up her blade just in time, acting as a shield as the monkey presses its weight, bearing down on her. As she was losing the strength to hold it off, the captain fires the gun again, shooting the air where the monkey was. It had disappeared from the clearing completely.

My eyes widen at the sudden silence. It's jumped back into the woods. Getting to my feet, I frantically search the clearing for it. But as I move, I hear the click of a gun and freeze. I see the same gun that this man was using on the creature was pointed directly at me. As X was about to raise the blade joining his superior in their new target (i.e. me), the monkey comes down again, taking all of us by surprise as it lands behind the captain, taking him by the neck and he literally squeaks before it jumps away again, his gun dropping into the mud only a moment later. Just as the silence was about to fall again, a blood curdling scream of pain reverberated out around us. Whatever the monkey was doing, it was making sure it was dragging out the man's agony as long as possible before the ear-ringing silence returns.

Panting, I was about to go look for my brother only for the monkey to return. Before anyone could make a move, it was a blur of yellow aiming at the girl, stopping just a hairs breath in front of her as she froze, resulting in her being flung and landing with a thud against the toilet block. It comes towards X with the same move it used on my brother not a minute ago, sending him sprawling on the ground. X feebly moves to get back on his feet to attack but the monkey was now focusing on me again. It stalks up a bit before running full throttle at me.

I couldn't run. I have no energy left. It took all my strength just to stand here like a moron.

Just as it was about to get me, my brother suddenly comes in from behind, rushing forward with his arm pulling back slightly to punch the monkey.

His fist lands right between the eyes, blood and bone crunching as it breaks under the force. Cody then pulls his other fist, slamming it into the front of its skull. He then pulls into a rounding hook, ramming into the side of its jaw, breaking it apart completely. The monkey staggers back as blood bubbles from what is left of its face but Cody didn't give it enough time to react as he went for the finishing jab in between the eyes again but ending with the skull breaking completely and the monkey drops dead. The dead silence all but returns, save for all of us gasping for the cold air like we couldn't get enough of it.

As X manages to get to his feet, my brother backs up towards me, becoming a shield from the two Suppressors left. He notices something in the mud near us and quickly bends down to grab the blade that the girl had dropped. As he pulls himself up, he grabs onto me to take some of my shaky weight and begins to leave. X makes no move towards us, watching us with tired eyes. For the first time I saw that his eyes were two different colours. One moonlit silver and the other molten amber. He gives a single nod, earning one from my brother before we both made for the forest.

Chapter Three: Sweet Dreams

- -

A/N: I took a break from exams for a bit (before I go nuts) and was able to bring out an update...not much of one but still...

- -

Chapter Three: Sweet Dreams

I'm finding it harder to walk as I lean more and more of my weight on Cody who was dealing with his own wounds as well but he ignores it, awkwardly holding onto my arm that was draped over his shoulder and the other at my waist that was gripping that blasted sword he just had to pick up.

I must have made a noise of pain as the next thing I notice, Cody goes to a nearby tree and pulls me round so that I was sitting with my back against the trunk.

Swallowing hard, I look up at him and find him sliding to a crouch in front of me, his fingers tilting my chin from side to side to get a look at my neck, "It really did a number on you."

"Look who's talking," I mutter back, pushing his fingers away while moving my head from his reach. It wasn't my stomach that it almost ripped open.

There was a silence as he reaches for my head again, forcing me to look him in the eye. "At least you don't have a concussion," he finally says after his eyes were searching mine. "But seriously...what was going through your head when you threw your shoe at it?"

...Was that what I threw at the blasted monkey? "I wasn't."

He sighs while pushing my mud and blood encrusted hair from my face, "Clearly. God there's a gash in your head as well."

"Well you're not exactly unscathed either. It was about to play skip-rope with your intestines."

"I'll live."

An exhausted breath leaves my lungs as I lean back, my energy almost completely drained. I'm so tired.

"We need to keep moving." He moves to pull me up. Almost all my weight went onto him this time as I found that as we begin walking again that my ankle was now hurting. Probably sprained it. Wonderful.

"They know you exist now," I said after a while as we trudge through the forest.

"Does it look like I care?"

I met him with silence. How am I supposed to argue with a pig-headed moron with mental movability of a brick-wall?

As we make our way through the woods in silence, we came onto a highway before finding an old beaten track that lead to a farm house that Anne had spotted this morning. It took a good hour for us to make our way towards it resting on a hill overlooking what was once a cattle farm but now overgrown and the forest was slowly taking it back. But the house seemed to be from the era that eve a tornado couldn't pull it down. It looked sad and lonely with faded chipped paint but it was away from everything and so far no one has even found it until now.

Making our way up the dirt driveway that was full of pot holes, Cody finally opens his mouth after almost two hours of silence, "Don't tell Anne about this."

I shoot him a look, "Have you met her?" One look at us and she'll know. She always knows. It was Markus I was more concerned with to be honest. As if reading my thoughts the front door slams open on its hinges and a ten year old whirlwind comes running down the stone stairs towards us. Markus crashes into my gut, making me gasp and cringe as he tries to wrap his arms around my back, knocking the air out of my lungs and squeezing my sore and battered body. I hold onto him as he sobs into my shirt.

"You're both idiots," Anne's voice came from the doorway as she looks out at us. Her sharp blue eyes took in both of us calmly.

"Why thank you ma'am," Cody half bows to our twelve year old sister.

Stroking Markus's back, I try to coax him from his death grip on me, "Come on, I need to clean up." Shaking his head, his grip tightens as he buries himself further into my gut. Seriously... "Come on, Makky...I'm here. I'll always come back."

He looks up at me to make sure I wasn't lying before letting me go and I could feel my legs turning to jelly but I had to ignore it. I had to make sure I look like I'm fine.

Anne must have caught my intentions and calls for him, "Markus, Kae's gonna need a bath. Can you go look from some clothes for me?"

Markus nods again and runs into the house.

I can feel Cody's eyes on me as I limp my way towards the house. "Are you alright?"

"Speak for yourself," I mutter back. "You're the one in a fist fight with it."

He scoffs behind me as I make my way towards the house.

Once in front of Anne, she looks up at me carefully, "The bath is upstairs."

I pat her head as I go passed, "Thanks, missy."

"What about me?" Cody pouts.

"You can jump in a lake," I retort while making my way through the house. Inside is quaint with wooden furnishings and a staircase covered in worn carpet. At the top, I found the bathroom easily enough and the white tub already filled with hot water. How you may ask? Anne's a psychic, psychokinetic bundle in a dress. I'm not joking. Her abilities are unstable and flux but she's been learning to control them and developing more and more abilities. It's almost scary what she can do and I'm terrified if the Suppressors ever got hold of her.

I strip off my clothes that peel off like a second skin and gingerly hop into the tub. My feet tingling as the numbing cold is suddenly attacked by heat. All the mud and blood colour the water immediately as I try to clean myself off. I notice bruises and cuts all over my body and wonder at the ones around my neck. My fingers trace my neck that's still raw, the memory flashes through my mind in an instant. Mentally shaking myself, I couldn't linger on the pain or the fear. Anne will see...she has already seen way too much and it has caused her to age far more than she should ever have. And that is not fair on such a little girl. This world is not fair on Markus or Anne. And I will not impose any of this on them. And that is exactly the reason why I run after Cody, to bring him back.

Finishing in the bath, I find a towel and some clothes left beside the door. A black hoodie that was big and thin, a pair of worn ripped jeans and a white shirt that was far too big for me. This was an interesting house to say the least. The Disaster happen nine years ago and yet the house and its contents all seem to be in relatively good condition. I make my way slowly down the musty hallway and found something that was too good to be true in one of the rooms. A bed. I collapse on the dusty creaking heap without hesitation. It felt like a cloud. A creaky musty cloud. But I don't care. I haven't felt comfort like this in a while.

"Thought you'd be here," Anne smiles in the doorway watching me. I notice that in her hands was a first aid kit. Our only one.

I frown, "Don't waste that on me. You should check Cody."

"He said the exact same thing." As she sets the box down at the foot of the bed, I grab her, pulling her down onto the bed with me, wrapping my arms tightly around her small body.

"Kae!" She whines but doesn't struggle.

"This is better," I say while closing my eyes, I want more than anything to sleep. Looking over at the doorway, I saw Markus standing there and I roll onto my back, freeing up an arm and a side. He doesn't hesitate to jump into my side, snuggling into me as my arm curls around him.

"Kae," Anne repeats.

"It's fine. Just let me sleep," I go back to closing my eyes. "You should sleep too. I know you haven't been."

"...Because you're not here," Markus voice was soft and almost strains with emotion.

I chuckle, "That's right. I chase the nightmares away."

"A lot more than you know," Anne whispers, burying her head into my neck. I almost wince in pain. Almost. I try to exhale as smoothly as possible to mask the cry of pain that was rising in my throat.

Since these two were small, they never seem to want to go to sleep as the nightmares constantly hounded them. That was when I said that if they stayed by my side I would protect them from the nightmares. If Cody protected us from the physical danger, then I would protect their dreams. Since then they always sleep peacefully if they wrap themselves around me.

As I drift off, I could feel Anne moving from me, probably to see to Cody. Later I feel the springs in the mattress creak with additional weight but it did not disturb me in the least. The four of us were squeezed onto this old double bed and I felt a moment of bliss even through the haze of pain. This was my family and I would do anything to protect them and make them happy.

My eyes snap open as ragged gasps leaves my sore throat. Swallowing down the blades I look around the empty dark room. Feeling that there wasn't any threat I relax a little. I had a nightmare again. Though I never seem to remember much of them. Cody began rubbing my shoulder from in front of me, meaning I had turned to my side in my sleep and Markus was between me and Cody. Anne had wrapped herself around me from the back, practically strangling me but I knew that they were peacefully sleeping so I put up with it.

"You're sweating, Kae. Do you remember anything?" Cody's voice was hushed but at least it didn't have that irritating arrogant tone to it.

"No," I answer back simply, my voice croak and sore. "Go back to sleep."

"It seems like you pay the price," he says after a time.

"What?"

"That all of us sleep peacefully but you wake up in fits every night."

"…It's a small price to pay if it means everyone else gets a goodnight's rest."

"But you don't."

"I don't remember anything."

"That doesn't mean anything."

I grin. A breathy chuckle rocks my body, a joke rising from my tongue, "Maybe that's my Cursed power."

"Huh?"

"I let people sleep." Fear me! I can give you decent night's rest. Lame.

"…I highly doubt it. You're the closest thing to a parent that they have…" he then adds softly, "…and that's what comforts them."

He must be half asleep to be so chatty.

I then felt him somehow manage to wrap his arms around my head, pulling me in close but without sqeezing Markus between us, his fingers moving some of my bangs from my face "Go back to sleep. Maybe I can protect your dreams for a bit."

I didn't say anything and let myself sink back into sleep. When this idiot makes up his mind, it's impossible to change it. Maybe it's alright to impose on him…just of a little while…

Chapter Four: Hexed

A/N: Hi, yeah sorry I had to pull it down. I had to fix something up on it that may have been minor-ish but I still needed to fix it anyway...

Chapter Four: Hexed

I awake alone the next morning and feel rather sluggish as I pull myself from the bed. My body is heavy but I also feel wrapped up in something. Putting a hand to my neck, I feel a bandage woven around it. Then to my chest, head and arms and my ankle. All had plasters and bandages. I frown while making my way downstairs and spot Anne sitting in a chair downstairs. I make out that it is a living room with a fireplace and an old TV.

I open my mouth but Anne interrupts me without looking up from her book.

"Cody did it."

But-

"Yes I told him you'll be angry and he said 'does it look like I care?'"

Then where-

"He went out."

"Stop reading my mind."

"Don't need to do that. You're too predictable."

Grrr. I make my way to the door and see a pair of old sneakers about my size and shove them on. "I'll go get him."

"He should be near the edge of the farm by now," she calls as I shut the door.

As I half limp half walk out towards the overgrown paddocks I could make out a storm brewing in the distance. My stomach gurgling could be the thunder at the volume it was suddenly playing at. Urgh when did I eat last? Yesterday? Eh probably.

A sudden incline through the grass and snow snaps me out of my thoughts towards food as I almost lose my balance, reawakening the throbbing in my ankle.

"Ow..."

Steadying myself, I make my way up to find another rise but this time more balanced and in the distance I see a familiar breed of idiot.

I found him, standing at the top of a cliff. Coming up to him, I saw that he was looking out over at the landscape far below of a ruined city that was once a major metropolis some ten years ago. Now it was just an empty shell of once was. In the very centre is a large white wall circling around the very remnant of the city still alive. A remnant of humanity still alive, sheltered. Still safe. Still deluded into thinking that it was safe for the rest of eternity. The fence supported a huge globe like structure made entirely from this strange blue energy force field which keep everything out, out and everything in, in.

Stopping beside him, I couldn't help but say, "It's like they're living in a bubble."

"It's only a matter of time. All it will take is one mistake," I hear my brother voice absentmindedly as if talking to no one in particular. "One wrong move and their deluded sanctuary will come crashing down around them and then they'll have to crawl around in the mud and corpses to survive like the rest of us that they've so conveniently forgotten."

I held in the usual sigh, instead look up at the storm coming closer.

"That isn't going to turn into a Miasma storm is it?" I ask. Better not be. I'm not in the mood for the whole 'screaming and running for our lives' at the moment. Normally Miasma takes on the look of blood red and purple clouds but you can never be sure.

"Anne said that there won't be any for a few weeks at least. We should be alright for a while."

"Well that's comforting..." I mutter. Just need to focus on the beasts, Fencers, Suppressors and anything else that wants to kill us. Oh and the lack of food and water, shelter, clothing, winter...yeah the list goes on.

Speaking of which, I'm starving enough that I could eat a hippo. Cody sorta like a hippo. Big mouth, short temper...

"Here."

I look over to him and see him holding out that goddamn black sword from yesterday at me. I look between him and the blade not exactly sure what's going on. He pushes it into me until I had no choice but to take it.

"What's this for?"

"You need it more than I do. Or even Anne or Markus for that matter."

I'm not sure how I'm supposed to react here. Dumbfounded, irritated and insulted I think is the appropriate mix. "Gee thanks…"

I can see him smirking at my irritation as I put it one hand and take a swing. This black crystal stuff shot up with the Miasma and the Disaster along with everything else that happened nine years ago. It's strong, light and durable. But it also has a spooky feeling about it and touching it feels like you're brushing up against electricity. Even the hairs on my arm are standing on end and it's got nothing to do with the cold.

"Hah it makes you look cool," I can hear the snickering.

"Feels more like I'm cosplaying," I mutter back. I glare at him as his amusement continues.

But then just as suddenly the bastard's tone turns into something completely serious, "There is a group down by the Deadside that I'll be seeing by the new moon."

I can feel my brow furrow, "This better not be that rebellion group." Met them once. Didn't like em neither.

He meets me with silence.

"Cody!" I exasperate.

"What?"

"What moronic grandeur dreams did they sink into that thick head of yours now? And when did this all happen?" This idiot…

He exhaled deeply, unable to meet my eyes, "Yesterday."

So that's why he went out ahead of us yesterday. I point the sword's tip at him, "You have any idea how much-"

~Cody!

Anne's voice shot through my head like an ice knife, splitting through my skull that I almost collapse in pain. The sheer magnitude of panic and fear almost bowls me over as Cody stands there frozen.

~Cody!

~Cody!

~Co-

Her telepathic voice cuts off violently, making me shake like someone went into my head and tried to rip my brain out. Cody's eyes switch over to me. I forget the lecture and the limp as we sprint back to the house.

We come up to the house and Cody barks at me, "Check inside! I'll go round the front."

I leap inside the house, frantically looking through the dated kitchen with vinyl floor, racing passed the small table that had breakfast already set up for us. My breath hitches when I see Anne crumbled on the floor. I dash before sliding on my knees towards her, abandoning the sword. Pulling her into my arms, I try to see if she's alright...still...alive...

Yes, she's breathing. I pull her in close, nursing her head, seeing a red mark surfacing on her cheek from where she was hit.

"Anne?" I try to rouse her and her eyes flutter open before she jumps from my grasp.

"Markus!" she screeches before running out the front door.

"Wait, Anne!" I stumble after her.

I look out from the doorway to see Markus clinging onto Cody's legs as Cody had an arm raised with his fingers tightly curled into a tight fist as

if he had just hit someone. His face was of pure rage as he was looking to something that wasn't too far from me. I look down to his line of sight and see someone who I have never seen before in my life.

The man is half crouching over as if catching his breath. He is heavy set and looks to be in his late thirties. His straggly black hair is balding in patches as it combines with a sparse beard and fro the smell and the state of his clothing, he hasn't seen a shower of a razor in months. His eyes are strange and predatory as they are fully set on Markus. I notice that his complexion is almost ash grey with feint black veins all over his exposed skin. ...Oh don't tell me...

A primal growl was spewing out along with drool that he couldn't contain, spilling out over lip and into his beard. His delirious eyes suddenly focus on me. Oh Great.

"You...smell so good!" He comes towards me, stumbling forward like a drunk. My eyes bulge as I move from the stairs and make my way over to Cody. His eyes trailing me with his neck bent out at an awkward angle.

A snarl rips through his throat and begins to run full throttle towards me. And I have absolutely no chance of out running him. Just as he is almost on me he begins choking and drops to his knees as grabs at his throat, his tongue lolling out as his mouth opens wide while he makes choking noises. I watch without feeling as branches shoot from his mouth, vines twist around under his skin, bursting through his veins and skin as flowers burst through, tainted with blood. The branches thicken from his mouth, blood spilling and skin tearing, until the trunk spews forward, splitting the meaty cage apart with his bones creaking and cracking with an audible snap until nothing but a tall crab apple tree in full bloom took his place completely. It continues to grow, the roots and branches begin attacking the front of the house, pulling apart the wall as branches flood the windows and the living room with brilliant pink plumage.

I turn and run to Markus, collapsing to my knees as I pull him into a tight hug as if to break his tiny body, "Stop Markus. It's enough. He's gone. He's gone."

"He hit Anne. He was going to-going to-"He gulps at the air as he begins sobbing, while clutching onto me tightly, the tree's growth slows down to a crawl, almost stopping completely.

"It's ok. You did the right thing. It's ok," I soothe, rubbing his back while rocking him slowly. I needed to calm him down quickly before he goes out of control.

Cody turns to Anne, who had also taken to hiding behind him. She sobs into him as he soothes her as gently as he can while trying to rein in his anger.

"What the fuck was that?" His voice is trembling as he turns to me, holding her head close to his chest.

"Hexer," I whisper.

I can feel the temperature drop around him as he frowns deeply. "...Since when can a Hexter talk?"

"I dont know."

"Why was it even here?"

Good question. I turn to the tree that has now taken out a good portion of the house. "They seem to be spreading out..."

"You would think by now they'd've all died," he hisses through grit teeth.

I share his irritation, "Not if there is a Keystone near..."

"Just how many are there?"

I shake my head, "How am I supposed to know? If anything I think they keep springing up." I then look down to see Markus has fallen into an exhausted sleep.

"Fuck!" Cody bites out as he pulls himself up with Anne still in his arms.

He makes his way towards the house, probably to put Anne to bed. I pull Markus up and follow him inside. Luckily the sofa is untouched as he puts Anne down carefully, who is still sobbing quietly. I place Markus beside her and grab a blanket to encircle them while I sit on the floor in front of them. Anne immediately clutches onto Markus and makes for my hand, squeezing it tightly and before long she calms down and exhaustion puts her to sleep.

As soon as he was sure that she was asleep, Cody makes his way for the door, "I'm going to search closely to see if there are any more around," his voice full of malice. Opening the door he ignores the gaping hole beside him and the flowers and branches filling it. "You." He points directly to me. "Stay put. I'll be back, so heel." Then he shuts the door and heads out to god knows where.

Am I dog now? Does it look like I can even move?

As his footsteps disappear I look up at the tree as petals begin to fall, mixing with the snow that is now coming inside. I'm beginning to worry. A Hexer has never tried to attack in broad daylight before. Something is different...

No.

Something is coming.

Chapter Five: Whine and Dine

Chapter Five: Whine and Dine

Cody came back a few hours later, finding nothing. Well, knowing his tactic of 'looking' would be barrelling through the forest like a crazed rhino completely tunnel-visioned in a rage. But all the same, I trust his judgement. Not like I have much of a choice here.

Anne believed that it was her fault that they were attacked because she didn't 'see' it. How can it be her fault? Normal people (like myself) don't even get an inkling as to what may happen in the future. It took a lot to convince her but really, I think she just gave up on me and continues to quietly blame herself.

Markus...went back into his shell. He wouldn't eat or talk for a few days. He completely refuses to sleep unless I was with him round the clock. Cody has also kept his wondering to around the house, completely on alert. Which is good in a way. I didn't have to go looking too far for him. But he also refused to breach the subject of him and the overly 'heroic' rebels and their stupid plans that they have in store that I just know will end badly. Not to mention that the new moon is fast approaching. There was only one day left.

I stare at him across the table that Anne has forced me to sit at while she's force feeding me whatever she finds. Which are practically wild vegetables and fruit that are strewn all over the farm. She knows I skip out on meals so that there is more on the table for them, so she gets on my case until I eat something. Though she does try to get 'creative'...and I'm staring down a plate of mashed potato mixed with carrot, cauliflower and...I think turnip and apple all lumped in together in a gooey mess. It doesn't exactly look appetizing but the way she's glaring a hole into my head... I picked up a spoon and take a bite...tastes like baby food but I am hungry and she's still glaring at me. So to be safe I take another bite and swallow.

Satisfied, my sister sits beside Cody with a cup of water. "When are you planning to go?" She doesn't look at him but the question is directed at Cody.

"...In the morning."

"Then we best get some sleep," she says into her cup.

"Uh-uh. You lot are staying here. That includes you, Kae."

I glare at him, "I am not going to let you go wondering off with those idiots. If I can't stop you, then I will come along and make sure you don't do something completely stupid."

"They're not idiots."

"Oh sorry. Idiots with guns and a pre-dated sense of justice."

"They're not idiots," he repeats.

"What proof do you need?" I mutter more to myself, "They invited you."

"I heard that!"

"Are you running away?" A small voice said from the doorway. It's been over two weeks since Markus had opened his mouth and his wide eyes were on Cody.

"No, not running away," Cody is absolutely taken aback with shock.

"Then why are you leaving us behind?"

"It's not safe."

"What? And leaving us here is?" I stare at Cody while motioning for Markus to sit next to me, pushing my plate in front of him and placing the spoon in his hand. He doesn't hesitate to eat, albeit slowly, but at least he's eating.

I didn't want to bring up what happened two weeks ago in front of Markus so I was hoping Mr Thick-Head with hooves across the table catches on. I suck as any kind of protector. Markus and Anne may be filled with mystical voodoo powers but they fluctuate and get unstable so bloody easily. The tree in the house is a good example. ...What happened to our original house and the surrounding suburb is another.

Cody bites his lip, gnawing on it as if it was going to bleed forth a comeback but he remains silent, mulling inside his head, at one point shooting a glare at Anne who in turns glares back. I look between them, completely unamused. I was about to order the conversation out but then Cody shoots up from his chair suddenly.

"Fine! Do what you want!" His voice fuming before storming out the kitchen door.

Leaving both Markus and I to stare at our now very smug sister, who simply says, "There we go."

"What did you say?" I blink as Markus shoves a spoon towards my mouth, another one who is going to force me to eat. But if he's sharing, that means he will have to eat. So I comply, opening my mouth the let him spoon feed me.

"I simply said that I will always be in his head. Every minute of every day. Every moment he thinks he's alone, I'll be there. Even when he's showering, even when he's sleeping I will see every thought so that if he even tries to sneak away, I'll know."

I think a chill just ran up my spine. This girl is turning into a monster.

"I learn from the best," she retorts back at me.

"Oi," I state. "Stay out."

She shrugs at me and finishes her water. "Markus, you should have a bath. I prepared it a while ago so it should be good now."

Markus finishes the last spoonful of the mush and hops up, "Ok. But Kae needs something else to eat."

"I could say the same about you, mister," I growl as he scuttles away from me, a grin on his face while I attempt to nab him but miss. Thank god I saw it again.

As I watch him make his way up the stairs, I make sure I heard the door shut to the bathroom before realising that Anne is staring at me.

"What?"

She shakes her head as she stands up and goes to the stove, as she touches it, the hotplate comes alive as she moves to take a pot and put it on top. "Cody found a cow. So we have milk." As she said this, she gets a bucket from beside the door and pours some of the milk in.

How did Cody find a cow? ...Birds of a feather...or cows of a paddock in this case...

"Something like that," she answers out loud.

I suddenly thought of something, "How come you can talk to Markus and Cody in your head but you can't with me?"

"You already know the answer to that," she says simply.

Yeah I do. Whenever she communicate and I happen to be in the loop ...well that pain I felt when she was screaming for Cody...

She nods as I remember, "I think your mind is really sensitive."

Gee thanks.

"I'm not trying to insult you, you know."

"Yeah but it points out that I'm the biggest burden though." Not like we need add any more to the list. Ah I shouldn't be complaining, she has enough on her mind as it is.

"Not really, it's just Cody repeating song lyrics in his head over and over to try and block me out."

"Which song?"

"...Something about some guy called Cotton Eye Joe?"

A smirk appears on my lips. "Oh well. I should check on Markus."

I managed to wake early enough to watch Anne staring at Cody who was look rather uncomfortable under her intense gaze.

"I said I won't already!" he cries out after a time after we all manage to get dressed.

"Good!" she states before marching out of the bedroom with Markus in tow, "We'll be downstairs."

Cody lets out a sigh, "Seriously."

"Why are you meeting up in Deadside?" I ask, folding my arms.

He looks up at me, "To check something."

"And that is?"

"Find out when we get there."

Cody is the master of pissing me off.

It took a good walk down the highway and onto a main drag before we reach a bridge that was the city's old limit. Deadside was in the middle of an old business district that was a mix of Chinatown thrown in. Those who were locked out manage to always find themselves in Deadside eventually. There is a small community but Cody and I thought it better to keep wondering. Of course that meant we barely made contact with others like us and when we did they were either crazy, scared, spiteful or just downright rude. Then there was Jack.

Eventually, while we walked, Markus tired of doing just that and proceeded to use me as his personal beast of burden. Coming into the street there is a large bonfire roaring smack bang in the middle with people strewn through it. Some together in whispers that pause conversation to stare at us, others inside abandoned shops and houses with fires of their own, minding their own business and those who by themselves warming up by the fire as the sun finally set. But they all lost interest just as quickly.

We move towards one man in particular with a rather overly serious look on his face while talking to some hooded person all hushed and shit. Probably ordering to do something insane. As always. Noticing us with a mere flick of the eyes, Jack grunts, "Cody."

Cody smiles as he walks up to the man in his mid-twenties. He wasn't a particularly tall and a little scruffy with scars accumulating over the years. But he was a man with character. And it seemed to lure Cody in like a fly to bullshit.

When Jack's eyes fell on me, his tone went to sarcasm, "My, my and you even brought Oddball."

"Jack the ass," I reply back. "Still as bent on your suicidal schemes and dragging everyone along with it since the last time I checked?"

"You still have that sharp tongue, I see." He then did a once over on my two younger siblings. "And these two..."

I frown at him but he didn't finish the sentence.

Cody knows that this guy winds me up quicker than he does and opens his mouth, "I have come here to exchange information."

"Of course you have. Why else would you have answered my call?" Folding his arms, Jack turns back to Cody, "There is something I want you to see. It's best if you leave your siblings behind."

"Like hell I'm leaving you with him without direct supervision."

"You really should buy the Mother Hen a leash. And muzzle." He then thought on it. "Whatever. It's your skin, Oddball."

I bite my lip, I can't drag Markus or Anne along.

"I can look after them if you want?" A small woman comes up to me, motioning to take Markus from my back. "My name is Yvette. I just made fresh bread and muffins if you don't mind?" She looks at Markus with kind eyes. Markus perks up at 'muffins'. Yep trust his cake and muffin tooth to spin him out of being shy.

Anne has been busy looking into the distance for a while before her gaze switches to me as if snapped from a dream, "It's ok if you stick to the eastern ridge. None of the military are there for the moment. We can stay behind. I trust that he isn't planning on taking you far."

"Interesting..." Jack mulls over at my sister. "You're very interesting, little girl."

Oh so help me-

"And you're dangerous," Anne retorts.

"I'll take that as a compliment."

It wasn't compliment. It was a warning. And I hope like fuck Cody heard it.

"Follow me." He simply state before walking off into an old, decaying and rather decrepit alleyway, Cody not far behind. I pull Markus from my back, "Uh thank you, Yvette. Markus, I'll be right back."

He nods, probably more interested in the muffins at the moment. I look at Anne before quickly going after them.

Chapter Six: Tyrannical Terrorism

C hapter Six: Tyrannical Terrorism

Wait. Did she say 'military'? What would the military be doing outside the Fence limits?

I quickly make my way through the alley, revealing the dead city on the other side. I have never really looked at or pondered on what has been left abandoned by those who made it into the defences of the Fence itself. It's all just rubble and dust. Echoes of a past that no one can relive. At least, not on this side of the Fence, anyway.

I almost lose my footing as some of the dust and rubble shifts under my feet. Just as I went down, a hand caught my arm.

"Should you be out here with that leg?" Jack's voice comes from behind me, making me jump.

"I'm fine."

"Of course you are."

I roll my eyes and pull from him as fast as I possibly could. Do not need him invading my personal space any more than necessary, thank you.

"We're not far. Should I carry you, princess?"

I grind my teeth and march away, not caring about the pain shooting through my ankle.

But all thoughts scattered to the breeze that suddenly picks up as we come closer to the towering monstrosity that is the Fence. It was big far away but up close it's something else. It towers above you, making you feel microscopic while having to crane you neck and squint, just to see the top in the far distance. That it was intimidating normally, began to make me wonder at the ring of military below. Like a black horde, a mass of soldiers, tanks, trucks and parked helicopters all faced out, standing as vigil sentries, with most heavily defending the tightly shut great white steel gates that were a third of the height of the wall.

Cody grabs my jacket, pulling me into a nearby collapsed building just in time as an armoured truck rolls passed. We watch as the soldiers all dressed in black gear and technological masks that probably gave them everything from night vision to filtrating toxic air. ...I wonder if they could even piss in them...

"What's going on?" Cody asks.

Jack puts a finger to his lips just in time for another patrol car to go passed. "We can't talk here."

I frown, watching the soldiers all on high alert. A sinking feeling pulls at my gut and I force myself from the wall. We shouldn't even be in a four hundred mile radius of this place in the first place. My gaze switches over to a group talking amongst themselves and pointing in our direction.

"Gotta move," I mutter, pulling on Cody and we all quickly get out and go back.

After some time, Jack opens his mouth, "Their movements have increased threefold in the last two days alone," he states. "We've tracked their patrols for days now, in the beginning they only went a few blocks around the wall but their reach is extending further with each day. It won't be long before their patrols include Deadside."

We all knew what that meant. That little community would be annihilated without thought or question.

"Can't you evacuate them?" I ask while Cody is helping me get up a sudden steep step.

"...It is their decision to stay or leave. But it does present an opportunity."

My glare fixes on Jack. Just what is he planning? This kind of preparation can only mean one thing and I do not want to get mixed up in all of this. We need to move and preferable by tonight. The farm house isn't secure enough for something of that magnitude. We need to move on.

"Opportunity?" Cody stares at Jack with intrigue.

Of course the bastard is hooked.

"Not here," Jack looks over his shoulder, probably to get another look at the wall.

The very last of the sunset left by the time we made it back to the bonfire and more of Jack's men had gathered. We shared a huge meal of soup with chunks of beef and vegetables that I slurped down like it was liquid chocolate.

Yvette had ensnared Markus's heart and he was eating like there was no tomorrow which was a good sign, considering. Anne ate little, just continually staring out into space as with more people it was getting harder to keep to herself. I sat next to her as close as I could to try and help her keep a sort of tether on her mental wonderings.

On my third bowl of soul and bread, I notice Cody's talking to Jack in some corner and get to my feet. Placing the bowl down on the bench, I tap Anne's shoulder, indicating her to eat it for me.

Coming in closer, I began hearing parts of their conversation.

"...not too far from here," Cody frowns as he talks.

"Their movements are at best sporadic. No one on the inside of the Fence here knows much about them." So Jack has insiders of the Fence of this particular city. Guess it made sense, how else did he have all this information on everything.

"I thought that the Suppressors had a foothold in all cities."

"...No. They don't have much to do with this place."

So they're talking about Suppressors.

"Ah Oddball, here I was thinking that you were completely distracted between your sister and the food."

"Shut it, terrorist," I pull myself up next to Cody.

"Oh, I'm wounded by your words."

"Play nice," Cody warns me.

"I will, when he does," I mutter back.

"So I saw your sister carrying a rather interesting object all wrapped up like a Christmas present," Jack switches topics. Cody had demanded that I take the damn blade with me, instead of leaving it a safe spot in the farmhouse like I had wanted. Anne agreed with him, to the extent that she even carried it and refused to give it to me. Probably because she knew I'd try and leave it behind. I'm always at a disadvantage with her and her Jedi mind tricks.

"I stole it from one of them. I thought you might need the proof."

"I wouldn't doubt your words, Cody. But rather, are you going to pawn it off? With that any one of my clients –inside the Fence and out- would pay dearly for it. Suppressors are like legends in this city and most of the higher-up love mantle pieces. And anyone out here would love a weapon that can cut through steel like paper."

Cody frowns, "I gave it to Kae."

Jack just chuckles, "He looks like he needs it more than any of us. Don't you, Oddball."

Strike one. Third strike and I'm finding a brick to peg at his head.

Cody let's a small smile cross his face but removes it when my head snaps over to him.

"But this information alone is valuable enough. They have tracked a Miasmic Beast out here. That is highly unusual. Last time I checked, none of the storms are severe enough to call them and there are no Keystones either."

Both of us frown at that.

"Something else you're willing to share?"

"...We were attacked by a Hexer a few weeks ago."

Jack's eyebrows shot up, "Now that is troubling."

"And it talked."

Jack was silent before opening his mouth, "What did it say?"

"He said that Kae smelt good."

The silence settles again as Jack takes a swig from a bottle sitting beside him. "They like eating flesh, I suppose. Driven mad by the Keystones. Who knows how their minds work? No one has much intel on them. Anyone that gets close enough turns into a raging lunatic...or lunch. What stage was the Hexer at?"

"That's what's troubling me as well,' Cody swallows, "He still looked human."

"Then the brain may have still been wired to speak." His gaze then fell on my neck, "Is that how you got the bruising?"

"No. He threw a shoe at a demon monkey."

"Are you serious? Oddball, I know you're a bit crazy but just wow."

I bristle at how stupid it sounds out loud, "Cody was too fat."

"Maybe you're showing signs of being a Hexer," Jack chuckles. "No one in their right mind would do that, except you."

Strike two.

Cody probably notices my jaw tick as he looks back over at Jack, "So I've shared my information, now it's your turn."

"That it is." Jack pulls himself up and leans forward, closer to us, "I've shown you the military outside the wall."

I frown back at what we saw just an hour ago.

"Now normally, there is maybe one or two patrols in one month as a formal thing to keep the frightened civs humoured. All part of the delusion they have going on in there to make them think that they are being kept safe."

"The Fence has worked for almost a decade," I mutter to myself.

He nods, "All part of the smoke and mirrors. However in the last couple of weeks the military has been building up and it has nothing to do with city defence against the Miasma or Keystone hordes."

"Then, what's left?" Cody frowns.

"What else is left?"

My breath hitched when I realised, "Other cities."

"What?"' Cody was stunned. "But-"

"The City-States have been unsettled with each other for a few months now. A war is brewing." Jack cuts him off.

Then we shouldn't be here. We don't need to be caught up like some helpless casualties. They threw the doors shut and killed us if we got too close, why stick around?

"This is a perfect time to strike."

Strike what? What's this lunatic gone and done now?

"While they fight each other, we bring down the Fence."

I shot to my feet, "Are you serious?"

"What do you think?"

"If there is a war coming, they aren't going to be hitting each other with plastic mallets. From what I remember you telling me, they have advanced in any and all technology. That includes weapons."

"And we have sat on the outside for far too long," Jack growls. "The city gates and that blasted Fence need to be destroyed. Before they begin the manhunts on us once again. And they will, this time far better equiped to murder children in their beds just because they can leviate a pot across the room."

My glare hardens, "I will not let you use my brother like some bulldozer."

"He would be a welcomed addition."

"And you think they'll sit by and watch you do this? They'll rain bullets down on Cody the moment he enters the fray, each side will think he's part of either sides' vanguard. This isn't our war."

"It is our war. We're starving out here while everyone inside live like kings. Think about it Oddball."

And you will do anything to achieve your justice. Sacrifice anything and everything to see a little wall brought down.

"You're not using Cody," I repeat between clenched teeth.

"That is for your dear brother to decide. Cody?"

Both our head turn over to Cody. Cody looks between us and then exhales, licking his lips, "I'm only here to give you information. That's it."

I feel my body going weak with relief.

"You're that scared of your brother?"

"You have no idea."

Jack chuckles, "You are a wonder, Oddball. What would you do if I asked to borrow you're other two siblings?"

"You're eyes still functioning alright?"

"Yeah."

"Cody, give me your fork."

Jack quickly leans back with a lazy grin and his hands up in surrender, "Point taken. I will not ask your family to join in. For now. We still have time. But do think on it Cody, you have been more than helpful over the years. Even with that little loud-mouthed terrier yapping at your heels."

That's it. I'm finding that brick.

Chapter Seven: Flawed

Chapter Seven: Flawed

Cody had wondered off a good way, probably for his 'alone time' to 'think'. I watch Cody, his mind somewhere else entirely. I didn't like the way the emotions flickered across his face and never seem to settle for very long. He wants to join. Desperately wants to get back at the world in any way he can. And Jack fuelled it with this made up 'opportunity'.

"It's becoming his conviction, in a way," Anne comes up beside me.

"And that'll turn into obsession. And it'll get him killed in the end," I look down to her, seeing that her eyes never left Cody.

"It's already an obsession," her sharp eyes now on my face. "It's all he's thinking about most of the time now."

And that struck a chord in me and I didn't like it. It was as if he was pulling himself away. "Cody?" I call for his attention.

He frowns as I interrupt him, "What?"

"Should we go?" I tilt my head a little in the direction towards the exit of the city. It would be best if we move on as quickly as possible. If there's a war coming, I'd rather be as far away as possible.

He looks between me and Anne before I saw something click in his jaw as he sets it. I mentally grimace.

"I'm staying."

"No," I immediately snap on impulse. "You already said you're just here to get information. And you have. We need to move on." Somewhere far, far away. Like another continent far away.

"I've changed my mind."

Of course he has. I can see the stubborn glint already but I'm not going to back down so easily either. "And what are you going to accomplish exactly?"

"The Fence falling for starters."

The fucking Fence... "Like that's going to help. There is a war on the doorstep and I for one don't want to get mixed up in it. Jack is only going to use you and he won't bat an eyelid as you're torn to shreds by machinegun fire."

"So what? At least I will accomplish something."

"What's that supposed to mean?"

"I'm tired of running and living in fear all the fucking time. I want to do something with my sorry life. I want to get back at the people who shut their doors on us. If it weren't for that, Mum would still be alive!"

I almost growl at him, "And tearing down this wall," I motion with a free hand towards the damn thing looming over us, "isn't going to bring her back! It'll only get you killed."

"At least it'll make me feel better."

"And I'm sure the wall and everyone in it give a shit about your feelings! I don't want to be even a thousand miles of this when everything comes down around us!"

"Then don't follow me!"

"Like hell I'm going to let you go off on your own!" I think we're shouting loudly enough to lure in every fucking soldier in the vicinity. But neither of us particularly care at the moment.

"I'll be fine! I've always been fine-"

"That's because I was there to stop you from doing something stupid."

"You're shitting me right? Half the time you go charging in and make more of a mess of it. If it weren't for you blundering in, it would have gone quicker and smoother. But instead you waltz in, screw us over and then have the hide to tell me it's my fault. Don't fuck with me, Kae."

"You would've ended up dead long before I intervened! You have no concept of danger or the people you're leaving behind."

"I leave you behind to keep you safe."

"The fuck you do! We are the farthest from your thoughts when you go blindly charging off all on your own."

"And what good are you? You're the only person outside the Fence who hasn't developed a single ability. You're no better than a civ."

Oh, he so didn't just go there. My fingers curl into fists at my sides, my nails beginning to bite into my palms as I try to control the emotion threating to spill. I don't deal well with emotional upheavals and I'm not going to have one now. That was the first time he used that used that term and it was directed at me. This was worse than heaving that gun pointed at my head. "Shut it."

"You're even weaker than Anne, or Markus, for that matter."

The reason I don't do well with emotion is because I go mentally blank, like I'm doing right now. Fuck.

A dry, cynical laugh escapes his throat, "You're so scared of everything! Scared of being useless. Scared of bring left behind. That's probably the reason why you don't want any of us using our abilities-"

"You're going too far-"

"The fact of the matter is that you are the weakest-"

"Shut up-"

"Useless-"

"Cody!"

"Person out here and a hypocrite who claims that he knows everything when he fucking knows shit all! You make decisions like you're Dad. But you're not and you will never be!"

He seriously just punched holes in all of my insecurities, "I have never once-"

"You have no right to tell me what to do, Kagen! And the fuck I'm listening to you now, you fucking brat! I'm the eldest. I'm in charge. And I say that I'm going. Do whatever the fuck you want. And it's my choice."

I almost spit out my remaining futile defence, "Right back at you, you fucking lunatic! As long as you fucking go on your own, I will follow you. I will bring you back. And that is my decision. Not yours. You have as much right as I do! So shut it!"

"Fuck you," with that, he struts passed me, knocking none too gentle in the shoulder as he does.

"Just where are you going now?" I whir around after him. He just bruised my shoulder. The fucking asshole.

"Away. From you. Before I smack you so high I might just toss you over that fucking thing," He motions towards the wall as he heads towards it.

What is he? Five? Immediately resorting to physical threats. I was about to snap back something but Cody had stopped, his back stiff.

"Makky," Cody whispers our brother's name, all of his built up anger now vanished, replaced with shock.

My eyesight falls to the front of him and saw it was Markus.

And the hear-wrenching look on his face as tears began to spill over made we want to burst out crying myself. It was heart-shattering and we caused it. Guilt immediately replaced my own anger.

"Makky," Cody repeated, taking a step forward.

But on the verge of tears, he takes a step back, "Why are you fighting?"

"We weren't-"

"Liar! You were shouting."

"We-

"Liar."

"Makky," Cody exasperates with a plea, trying to get closer to him.

"Liar! Liar! Liar! You said you wouldn't leave! You lie! You hate us! Always hate us!"

"Markus...no. I could never," Cody's hands were actually shaking as he reached out to him.

But Markus shakes his head, "No!" He takes a step back from us. "No!" he repeats between gasps and sobs. "No!"

I take a step towards him and he backs off. Oh no. he's going to run.

"No!"

"Markus?" I ask quietly.

"No!" and with that he spurs off into the night, down a street and into the dead city.

Shit.

I shoot a glare at Cody as I run passed, trying to catch up to Markus.

Cody catches up to me and for once was silent. Good. If he's going to give me the cold shoulder, at least he'll be quiet about it. By the looks of it, he was heading back towards the bonfire in Deadside. Maybe he was seeking out Yvette? No. Like Cody, he goes into a blind rage and has no idea where he's going. Just as I thought, he slips passed everyone who was staring blankly at us, probably hearing our fight in its entirety. Wonderful. Let's add melodrama to tonight's menu. Jack would love that.

"Markus!" I call again, trying to catch up to him. When he wanted to, he can be slippery and hard to catch.

And like that, he was on the other end of the camp it five seconds. Shit.

Just as was about to turn, Anne comes up beside me, "He's going down a dead end."

I nod, spurning to my left to cut him off. I saw the alley he was heading into before, and I could catching if I went through a broken house. As I did, I felt something very wrong, but ignored it. The silence. The fear. None of it mattered to me at the moment. Markus mattered. If Markus got hurt…

I stop just in front of him and he balks and takes a hasty step back from me, "Don't touch me!"

Ok, that hurt more than being called a 'civ'. I swallow the hurt and take a step towards him, "Makky."

"No! You'll lie."

"Have I ever lied to you?"

The question seemed to have stopped him. His desperate mind thinks and think until eventually his lips formed the word weakly, "No…"

"Makky. I'm not going to-"

A loud bang from a gun sounded behind me, just as Markus's eyes went wide with fear. A wet, dark patch begging to pool from his shoulder as he stands there, frozen in shock. No! Oh No!

"Kae!" I hear Cody's voice tremble behind me just as a sickening thud reverberates behind me with the sound of something cracking against a wall with a clouded grunt.

"Makky…" I begin, my eyes never tearing away from his frightened form.

He then looks up at me. A fearful squeaks from his lungs. His mouth tries to work to form words but nothing coherent escapes as he points to me. I frown, confused. That was when I felt something burning through my shoulder like a hot iron trying to set my blood aflame. I reach up to my shoulder and found my neck was covered in something thick, sticky and warm.

I pull my hand away and sure enough, it was covered in dark blood. The starlight giving it a shiny, slick surface. I look back at over at him, my own shock beginning to make my hand tremble. But that didn't matter as I realised the shock that had masked Markus from his own pain was wearing off.

His eyes bulge as he realises what's just happened to his body. He places a shaky hand up to his shoulder. His hand comes down to his face and he sees what I had never. Never. Never in my lifetime ever wanted him to see. He begins screaming as pain courses through his system. Pain, fear and shock override his mind. He takes off into the night. Blindly. Horribly.

"Kae!" Cody comes but behind me, supporting me as I realised that there was suddenly no stengh in my legs. "Kae talk to me."

"Markus," I whisper hoarsely, "We need to find Markus. Now!" I take a step forward, ignoring the pain and the blood seeping from my left shoulder. My legs are shaky but they manage to hold me. In the pit of my stomach I knew that if we didn't get him now, the war that had just started would consume him in hellfire.

Chapter Eight:
Everlasting Light

A/N: What is this, two chapters in one day!? Hmm...sort of got momentum at the moment so I'll try and get as much written as I can while I can :3

Chapter Eight: Everlasting Light

We clamber our way through the once dead silent city. Now awash with bullet barrage and the screams of the dying and so called glory. The loud jets and helicopters from overhead poured gunfire with blood spewing shrapnel and debris, lighting up the sky with a haze of orange glow with an intensity that threatened to melt the stars. The pungent scent of entrails and burning flesh fill my nostrils as I want to gag, my uninjured hand is pushed hard against my mouth before I vomit.

My damaged hand clings as tightly as it can to Anne, we became each other's life line in this mess of sound and vivid fire. A bomb falls to the sky, a ways off from us but I am not at all comfortable as it plummets down.

The world shudders while the first of I'd say many, mushroom clouds that light up the sky and rain death.

Anne began to take the lead on me, pulling me along the back streets, knowing where to go to avoid any and all confrontation as we run after Markus. My grip was slippery with the blood that's travelled down my arm but Anne keeps a firm grip on my sleeve. She was silent, her eyes forward. I could tell that she was trying to swallow down her fear.

This glory of war that everyone talks about. I don't see it here at all. I see faceless shadows yelling and screaming and dying. I see no comrade as one has his leg blown off and his friends run in the other direction, only to be shot in the head. Just who is who out there?

"He's gone down there!" Anne pulls me out of my thoughts, pointing towards something that looks like it was a shopping centre. Breathing heavily, I realise by the way my lungs ache that we've been running for way too long. I have no idea where we are.

As we go through the smashed front doors, I saw it was impeccably dark in here. There were a pair of escalators in front of us that lead straight down and the floor swallowed up by the darkness beyond. A glass railing with gold lining once parred the gaping hole that was always in the centre of these types of places. The shops that lined the sides were sad and broken with glass everywhere and dust collecting that we were disturbing.

"This way!' Anne tugs me down the unmoving steps. Of course down. Let's go down somewhere practically pitch-black that has God knows what down there. As my feet hit the solid concrete surface of the next floor, it was met with a wet, splashing sound. Water. The entire floor was flooded. I can hear Cody not too far behind who let out a grunt of surprise as his feet also hit the water. At first, my sight was met with a wall of darkness but slowly I begin to see that it was a dim walkway. Anne pulls me down along, so sure of where she was going while I was blindly stumbling behind her.

Anne didn't let me time to inspect my surroundings. Down the passageway, there was adimly lit area up ahead. As we came upon it, it was a spacious area that would have been the food court. It was like a massive empty ballroom now. The ceiling was damaged and a huge gaping hole looked up at the moonless night but still managed to be illuminated by starlight and the hellfire razing in the distance.

In a small corner, I see Markus and immediately run up to him as he clutches at his shoulder, his eyes wide and almost feral, like he didn't recognise anything around him anymore. The last time he was like this...

"Markus," I call to him, stopping just a few metres away.

"Make it stop," he whispers to himself. "Make it stop!' He repeats the sentence over and over, more and more panicked. Almost like a rhythm, speeding up. As he did, he clutches at his head, digging his fingers griping his hair. "Make it stop!" Over and over.

I was stunned. This...he...

He suddenly stops, his eyes now locked on something in the distance. All emotion gone from his face. Like he was a doll. Then the words echoed from his lips, "Make it stop."

Anne pulls on my arm, "Get back!"

Just as she pushes me back, branches erupt from Markus's back. Wooden vines peel through his skin as his body transforms. Flesh becomes root. Bone becomes branch.

"No!" I run forward. He needs to stop. Stop it now! "Markus! Stop!"

As he becomes consumed, his eyes fell upon my desperate face. His face was calm. Almost serene. A small satisfied smile touches his lips. And he was gone. My brother. Where a ten year old boy once stood was now a tree. I skid to a stop, my fingers trace and claw at the smooth bark, trying to fine him. "No. No. No. Markus…"

He didn't. He couldn't.

"He's gone," Anne's voice echoes as she collapses beside me. Placing her hand on the trunk, she begins to stroke it, her lips trembling as tears spill that she was trying so hard to contain. "Markus…is gone."

No. I look up at the dark branches, see that magnolia flowers began to open up. Pure white magnolias fill the air with a heavy scent that was almost intoxicating. The held a blue glow that were softly luminescent and the centres were rich golden in colour.

"He can come back. He's still here," I try to reason. "He's right here."

But Anne shakes her head, "This is just a tree. Markus isn't here anymore."

I pull her into a tight hug, not caring for the water lapping at my legs. I was beyond pain, even with the new wound in my arm. Anne pulls on my clothes tightly as she sobs into my shirt.

I look up, over at Cody that was staring at his feet. His fists had curled up tightly at his sides. I felt hollow. Just…Markus was there and now…

I tighten my hold on Anne. Was she always this small? My eyes stung as I look up at Markus once again. But it wasn't Markus. I close my eyes. He can't come back, can he? He's gone. Gone and turned himself into a tree.

I have never felt so helpless in my life. What can I do? What can I do to bring him back? To rewind what had happened. What was there? Why? Markus…just why?

"We can't stay here," I said finally. My voice was dead and sounded hollow, completely devoid of emotion, even to my ears.

But how can we leave him? Markus was a tree. How do we move a tree that towered over us enough that it just reaches the ceiling some twenty odd metres above us?

I stand up, helping Anne to her feet and look over at Cody, expecting him to say something next. But he remained silent. He was probably as unwilling to leave as I was. But we can't stay here.

The screams and machinegun fire outside attest to that and it'll just get worse from here on. And we couldn't afford to stay here.

But this was Markus.

I look back at the tree.

Just as I was waging an internal war with myself, the place shook around us. Another bomb had fallen and it was way too close for comfort. I look up in time to see a spray of debris hitting the air, landing in the water around us. I pull Anne closer to me, to shield her from the falling shrapnel and dust. A column collapses near us, sending wave after pounding wave of water against our side.

When the water begins to settle, a sound from above makes my inside run cold. A rope falls down into the hole. Then another and another. Until eventually there were eight lines and men dressed in heavy army gear coming down.

Cody pulls himself between us and them. Without giving them much time to think, he charges forward and without mercy he smashes a fist into one of them, cracking the ribcage and drops dead in the water. Cody then pulls on a number of robes and each strain under the new found tug of war with each having at least three people still on them trying to come down. But

Cody was angry and he pulls harder until the lines snap and they came tumbling down to their death. Each body hitting the shallow water and concrete underneath with a wet slab that was sickening to the ears. Cody then twisted around to meet a soldier who had successfully made it down and was raising his gun. Only to have his head meet with my brother's fist which slammed him into the air and landing harshly into a wall, the back of his head slamming along with it. But Cody wasn't done. Just as quickly, he comes at him again, still in the air and forces his skull through the wall, cracking it and destroying it along the way.

Another two had made it and began raining bullet down on Cody. But Cody uses his strength to power his legs, giving him lightning speed and he pulls one up by his wrists and punching the other in the gut, making him sprawl across the floor like a skipping stone. Cody then looks up at the man he had a hold on. He had pulled him up so that his feet barely touched the ground and pushes his fist into the man's gut who collapses onto the floor like a sack.

A silence returns to the area for a moment but more sound illuminated the surface above us. I could see Cody's jaw tighten and a madden stubbornness was taking over his mind. "I'll kill them," he growls before launching himself up to the twenty metre gap up top. Surprised shouts and machine gun fire soon sound afterwards.

I immediately make my way towards the passages back up to the outside. No way in hell am I going to lose him too.

Anne came up beside me, "We need to hurry. He isn't bullet proof."

I look down to her, a thought nearly made it to the surface but she cuts it down.

"I'm coming."

We slushily make our way towards the escalators and with a heavy grip, I somehow manage to pull myself up to the top where Anne was impatiently waiting for me.

"Why are they here?" I ask as we manage to get outside.

She leaves my question unanswered as her head whips over to the sound of an explosion up behind a half collapsed building that was being held in place by a broken wall that it was leaning on. She then runs towards the sounds, "Cody's over here!"

As I stumble towards her, I try to pull her back, only to miss and my vision starts to go fuzzy. Shaking my head, I try to focus again. I think I've lost a bit too much blood over the past few weeks and running around like an idiot with a hole through my shoulder isn't exactly helping either. Anne squeezes through a hole and I follow behind. Coming through to the other side, it was a horror scene and I just happen to walk through a curtain to it.

Surrounded by corpses and blood staining the ground, Cody was in the centre, wiping the blood from his chin. His eyes were feral. There was a glint in them as they landed on us. As they did, he runs up behind me and lands a solid punch on a solider that was about to point a gun into my back.

Cody was almost enjoying himself. And that left me feeling a sort of sense of dread.

"Cody!" I call to him but it falls on deaf ears as he pulls me to the side as machine gun fire explodes into the air, landing into the concrete just where I was standing before.

Fucking hell.

"Get to safety," Cody looks me in the eyes, "You need to get to cover."

"I'm not going anywhere without you!"

A grin spreads across his lips, "Try and stop me."

And with that, he leaps from my side and towards the ones shooting at us. What a fucking lunatic.

Chapter Nine: Insanities

Chapter Nine: Insanities

Cody was rushing through the torrents of fire and bullets like a mad man. He didn't distinguish between the two sides that had started this war. But why would he? They were both the same as far as he was concerned. And now that he had figured out that he could leap high into the air with the strength in his legs, he could leap up and smash through any sort of aerial machine within reach.

Even now as I was running as fast as I could along the ground, I saw him leap up to an armoured helicopter and take out those inside and getting away at the last second as it tumbles to earth, ending up as a giant fireball.

He began hopping between rooftops, increasing his distance from us, until eventually he was completely out of sight. But I knew exactly where he was going. The Fence. Even after everything, he's heading for the goddamn Fence.

"Next street," Anne calls beside me.

As we turned down an alley that lead to a street over, I hear an explosion with a wall of heat lapping at my back and a wave of force almost knocks me off my feet. ...I'm not even going to think about how close that was. As we head down another avenue, I realise that we were back in Deadside. I look around and saw that nothing was the same.

Something like a bomb must have gone off as everything looked like ground zero of a tornado. The ground was scorched and the fires raging around us lit it up just show it was nothing but black. Gone were the living. Now only reigned by the dead. Bodies of soldiers and those who lived out here littered the ground. Some were bits and pieces and others were whole. But I couldn't tell who was who or what was what. The smell of engine oil and god knows what else filled my nostrils as my eyes water at the smoke trying to blind me. I almost stand on a decapitated hand while slowing down to look around. It was hell. Pure hell.

I move to cover my face but the tug on muscle reawakened the pain in my shoulder that still has yet to stop bleeding. And running around the countryside isn't exactly helping. I put my opposite arm onto my shoulder, stifling a scream behind tightly shut lips, I look over to find Anne rummaging through some of the filth.

I make my way over to her and see I moment later she was tugging on something from under a soldier's body and was having difficulty. I kneel down beside her and help her pull it out with my injured arm. As I did, a piece of pure midnight slip from under the body and in my hand now it that fucking blade. I swear...

"You're going to need it," Anne said tightly. While looks at the blade, we both hear the body we just moved, groan. Anne takes a frightened step back as the solider raises a gun at us. And without a second thought, I bury the blade into his throat. The gun immediately drops form his gloved fingers. As he twitches and gurgles on his own blood, I stand in shock at what I just did.

Anne smacks into my back, "Don't think. You don't have time to think. Move!"

I shakily take a step back, the blade retracting from the man's throat. He was still alive and the blood pours faster now that the hole wasn't blocked by a blade. I severed the windpipe and the air escapes as chortled blood burst through.

"Kae!" Anne snaps at me but my mind is still too far away.

That was far, far too easy. To take someone's life like it was…it was nothing. I don't know the person under the mask. I don't know his name, his age or even if he has a family-

"Kae! Move now! Crisis later!"

Man she's snippy. I force myself to look away as the nameless solider finally stops choking on his lifeblood. I can still feel how easy the blade slid down into his throat like it was butter. I think I'm gonna be sick.

Anne must have been fed up as she grabs hold of my wrist, slimy with grot and blood and forcefully pulls me along. I look around with new eyes. Before I hadn't really thought much of death or bodies or killing. Because I had never been the one to have been a cause of it. Cody did it so easily. But looking around, I only see people who were once like everyone else. Living everyday like it was how they were supposed to. But now…they were nothing more than meat bags lying around, no better than a dead animal on the side of the road that had been hit by a truck.

"Think of them like that," Anne retorts at me. "You didn't cause this, Kae. He was going to kill us and you reacted. That's how it goes. They aren't people anymore. Just road-kill."

Anne is way too calm about this. I should be the one comforting her. I should be used to this.

Anne's grip tightens on my wrist.

Looking in front of us, I see the looming wall coming closer to us. It's still standing!? How is that possible? And where is Cody?

As we came closer to the major battlefield, I see people from the military attacking each other and those who I assume are part of Jack's brigade attacking as well. One threw a fireball that exploded a tank from underneath and sprayed the air with dust and metal that flew off and hit a number of soldiers around it. All knocked down dead. I let out a breath as a jet from above retaliated by dropping a rocked on top of friend and foe alike and the earth erupted once again.

I watch another missile heading straight for our direction and clutch onto Anne and leap at the last second. I tumble and land on my bad side. I land with the air squeezing from my lungs as a pained hiss and my ears left ringing. The dust and muck pelts into my back as I'm left in a daze. Urrgh why is the world sideways and moving? Trying to shake the feeling, I feel a small hand touch the side of my face and realise it was Anne trying to get me back to my senses. But really I prefer lying down at the moment. Can't I sleep for a few minutes? Not like anyone cares about one more body on the ground right? I wanna throw up my guts right now. No. No I don't, I had skulled down three bowls of stew. I don't want to regurgitate it all back.

My sight goes beyond the blonde mess in my face and I can't help but be fixated on the clouds that were in the sky. Yeah sure it was night and shit and clouds are always around but...even with the fireballs and bodies flying everywhere those clouds look awfully purple to me...I blink. Oh hell.

A rumble from under the ground makes my body all jittery. It sounded like an earthquake. But I don't remember there ever being earthquakes in this territory. Just as Anne manages to force me into a sitting position, a disgruntled roar tremors from under the ground and just as the vibrations became violent, an impossibly large body of something like a giant snake-worm thing erupts from the earth. A Wyrm. The fuck!? Is this an all-out total war tonight or what? Can't catch a break for one second here can we? The colossal trunk that easily towers over the wall and ten times as thick, bends slightly. The off purple colour of it immediately makes you think it was slimy and just as it bends down, the tip opens like petals on a flower, all lined with rows and rows of gigantic white jagged teeth. It lets out an impossible roar before smashing itself back into the ground, hiding under the surface once again.

The fighting didn't immediately stop between the groups but as another Wyrm makes its way to the surface, taking out several tanks and jets on the way up, all metal and bodies disappearing into that gaping abyssal mouth began to make them think twice.

"It's hungry," Anne watches as two more shoot up. 'They're all hungry."

This is impossible. Just crazy impossible. I'm deluded. Yes. The blood loss has made me delirious. That is not a Wyrm. Those are not crystal pillars beginning pulling out of the earth. This is not happening.

A group of jets fire rockets at another Wyrm, lighting the body up like some Christmas tree before it explodes into liquid fire, cascading down to the earth in a rupture of echoing shrieking pain. And my ears were already ringing.

"We need to find Cody, now!" Anne screeches at me, trying to get me to stand.

Now that my body had experienced lying down, it was a lot harder to tell it to do otherwise. Anne even forces the damnable blade back into my hand which had flown out of it when we were shell shocked early. How we manage to stay in one piece so far was mind boggling enough as another bomb goes off a few streets behind us.

Getting to my feet, I stagger towards the Fence. It was the only place he was going to be in all this mess. We need to get out of here before the Miasma Storm starts. And it was going to be big if it's called Wyrms here.

I zigzag towards the Fence, trying to lead Anne through the safest passage as the confusion of war has made everyone attack everyone. This sheer madness was beyond any scope of reasoning. It was almost like Hexers were let loose... My head swipes back to Anne.

She keeps her eyes forward, avoiding my questions completely. I turn down another alley and find us directly in front of the damnable thing. A thick road acted like a moat around the Fence. I have never been this close to it but...that sinking feeling you get when you look up from the bottom of a giant dam wall? This was far more terrifying. How could anyone stand living anywhere near this thing?

We head for the weakest point of this monstrosity, the gate. Even someone as thick-skulled as Cody would know to attack that point. As I manage to build up momentum, a large armoured vehicle comes sliding in front of us, crashing into the wall. I look up the street it had come from and there was Jack. Electricity pulsating from his body like he was some kind of lightning rod. Well he was a rod. A big one. A man from the crashed truck stumbles out and raises his gun in futile defence, only to be scorched alive by blue lightning.

I turn to see Jack, his hand raised and a smirk plastered on his face.

"Oddball. Fancy seeing you here. Nice night isn't it?"

"Save. It. Where. Is. Cody." I punctuate between clenched teeth.

"Oh. He and some of my men are headed for the gates. Should you be out here? Or are you using your sister as cover?"

My insides run cold.

"Where's the smaller one? Did you use him to?"

I grab him by the scruff of his collar, "Keep talking."

He grins at me, we were of almost equal height. He raises a hand, electricity sparking from it, "Careful, boy. Or I will electrocute you."

"Let's see who's faster. Me? Or you?" I growl as I had pointed the blade to his stomach.

"Kae," Anne pulls on my arm and I lower the blade and took a step back. "Let's go. Ignore him."

And at her insistence, I turn away from him completely all the while he's laughing at my back.

Chapter Ten: Torrid Skies

Chapter Ten: Torrid Skies

As we end up in front of the gate, I don't see Cody anywhere. Actually, when you think about it...no one was here. All the trucks and soldiers weren't anywhere to be seen. Did they abandon the gate? Frowning, I take a step closer to the solid thing.

Everything seemed so far away as I stand in front of something that separated those inside from everything horrible and blood-thirsty outside. Had they ever thought about the outside world? Did they consider themselves the glorious chosen to be saved by some God just because they happened to be on the right side of the wall when it went up? Did they feel safe while the rest of us were left outside to be slaughtered? The thoughts made me grit my teeth as I let myself touch the wretched thing. It was...cold. Even with the fire and explosions it was still cold. Not like ice but...similar. And somehow warm as well. I almost close my eyes to feel a pulse under my palm.

"Get down," Anne calls to me.

I flinch to the side just in time for something to come crashing solidly into the gate. It let out a loud rumble akin to thunder in a steel drum. It was Cody. His fist had sunk deeply into the Gate, leaving a twisted imprint into the metal. But it still stood.

"Fuck!" He mutters as he takes a step back, his fist leaving the dent that he had created. This was probably the first time that something didn't break under his sheer force.

"Cody!' I hiss at him.

"What? Kae!?" He was genuinely surprised to see me.

"We leave now."

"Not until I bring this down."

"Cody," I exacerbate his name with a breath.

"You go ahead, I'll catch up."

Like fuck he will. I glare at him and then looked up at the gate then at the dent he had made. I sigh and look over at Anne. What should I do? We need to find cover since bozo here isn't going to move.

"How'd it go?" A boy comes running up with a few others that I had never seen before. There was maybe about eight of them and all ranging in age between Cody and me.

"No good. I'm gonna have to try again." Cody doesn't look away from the wall. "How's your end?"

The boy in front wore a grimy white hoodie that he kept over his head far enough so that I couldn't see his facial features clearly and I presume he was the leader of this ragtag team that Jack must have organised as Cody's 'back-up'. "All clear."

"Good. You lot stay here and look after Kae and Anne while I try again."

"So that's your brother and sister?"

The question's tone sort of irritated me, like he was dissatisfied with something. Well sorry I don't look like a hulk that can tear down buildings like the jerkward beside me. Cody was going to have to go some distance to let himself get a charging start. I growl as he basically ignores me when he turns around to start again, "Have you thought about what'll happen when you tear this down?"

"Nope," his tone uncaring.

The air hisses between my teeth. "What happens if there's an army on the other side?"

Shrugging, he steps away, "That's an issue for when it comes down." This bastard-

"More are coming," Anne looks dead ahead as army trucks and soldiers began pouring into the streets surrounding us. Terrific.

I pull the blade down to my side. Slash and stab. That's about as much as I know about using this thing. And I guess that, in the end, is all you need to know. They come at us with guns, pushing us against the gate without much room to move. We're seriously outnumbered and all routes have been cut off but it wasn't like there was anywhere we could go to at this point. Cody did his best to keep them away from Anne and myself but there's only one of him and he couldn't be everywhere at once. A solider even came at me, his gun turned club came swinging at me now that it was out of bullets. I pull to the side, the blade steady in both hands as I cut him down by swiping through his gut and forcing him to collapse to his knees and finished him off by decapitating him. The held rolls off, still with the gasmask attached and his body flops to the ground in a cascade of blood. I wasn't able to think about being sick as another solider came up just as quickly to replace him, all the while I'm fully aware that were are all being pushed back into the Fence.

We were losing and fast. I cover Anne as best I can but how are we to get out of this?

As a solider comes rushing at me, I hear something whistling in the distance and getting louder with every second. Just before the solider made contact with me, I look up and saw a rocket heading straight for the gates. I twist awkwardly, trying to cover Anne but never make in time as the world around me was engulfed by fire and sound as I was thrown tumbling across the ground.

As I come to a rolling stop on my stomach, I could see that the missile hadn't even left a scratch on the door, causing the explosive impact to be rebounded and land on all of us that were fighting in front of it. My vision flickers as my body was numb, beyond any realm of pain. My hearing echoes like I'm trying to focus on something far away, shattering in an echo inside a tunnel. My body wasn't listening as I try to move, my eyes couldn't focus on everything, as if none of this had substance, everything was surreal. Time was moving much slower than I was used to.

"Anne...?" I groan weakly as my eyes land on Anne but I couldn't distinguish what's happening. She looks frightened. Panic and desperate as she stares right at me. Her hands, all bloody, reach out towards me. Her voice didn't seem to surface as the buzzing in my ears was louder than sound but her mouth was open, like she was screaming. I wanted to tell her that it was ok. But even twitching my fingers is hard. Tears had left tracks down her face that was covered in grime. She was getting further and further away from me. She was moving backwards on top of some weird greyish mass that was pulling her towards some blurry thing that had landed on the ground. I think it's a helicopter but I don't remember them making such an awful chopping noise as the rotating blades on top of the black body disturbed the air at a slow pace. It even left a ghost trail on my sight. Why could I hear that? It was like a heartbeat. Maybe my heartbeat?

And she was gone. Where did she go?

"-ae!"

Somewhere above me a large irritating mass was screaming down at me.

"Kae! Get it together."

Something wet landed on my cheek. A raindrop? And time sped up again with a force that almost knocks me out. Crackle of fire, jets overhead, bestial roars, and screams of the dying and the cry of thunder all reverberate through my ears with that awful buzzing noise. I think I'd rather go back to being deaf. I also realise that the shadow in my face is Cody leaning over me. I'm still not all with it as I stare blankly up at him. There was a huge gash in his head, covered in dirt and burnt at the edges. It made me want to reach up, to see if it was too deep. If it is, I'm going to have to clean it before it heals over.

"Don't move too much. Fuck, there's so much blood." So now I have his full attention? Lucky me. Next time I want him to shut up and listen, I'll just drop a bomb on myself.

Just as he struggles to get me up onto my knees, my body leaning heavily on him, I feel his body flinch as if something had just stung him. I see something sticking out of his back which I never seen before. It was shaped like a dart but the middle had some sort of clear flask like look. I blink, realising whatever was in it was emptied into his system was making Cody lag in breath and his body strains to hold me up. But the stubborn fool still manages to hold onto me.

"...Cody," my voice was a hoarse whisper and died before I could tell him to let go. Whatever was in that dart was affecting him. But obviously not his stupidity.

"I've got you," he hisses at me.

But just as suddenly, his warmth is snatched from my front and without it, my torso crashes back to earth. I look up in time to see two greyish blobs had a hold on Cody's shoulders and dragging him into the back of a truck. He pulls against them, a hand breaking free and throws it out to me. I weakly reach for his hand, seeing my own arm was covered in blood, dirt and lacerations. Our fingers almost touch but then his hand moves away, the truck taking off.

"Kae!"

I was unable to support my arm and it drops.

"Kae!"

His face gets smaller the further he goes into the distance.

I see one of the soldiers that had taken him push something into his neck and Cody weakly drops. Even at this distance, I see his eyes, the same cool colour of Anne's looking at me in such a desolate panic. His lips form my name but I couldn't hear him properly anymore.

Then he was gone.

The rain also had the insensitivity to pick that moment to start dripping down.

A/N:

-------------> Palm of Your Hand by Speed Limits and Jaco ft. Joni Fatora

This song has been stuck in my head while I was writing and liked the lyrics (that start about a minute in) and thought that they kinda suited the chapter

Chapter Eleven: Wished Denial

Actually i'm quite nervous about this chapter. I wasn't sure which way to go with this but I guess we'll just see how it goes....

Chapter Eleven: Wished Denial

I manage to drag my body into the nearest building which happened to be some sort of corner diner or café that was close to the Fence. The polished timber floors are scratched and marked, covered in dust and broken glass. I was on the floor and somehow managed to roll onto my back, just inside of the broken down front door, the tiny bell was near my feet, the middle rusted out. The ceiling was a dull greyish white with a ceiling fan still firmly affixed to it. The blades are wooden and I wonder if they're rotting.

I feel like a train decided to run over me and breathing brought on a so much agony that at first I tried holding my breath but when I gasped it hurt so much more. The rain's gotten pretty heavy all of a sudden too. I just made it in time, it seems. Now...I'll just have to wait and pray that the hordes don't find me. I press a hand to my stomach, there was a large gash that had cut right through the fabric of my clothes and bit into my skin. I'm too scared to see just how deep it is. But my intestines aren't hanging out so it shouldn't be that deep at least.

The ringing in my ear had quietened a little from before, but breathing brought on a headache that pounded behind the eyes. I'm probably going to die in a café, next to the Fence. Hah.

I almost laugh but it came out as a cross between a cough and a sob. Ah shit it hurts. I'm hoping to pass out pretty soon. Lightning illuminates the café for a moment and darkness returns the thunder's call. Not long now the hordes will spill forth and I'll end up as chow if they find my corpse. I wonder if they will manage to break through the Fence and destroy everything inside.

My eyes sting and shutting them made something spill from them. Huh? Ah my eyes are leaking tears. They were burning hot as they slide down. I raise my other hand to cover my face. Fuck, just hurry up and let me die or something. I've lost Markus. Cody and Anne were taken away and now... Now I'm left here by myself to rot away. And it was frustrating as fuck. And lonely. I bite back a sob. Shit.

Another shot of lightning brightens the room with the trembling roar vibrating underneath. A million and one roars soon fill me ears and my dread almost makes me flinch. It's begun. The Miasma will consume this place in no time. And with it, the night parade of demons had begun.

It wasn't like I was particularly afraid of it now that I'm in the middle of it. And losing so much blood that I was probably delirious enough to think of everything so calmly while wanting to cry my heart out at the same time, probably helped. I had seen a Miasma storm from a distance before. It calls all sorts of monsters and then they take over whatever the storm had landed on. Sometimes a thick blood mist would envelop the area but other times you see it. Thousands of monsters running through the night like a black swarming locust plague. I had watched them take over a city once. The city was somewhere to the west and the horde rained down upon it like insects to a carcass. And picked it clean to the bone. The thought made me shudder. There was a small community, much like Deadside and they were consumed utterly and completely. Hopefully it might take out the armies while it's here.

I hear something shift and the clinking sound of broken glass being disturbed. I open my eyes and turn my head in its direction. There was a hulking dark mass standing in the doorway which must have been another entrance. My eyes widen as it steps closer. Ah shit. Swallowing my spit which tasted metallic, I see that it had blue-green stripes that were soft glowing, all over its body. Bioluminescence...I think it's called. It resembled a tiger's stripes. As it gets closer to me, I realise it was a flipping tiger. Though black like midnight, so I would have mistaken it for a panther or something if not for the glowing stripes. The neck was too short for a panther and has those fluffy tuffs of fur on either sides of its face. It's fucking huge. I mean tigers are big but this...its mouth could probably wrap around my body without much effort. I was bite-size. Three chomps and I would disappear into its belly. Great. I was monkey chow a few weeks ago, now tinned cat food. Oh well, at least it sounds better to be eaten by a tiger instead of a monkey.

Its head comes close to my chest its lip twitches, revealing its sabre white teeth but it doesn't go in for the kill, instead it presses its nose to my stomach. Before I realise it, my hand's moving. What the hell am I doing? My hand lands on the bridge of its nose as its amber black eyes stare back at me. The fur was fine and soft, just like a cat's. In my mind I could feel something like an unsettling pulse that was overrun by fear and confusion but as I weakly stroke its fur, the feeling becomes softer and almost satisfied. A feeling of complete relief.

My eyes finally close as the heaviness of sleep finally caught up with me.

I wake with sunlight stinging my eyes. I blink, trying to understand where the hell I am. Why is it so hard to breathe? Then a crushing weight on my chest became apparent, the air squeezing from my ribcage makes me gasp. My eyes try to focus on what's in front of me only to see a big furry face lazily staring back at me. The tiger converted me into his personal pillow. What the hell am I supposed to do with this? It's stuffy and I can't breathe.

As if catching onto my thoughts, the tiger lifts its head and shifted so that it was facing me properly. I feel my body cry out in pain. I hurt everywhere. How am I still alive? I was bleeding all over the place and it's not like I wasn't alone here either. This man-eating tiger with glowing stripes looks pretty hungry to me.

The morning sun had filtered in through the broken windows and from the door, making the reality of the night more apparent outside. I struggle to sit up, my bones creaking in the process and my sore battered body screams at me in protest. I pull myself up to lean my back against the cashier counter. I'm heavily breathing and exhausted after the ordeal of sitting up.

Outside was, if it were possible, more desolate than I remembered. There were now gaps of nothing between and behind the broken bodies of the old buildings that were still barely standing, all around. Large black crystal pillars skewered a number of them, jutting out at all different angles like black teeth with food still stuck between them. The ground was also given the same sort of treatment and from here, I could tell that these were only the small ones. The huge obelisk like structures only got worse closer to the centre of the Miasma's storm eye.

Putting a sore hand to my gut, flinching at the stinging pain it leaves but still apply force. How I managed to survive is beyond me. Looking up at the ceiling I had to wonder; did the wall survive? I couldn't see properly from here. Can I even stand?

I put force into my legs and slide up the counter, my other hand reaches the dusty top of the counter, trying to take some of the weight. Just...barely. Holy shit, this...it hurts like fuck. But I need to see. The tiger was watching me the entire time and stood up to come over to me, pushing its head into my stomach. Oh god. It standing, I could see its proper height, its shoulder blade came right up to my eye line.

I freeze as it rumbles at me, my hand that I used to support my stomach moves out the way as the tiger presses gently further into me, almost making my collapse on top of it, my hand supporting me on the bench top reaches out to its head to support myself before I completely fall over myself. The tiger rumbles at me again as if to approve of my actions.

I have a strange feeling overtake my senses in my brain; it was feral but also quiet like a calm after the storm on an ocean and that strange content I felt last night. I stare down at the pair of amber eyes. That's...you?

An emotion of approval surfaces above the tide.

Holy shit. I have a tiger in my head.

Disagreement, like a frown. And yet not so. Agreement.

"I'm in your head?" I ask out loud, my voice my voice raspy and cracking in whispered fits.

It simply blinks at me, its ears twitching at the sound of my voice. Doesn't understand human speech. I then tried thinking, I am in the tiger's head.

Disagreement. And yet not so. Agreement.

Erm. Ok so we're in each other's heads. Apparently. ...Let's roll with that then...Will you eat me? How is this supposed to work?

Confusion. Knowing. Dreams quiet. Bright and soothing. Warm. Relief. Dreamer no more? Fading light. Cold. Sadness. Dreams no more. Darkness. Despair returns.

I'll take that as a 'no'. I frown, trying to comprehend the mixture of colours, sensations and emotions flooding my brain.

Swallowing, I cling onto its fur near the shoulder blade as the tiger in turn moves so that it was now facing sideways.

Desire?

The emotion question comes into my mind. I think it was asking me what I was wanting. To be honest I want to collapse onto the floor but I need to go outside. ...I need to see.

Disapprove but acknowledge.

"You're as bad as Anne," I mutter.

The tiger's ear's twitch again at my voice.

"Never mind."

Chapter Twelve: Abandoned Wonderland

A /N: A couple of days late...sorry about that. Two things happened to me; gym and writer's block. I was drawing a blank for a bit but still managed to pull through...somehow...

and I was forced to join a gym (becasue I am seriously unfit...) and thus far am proving that exercise kills people. I couldn't move for three days and I'm still limping...

anyway, new chapter!

Chapter Twelve: Abandoned Wonderland

The sight before me after leaving the diner left me feeling unbearably hollow. The wall was smashed to pieces. Full sheets suspended in mid-air by the thick black crystal, including the gate. The gate that not even Cody could take down. But there it is; dangling far above my head like a piece of meat on a skewer. It even swung slightly in the light breeze.

I limp forward a little, the cat seeming to be content at the snail pace I was attempting to hobble at. Another step. Another step. I bite my lip, supressing the waves of pain that rankle my body.

The tiger's thoughts form almost coherent words, Continue? Confusion. Hurt. Pain. Why?

I tighten my grip on its fur, I need to keep moving. If I stop, I won't move again. I need to go forward.

Irrational. Foolish.

Just as I was about to say something back, something shiny hits my eyes. I look up. And there was the goddamn blade. Again. It is seriously turning into the proverbially 'bad penny'. This time it was sticking out of what I presumed to what was once a wall. I should just leave it there. My tongue clicks as I reach for the damn thing. Curse me and my sentimentality. I hate this thing. But I'm probably going to need it. It saved my ass a few times. The blade slides out of the concrete easily enough with a hiss. I couldn't even hold it up as the point hits the ground with a dull tink and I find myself leaning on it like an old man with a cane. My hands shake, remembering last night. It was so easy to kill. Don't think about it. I feel like I'm going to be sick.

I lean on the tiger a bit more, pressing my head into its shoulder and shut my eyes to fight the wave of nausea rising from the pit of my stomach. Quite frankly, I feel like I was going to vomit blood. It hurt so much. But I need to keep moving. My feet seem to have a will of their own as they slowly take me towards the wrecked monstrosity of what was left of the wall.

I look up the street that lead into the once called 'haven' from the outside world. A place that was supposed to be paradise compared to out here. A place that threw us away. I could barely see the skyscrapers and streets. All in ruins. The crystal pillars shooting out everywhere. But I was curious. What was so special on the other side?

Feeling a little dizzy, I still manage to take another step towards the place that had been 'forbidden' to us for the last ten years. My heart is seriously ponding wave after loud wave of pressure in my ears. It was a place that everyone outside desperately wanted to go. It was a place that everyone inside wanted to keep locked up.

Walking up to the gate, both me and the cat manage to squeeze past the thick obsidian crystal through to the other side. And what greeted us was something that was a replica of the first Disaster. The entire city was at a standstill. Fire still burned some of the buildings, cars littered the streets, some crashed into each other in a panic. Stores destroyed and glass and debris spread like glittered reflections of tiny stars in the morning sun. Towers of crystal jutted out everywhere just like outside. Walking down what I could only guess be a main district I saw a huge plasma screen spanning an entire building's side that was still working, despite a crystal poking out the middle. But it only reflected black and white static. Despite all the destruction and panic that I had assumed only happened hours ago, it was quiet. Like the dead. And there weren't any bodies either. I even check a crashed car with a glance; abandoned, the keys still in the ignition.

"Just...what happened...?" I mumble as I find myself being pulled down the street. Yeah sure there was a storm but this sort of destruction doesn't just leave no bodies behind. I find myself walking passed something that I had always wanted to play as a kid; an arcade. But I didn't feel any pull towards it, instead I still trudge down the street. I see traffic lights ahead that where still functional, showing a bright red glow the flicks green within a second.

Something was terribly wrong. I mean...not just the missing bodies but...even with all the debris and fires and sirens going off, it's far too...freakishly quiet. The air is stale. I could taste dust, like it was only just disturbed. I frown, how is any of this possible? Did something happen here? But Jack mentioned contacts.

No. Even if he did, that doesn't mean it was real or he kept in constant communication with them. Besides, with the military being all anal about this place... Were they trying to keep this place contained or something? But then the others wanted to get in? It was strange that they knew exactly where to find us now that I think about it. I mean, who comes after a bunch of kids in the middle of a war? ...I feel like my brain is overheating.

That was when I feel like I see something shift from the corner of my vision. My heart lurches. Please tell me that's my imagination... When my head snaps in that direction; of course, nothing. I grip both the tiger and the sword-cum-walking-stick a little tighter. I so don't need this right now.

Next I have the cat in my head and from the emotions and colours it was emitting at me I think I could understand it was saying; 'Should move. Leaving is good.'

But something was still pulling at me in here. And like any shitty horror movie idiot, I listen to that tiny feeling nudging me on. Turning down a wrecked street, I almost gasp at the huge golden thing that is, I presume, in the very centre of the city. It looked like some sort of sparkly gold and crystal tower-thing with weird-ass look wing things at the very top, encircling it like they were half opening to protect some weird structure at the top. What is that? I feel like I stepped into something really weird. At the base of this tower (that was amazingly untouched) was black crystal but it was strange, like a wave caught frozen as it attempted to take the tower but was unable to touch it.

This is just weird.

Weird-ass tower. Weird-ass crystal. The pillars all stop to encircle what I imagine the water feature moat that surrounded the area the tower was in; sunken into the ground. What was once and immaculate symmetrical park surrounded even that. But the grounds were untamed in the time it had been abandoned. The lawns now over grown with tall grass, the flower gardens all struggling with weeds, the bushes and trees had branches sticking out every which way they were supposed to. Just...This place is really giving me the creeps.

This wasn't what I was expecting at all. Other than the weird-ass gold crystal tower thing, this place looked so...normal. I was expecting something taken out of a futuristic space-age film –all metal and neon lights. But it was...warm. The morning sun tinted to world golden. This place that was shut off from the horrors of outside. But what was happening in here to make it like this? I mean excluding last night's events, no one was here. No bodies. Nothing. It's disturbing.

I want to know what that tower-thing is. I've never seen anything like it before. I want to get closer.

Another flicker in the corner of my eye and again when I turn to see it; nothing. I try and focus on moving forward again.

'Something wrong.' The tiger stops, its ears flicking to the left.

I turn my head in that direction. Nothing.

What is it?

'Something wrong.' Bad dream. Dread. Corrupt. Should not be. Should never be.

I shake my head, the tiger leaves a fuzzy feeling in my head. Or maybe that's the exhaustion..or the dehydration...or the blood loss. How the fuck am I still standing?

That was when I heard a hiss like growl and my back goes rigid. A shuffling noise, like it was carrying something too heavy to hold follows. The sound of glass rubbing against stone.

I bite my lip as I look to the left. A Hexer.

This city was infested with Hexers. Evolved Hexers to be exact. Which means that this place hass been infested for a while. At first you'd think 'zombie'.

"Zombies with super powers," I muse to myself as I see another coming up from a main street just down from the other one.

Evolved Hexers have chucks of crystal growing out of them. The first one had its entire shoulder bulging with crystal spikes and lumps, taking over its arm as a giant over-sized shiny black claw that was too big to carry normally, making it limp and drag it over the ground. The other was missing a part of its face behind a black clump and spines of crystal growing from its back in random spots. The greyish skin and freakish black veins were heavy, especially the flesh around the crystal clumps.

...I'm now understanding why there weren't any bodies...

Then...that Hexer that attacked us a few weeks ago at the farm...

I've just walked into Keystone territory...and nest.

Chapter Thirteen: Finding Heaven

Chapter Thirteen: Finding Heaven

I glance between them, pushing myself and the oversized cat to move. I didn't know where to go but the minute the Hexers charge, we're dead. Well I'm sure Mr. Tiger here can fend for itself. Actually is it a 'he' or 'she'? Aaah don't have time for this.

Keeping down the untouched streets, I could hear them growling and gasping not too far behind us. I notice as they stumble forward with a sort of clumsy grace that lets them stay in our sights; they are avoiding the crystal pillars that had come with the Miasma. If maybe we go somewhere where the pillars are at their peak...?

Is it just me or ar there more of 'em?

Agreement. The tiger beside me growls a little, trying to steer us down a narrow street that was filled with cafés and takeaway shops, pushing me just a little.

As we emerge from the street, it open up into a construction site. I feel really uneasy as we walk through the unmade building. Why aren't they attacking?

I then realise something. We were being herded towards something. Why? And where?

Steel beams and pipes jutted out from bare frames like skeletal remains, plastic flapping slightly as they hung from the naked higher floors and beams as makeshift walls. The floors were a mix of concrete slabs and rubble mixed in with red dirt.

Look above.

The tiger hits my thoughts like a train and I suddenly feel the world turning sideways as the tiger knocks me to the side in time for a Hexer to come down from a higher, unmade floor. I landed on the side of a truck in time to see the damn thing staring at me.

Well, I think it's staring. It was far more along in the transition into whatever Hexers eventually become. Its entire top half of the head no longer looked human. It was so alien, shiny and black that it did resembled a head but it was clear of any features or hair, save for a strange smooth like dome that you would swear was a giant helmet with a visor. Except that the bottom jaw was still human, the skin peeling around the embed biker helmet that was now its face. The rest of its body has become elongated and streamline, the black shiny crystal-like skin taking over its nape and its back. Actually the only thing that seemed to remain remotely human-like was the skin over the throat and over the front of the ribcage, the bones sticking out under the thinly stretched pale skin. But that skin was peeling as well. It was creepy, disgusting and I really want to get out of here.

"Sm....eh...eh," the thing gasps in a thin raspy voice like it's never been used in years. It points a long stick-like finger in my direction and I feel my blood reversing in my veins. "Deh...leh...sssh-ssh...Sme....Mu-uh-uh-sss-ssst....D re....Eh..."

I don't think I wanna even try piecing that weird ass gurgling together. I shift, earning it to step forward, its limbs were strange and long as it slightly crouches, its arms practically scraping the ground. It almost reminds me of an insect. This is really creeping me out.

The tiger, steps between us, crouching down, its shoulder blades pulled tightly together.

Run.

What?

Get away.

I stare at the tiger's back. I...I don't understand why he's going out of his way to defend me. Running away, leaving me behind to make its escape would be the more logical answer when dealing with survival. I'm nothing.

Disagreement. Dreamer is...

The combination of colours and sounds mixing in with raw pure emotion flood me to the extent that I couldn't even begin to even to comprehend what the tiger was try to say.

Go away!

With that, the tiger opens its jaw, roaring out, taking a swipe at the helmet Hexer who took a skip back and shrieks back at the tiger; both of us cringing at the noise.

Go away!

The tiger's emotion form an almost physical force that pushes me along the wall, making me take a staggering step back. I look at the tiger, unsure what to do but...my feet move again, taking me down another tiny space full of construction but too narrow for more than one person to squeeze through at a time.

I couldn't stop myself or turn around. I was going somewhere and I don't understand the pull of it either. It was a small nudge outside the Fence but now it was turning into a stronger pulse, egging me on, dogging me until I find out where it's coming from.

Squeezing over, under and through pipes, machinery and half-made buildings, I breathe hard, my limbs shaky as I look up above at the tall skyscrapers and oblisks of black crystal, trying to find some direction. The tower pointing to the clear azure sky now not too far away. I was being pulled towards the tower. Dawning on that realisation, I hear the screeching and shrieking behind me and whip my head back to see a number of them clambering after me. Including the helmet one who was far more poised and graceful than its stumbling deformed comrades. I turn back to my front, moving as fast as I could while they were still stuck back there.

I move further along until I hit a wide open slab of flat concrete area that I felt was far too exposed for my liking but it was the only space between me and the city and the park and most of all the tower. As I step forward, I see that it was in fact a roof and that the city was quite a distance far below. But I couldn't turn back, I had to walk along the edge to see if there wa a ladder or something that I could climb down.

The helmet Hexer was the first one through and as it steps out onto the roof, its feet click on the ground, stoping just at the edge of the roof and I stop, watching it slap the ground with its hands. At first nothing happened but then the solid ground below my feet began to shift and tremble. I look back at it, my jaw almost unhinged as I swear it was grinning back at me. The rumble of concrete cracking and starting to crumble made me scamper for the far side that was attached to a steep hill.

But I never made it more than two steps.

The ground beneath my feet fell away and I along with it. The rush of dust and rubble crashing beneath and all around me made me feel shut inside a tunnel of white noise. I land on something on my side first rather awkwardly as I realise that I was caught in some plastic which pulls taunt against my weight for a moment, halting me for a split second but ripped and fell away, wrapping around me and joined in my continual descent.

Finally, I hit something hard. Landing on my back, making my back arch and my breath lost as my lungs condense in my ribcage, paralysing me with shock. I...didn't feel any pain. I was beyond pain. My breath was ragged, winded, my mind clouding with the fear of not breathing. I couldn't move, it took everything to try filling my paralysed lungs.

I watch as the damn helmet landing on its feet gracefully, taking in what it's done and how it's caught me with the wind literally knocked out of me. You know, just once I would like to catch a break and it slipped and broke its neck or something.

It slowly walks towards me, taking its time as it knows I can't go anywhere. It even drags its stick fingers along the plaster boards, leaving a cutting trail, Freddy Krueger style. Oh wonderful. I grit my teeth, trying to will myself to at least attempt moving, but my body doesn't like me. Well I wouldn't either considering what I've put it through in the last 30 hours.

As it came closer to me, I hear something come crashing in from above and I have never been so relieved to see a giant glowing man-eating tiger in all my life. As it lands, it leaps towards the thing and crashes into it and both tumble to the ground. As they hiss and skriek, claws and talons and teeth biting into each other, I see the blade buried under some rubble not too far away from me. I turn onto my stomach and force myself to wriggle my way towards it.

My fingers touch the handle as I hear Mr Tiger crash and skid along the ground, landing just away from me in a daze. The helmet then lets out another shriek that I swear was making my ears bleed as it charges for me, leaping forward as I twist around, the blade now in my hands. The helmeted Hexer lands on me, impaling itself on the blade but not before its teeth sink into my shoulder.

I bite back a scream of pain and instead channel the last of my energy into pushing the blade deeper into its gut and pull up, tearing into its ribcage.

If I was going to die, then I am damn well dragging this bastard to hell with me, kicking and screaming.

As its weight was digging the handle into my gut, the tiger go to its senses and swiped the Hexer away pushing it into a far wall while biting into it, ripping the ribcage apart from the slash that I had made in the torso.

I feel like I'm in some sort of dream. My eyes and mind unable to focus on anything anymore except for one thing; I was bitten by a Hexer. The thought didn't disturb me as much as I thought it would.

My breathing seemed to have calmed down as I struggle to pull my body up. Well at least that damn Hexer saved me a trip down.

I go to sit up but something slams into my brain with enough force to stun me for a few moments. Pressing a hand to my head, I look around and saw for the first time that this building wasn't completely concrete. Thick black veins climbed along the floor, twisting through the walls and ceilings like veins choking the life out of the steel frames, getting thicker the further I look in. Squeezing my eyes tighter, I could just see that there was a passage way that led to a ramp, down to what I could only imagine to be an underground parking lot. We were in a building for parking, I realise.

With a hand on my shoulder that was now ripped open (again). I reach for the blade to steady myself as I try to stand and somehow manage to get onto my feet that felt like jelly. I was barely standing but there was no mistaking it. Down there was a Keystone.

Mr Tiger limps towards me, slowly. The thoughts it was trying to give to me were all disjointed like trying tune into a radio channel but only getting static. I reach for its head and pet him/her. "Thanks for that."

I take a shaky step forward, almost unconsciously, towards what was below.

Don –St-F-. Dark- White-A cut-off scream-Dark-Cold.

I didn't have to step far as my feet land on a slippery smooth surface and I fall down, sliding down the ramp into the darkness and I came face to face for the first time, a Keystone. It was described to me before. Cody never took it seriously, claiming it to be bullshit as no one who got close enough came back sane. But this...this...

It was...

A black mass of jagged crystal grew from the ground, reaching the far corners almost like a tree with the very centre dripping with what looked like oil, oozed onto the ground and globs creeped along the walls. The great wall of crystal spines stretched far and inked out almost everting. It all came from the ground. No. Not the ground. Just faintly, I could see something lying under the giant black mass; a small hand that resembled a child's.

Keystones were once human. This was once a child.

A/N: Hah, yes I was able to deliver as promised!

Don't forget to check out my new work Hollow Moon and tell me what you think as well! It's sort of like Vivd but they are completely unrelated

Chapter Fourteen: Numb Delirium

- -

Chapter Fourteen: Numb Delirium

I was frozen to the spot completely. It took over everything.

Everything dropped from existence around me.

It became my world.

Inane whispers penetrated my mind. They were disjointed, soft and harsh with no real focus or meaning. It was singular but many. One voice but a crowd. Together but not in chorus like they were piling on top of each other. Loud silence. Maddening. Frustrating. Never ending. Shrilled sweetness. Suffocating. Insanity. Blinded euphoria.

I push my hands harshly to my ears, blocking the aural violation.

'Make it stop'.

Something catches my sight. My vision locks onto something thick and black oozing down my arm. I bring them in front of me. I watch in horror as my flesh melts from the bone. Shaking, darkening.

'Make it stop'.

A scream rips through my throat, crackling the vocals cords, straining until I could feel them snap. Bubbling. Liquefying flesh turning black, dripping slowly like wax under the intensity of a candle wick's flame.

My sight flickers between white, red and black in a continuous loop, fraying on the edges as I feel like I'm falling through vertigo. But nothing is moving. The whispers becoming more aggressive but I still could hear them.

'Make it stop'.

Something like a bullet shots through my skull and stuns my brain into suspended animation. What was left of my arms roll to my sides as I sit there, the strings to my body cut. I was limp. Lifeless. Liquid fire tears burn my cheeks. Why? Why am I not dead?

'Make it stop'.

Why doesn't it stop? This madness.

'Make it stop'.

Over and over. Those words. Are they my words? Over and over. Shut up.

Make it stop.

Shut up.

Make it stop. Make it stop. Make it-

Shut up! Shut up-shut-up-shut-up!

Make it stop.

Make it stop.

I glare at the mass in front of me. If it's going to drag me under-

I do not know how I could grab the blade beside me but my fingers curl around the contrastingly ice-cold handle.

-then I will fight it to the last shred of sanity.

I shakily get to my feet, something metallic mixed with something disgusting pours from my mouth, pooling on the floor as a mix of red and black.

'Make it stop'.

I sprint with the blade poised straight in front of me, I yell with everything I had. I stab the blade through the middle, a piercing glass on glass contrast ringing out. At first nothing happens. Frustration makes me see red as I drop the blade, clawing and punching at the giant pile of crystal, the jagged edges bite into my flesh. I punch harder, not caring anymore if my fists turn into a bloody pulp, the bones broken and crushed beyond recognition. I don't care anymore. Just shut the fuck up.

Tendrils of that darkness explodes from the centre climbing my arms as I struggle against it. The black liquid consumes my body as I sink to the floor. The oozing darkness swallows me, enveloping me like it was going to eat every bit of me as it drags me under. I struggle under the weight, still trying to get at the crystal. If it's attacking then that means that I'm making some sort of progress.

I gasp, as the slime climbs my neck, entering my lips. The same taste as before. It overruns my mouth, choking me as it still climbs further to my eyes that I shut tight. I feel myself sink into the darkness.

'Make it stop.'

Oh my god. You're still going on about that? Shut up already.

'Make it stop.'

...You're really a broken record. Can't you just be quiet long enough for me to die?

'It hurts so much.'

What does?

'It just won't stop. I scream and scream out over and over but- not listening.'

Probably because you won't shut up.

'Keep going. Keep going.'

Can't you continue the self-monologue after I die?

'Why does that light not fade?'

I'll take that as a 'no'.

'Those who hear me change. Change into something else. It doesn't stop. Always on and on. The light is still there...never stop. Not stopping.'

Like your speech apparently. Hang on... are these the thoughts of the Keystone?

I feel myself stir a little like I was sleeping submerged underwater.

'Every sun rising. Every moon setting. I wait. Wait. Wait. Take the light. That warm light. Wait. Wait.'

"Why?" I feel myself say.

The darkness freezes. 'Why?' It stops for a moment, almost contemplating my words. 'Wait. Wait. Day. Night. Wait. Wait. Change. Change. Change.'

I grit my teeth, "You're really running off your mouth aren't you?"

'Change...light. There is light. Give it to me. That warm light. Feels nice. Extinguish it. Smells nice. It's mine.'

I felt something squeeze down on my throat as the darkness slides down further. This really is a shit day. I'm being strangled and drowned, it's not comforting. Coughing, I struggling against the darkness. How am I supposed to fight something if it's everywhere? Surrounding and transparent like mist but thick like mud?

'Mine. The dreams are mine!'

"Enough," my voice was strange. Irritation bubbles up through my chest. More than fear. More than any other emotion that could flicker through my spectrum, I have had enough.

"You keep going on and on about yourself. All this shit about tainting light and shit. The need to be saved. Fine."

I saw it. A small flicker in the middle of all this muck. I poise my arm to reach for it the next time it appears.

'On and on. Give it to me! You are mine!'

There! I strike forward, my fingers straight as I reach for it.

My hand slips through something solid, the darkness gasps in surprise and recoils from my body, twitching as if it was dying painfully.

The darkness weakens and slips away, revealing what I had struck. It was buried deeply into someone's chest cavity, right through to the other side. Staring right back at me was some who couldn't be more than two years younger than me. I look at my arm and back up at him, my brain unable to process what's happening.

"Wh-wh..."

"Thank you." Blood starts to appear from the corner of his mouth. I do a double take as he's smiling, relief colouring his angelic features. Soft blonde curls covered more of his face, his big bottle green eyes glowing against his pale skin.

The darkness disappears around us, revealing a white room. A box with only four clear white walls. No doors. No windows. A smooth stone floor. And we are in the very centre.

"...You're the one that called me here," I state.

His smile doesn't falter, "...Yes. I call out, hoping you would hear me. ...But I forgot why until you...saved me."

I stare back, unable to move, a question escapes my throat before I could stop myself, "You have never thought of saving yourself?"

"There's no way back."

I glance around. He was right. It's a big white box.

"How did you get here?"

"I...always came here when it hurt. It was safe and away from everything but now...now I can't go back."

I frown. Am I causing that pain now?

He shakes his head, "The others. Before. They kept injecting stuff into me. Do tests...endless pain. Always. Always. They never let me sleep."

"Who?"

"I..." pain and hazy confusion flickers across his face. "I-I c-can't...I'm sorry," he whispers.

I shake my head, unable to supress my own sad smile, "It's ok." I've just killed him and now I'm demanding answers? Am I an idiot?

"You're...a strange one."

Gee thanks. "I've been told that a lot."

"...You shouldn't be here."

What? Inside this weird mind room? Is this what Anne see when she peaks into someone's head?

"I'm sorry," he mumbles again.

"Why are you apologising?"

"It's my fault."

I frown. I don't see how.

"I'm sorry...I...don't know why. But I can't remember a lot of this. My memories are hard to comprehend or grasp but I know it is my fault."

"I don't think so."

The sadness in his smile doesn't shift. "Thank you. But..."

I feel him reach for my free hand.

I feel a shock tingle through my fingers as his entwine with mine.

"You're...not like us...I'm happy. I can...let go. I was afraid but...you're here. I can finally let go."

"You said that-"

"I can't return. But I'm tired. So tired. Too much pain. Never ending. But you can end me. You...already have...I've waited so long."

How can he smile?

"Because you came. Because you made me realise that I can escape. Made me remember."

"Remember?' my voice cracks.

"Yep. You can't even imagine the relief I felt."

His free hand touches my arm that is piercing him. "You can hear them.. .you are them. You are what we shouldn't be."

"You're not making any sense." There's something strange about my arm. And I don't mean its imbedded in this guy's chest...

"Don't be afraid. I'm...sorry." As he whispers those words, his body begins to disintegrate, disappearing right before my eyes.

"Wait! Name. What's your name?"

He falters for a second, "...I...can't remember." But the smile returns, "But that's ok. You...got to see me like this as well. At least you can remember what I used to look like."

And he was gone. I collapse to my knees.

Like Markus.

Like Anne.

Like Cody.

Again. I can't take this anymore.

I'm left alone in the little white room as it fades away around me.

Chapter Fifteen: Spiralling Void

A/N: ...Ok, last chapter was a bit morbid but I did have some time to do a double update for the long weekend (becasue I'm avoiding my assingments to the last second).

Chapter Fifteen: Spiralling Void

I open heavy eyelids to the sound of fighting and roaring around me. They open to the world that I was in before. The hard cold concrete against my cheek attested to that. I could feel something in my hand. Looking in front of me, I see I was holding a hand that wasn't much smaller than mine. The only thing that remained remotely human of the Keystone. A kid who couldn't even remember his own name. The rest of his body was nothing more than a split open rag of skin. Black veins, now shrivelled up poured out of the skin rag, crossing the ground and the walls like dying vines.

I hold back everything. I remember it all. He was trapped in his own world because someone turned his body into something that he couldn't call his own anymore. Mutilated. They destroyed it. I've really had enough.

Mr Tiger's roar drew my attention as I realise that there was a full on Hexer army surrounding him. Apparently taking a holiday is out of the question. I struggle to my feet, seeing that the tiger was struggling to protect me. I don't know how long I've left him all on his own. But he looks exhausted, battered and ready to fall over in a heap any second. I manage to just raise myself. Why? Why can't they just leave us alone already?

Emotion bubbled in my chest, rising but caught in my throat, making my eyes and nose feel congested. It hurts.

Can't I be left alone for five fucking minutes? Fuck!

A sudden impact rocked the world as dust and debris flung out around us, allowing the pale morning light to filter through the dust and snow slowing falling around us. Everything stopped as we all look at the centre of this...what? Meteorite that managed to land in front of me and the tiger, taking out a good number of Hexers.

In the middle of all this was a slumped over carcass of a small Wyrm, leaning in from the hole, the rest of the body still arching in from outside. Well when I say 'small', I mean it was the size of a semi –trailer. Where the fuck did it come from? Black blood poured from the mouth cavity and the deep cuts that wracked most of its body. Something beside it moved, I caught a glimpse of white gold that moved like lightning, disappearing like a figment of my imagination.

I mentally groan. What now?

That was when I realise that the Hexers suddenly go in a panic as white gold flash through them, taking them all out, cracking through their crystal encased bodies like brittle glass until none were left. I look up to feel my jaw drop as the white gold lightning came to a sudden stop in front of me. Mismatch quicksilver and burning gold eyes stare back at me. X.

I feebly reach for the blade that was (still fucking) beside me, raising it at him, even though I knew it was pointless.

A small grin and an amused grunt escapes his lips before he crashes to his knees, blood spurting from his mouth as he coughs and chokes, falling to his side in a crumpled heap.

I sat there, too shocked to move. I notice that he was fully covered in wounds, all deep gashes and his breathing was slowing down.

Is he dead?

Fading.

Ah and here I was missing Mr. Tiger in my head. I scramble my way towards him and place a hand to his wrist, then his neck. My eyes widen in shock as his pulse was getting so weak that his heart was going to stop any second.

"No…" I breathe as I press an ear to his chest. It stopped.

"No. No. No." I quickly move to place my hands on his sternum to do CPR. "Can't die," I feel I was going to lose it if he dies as well. I can't…I can't take it anymore. It'll destroy me if he's gone as well. No more. No more. I've had it. I'm tired of sitting on my ass and watching everyone else fight and protect me because I'm so fucking useless.

A wet drop falls onto X's coat and I realise I was crying and panicking. In this state I wouldn't be able to save him. I press my ear to his chest. Nothing. My hands move to cup his face.

Please.

Anything.

Anything at all.

I'll do anything.

Just-

A burning sensation crosses my cheek and all over my body. My bones feel like they're snapping as I hold tightly to his face as the world stops spinning. Red drops mix in with my tears. The scratch across X's cheek...its closing up like it never happened. Perfectly clean, unblemished skin, there wasn't even a scar.

My eyes widen in shock. I...if I'm doing that...please. Just please...even if I die. Save him.

My body jolts as a sting pricks at my gut. Looking down, I see X had punched something into me. His hand moves, letting me see the glass dart-flask that had gotten Cody protruding from my stomach. I look back at his face in shock. His eyes were wide open and intensely staring at me.

He's awake...Then, he's ok. That's good.

The world fades, becoming fuzzy as my focus no longer holds and neither does my body. I feel myself fall but never feel the impact as I fall into a deep sleep that I half hope I never wake from.

<<<<<<<>>>>>>><<>><<>>><<<<<<>>>>>>

The sound of a van is the only thing ringing out in the still midday sun of a long dead city. Coming up to the entrance of a car parking lot, the team moved in with as much haste as possible. He disappeared during the middle of the storm, only to wind up in Section 1.4.2 of the second district. Fenir looks at the tracker system one more time to check. How he ended up in the path of a Keystone, anyone could guess. But they needed to pull him out before the saturation becomes toxic.

They pull up just outside the second level, ready for the worst. With gas masks on, Fenir moves the team out with hand signals. They needed to be careful in this type of area. A nest is never a good place to land.

And that idiot had to land smack bang in the middle of it all.

He glances over his shoulder, motioning for Hanna to move in first. She was the only one who could help him if he needs a 'kickstart'.

Hanna moves forward, taking the lead. She checks the monitors and blinks in surprise, saturation was lower than 15%. This has never happened before. She taps the small device, just to make sure but nothing changes. That's impossible. Alphas have been sighted here before. Perfect scions can only form from a Queen body.

Fenir notices Hanna's confusion, tapping her on the shoulder. She needs to refocus. They weren't here for her little science exploitations. They needed to recover the Monster before he goes berserk. She nods to him, showing she understood and stepped forward, eyes still on the monitor. The saturation radiation didn't climb as she got closer to the Nest.

And she was itching to know why.

Fenir rolled his eyes as she steps forward. Shaking his head, he looked back at Rain and Mist. Both were wait in position with black bullets in case a freaking army of Black Beasts decide to greet them. If the Monster forgot some. He normally didn't, he was very thorough when it concerns his own kind.

<>\<<>><>

Hanna makes her way up a ramp, noticing the clear signs of a Keystone taking root long enough to become a Queen. The veins covering the floor and ceiling and any walls within reach. Climbing like vines, thick enough that they were climbing on top of each other, leaving not spaces, feeling like she was entering some weird organic chamber. But the veins were dead. The crystal clustering has even become brittle. This…was impossible. Ever for X, he has never been able to get close to a Queen, let alone touch one to destroy it.

Is…is it possible for a Keystone to implement an ordered death? No. She understood the programming enough to know that a Queen cannot terminate its own role. Then an Alpha? It's true Alphas carry the capacity to become a Queen but it would need time to take root and establish the Nest. But that's inconclusive. Alphas and their scions aren't pure copies and take longer to fully transmute. Some of the Lesser stop formation altogether. Besides, she has never heard of a Nest killing its own Queen. She felt a small thrill in her stomach. She was about to see something interesting. Oh and of course X. He probably needs some medical attention.

Bracing herself, she was ready to see a destroyed Keystone for the first time.

The shattered remains of the Keystone scion were scattered about like discarded sand. X's doing no doubt. She was a little annoyed that maybe just once he could leave a complete carcass for her to examine. Next, there was a body of a juvenile Wyrm taking up a giant hole in the middle of the ceiling. Both probably X again.

"Hanna," a weak voice calls her attention down to the front.

She blinks, realising that it was X. But he was holding onto someone. Frowning, she steps closer and realises that it was an unconscious boy who could have only been about sixteen.

She knees down to take his pulse. They said that this city was abandoned. No human could be here. …Unless, this was an Outsider who was too curious for his own good.

"Can I call the radio silence off?" Hanna looks back at X. He was fine. This was the most stable she has seen him post-'killing everything in sight'.

He nods, staring back down at the boy who he seems quite interested in. Which is unusual in and of itself.

Tapping the ear piece, she opens the radio-way, "Fenir, it's safe. The levels of saturation are still low and stable. The Nest has been destroyed."

"Roger. Stay there, we'll bring up the van. Is Monster ok?"

"He's stable but there is someone with him and he's not going to last much longer if we don't get him to a Station in the next twenty minutes."

X stands, pulling the boy up in his arms easily enough like he was cradling a toddler.

She glowered at his in-human strength.

"We don't have that sort of luxury," Fenir grumbles over the radio.

She rolls her eyes, "Then it's lucky that the Tower's still functioning, isn't it?"

"You will need to bring another," X, who rarely opens his mouth, spoke. His voice was something alluring in and of itself.

"Huh?" Hanna took a moment to register what he just said.

He motions towards a giant black tiger with glowing blue stripes.

"Is...is that what I think it is?" Hanna could feel herself tremble. If that's what she thinks it is, she will forgive X for all the misgivings he's ever given her. She could kiss him. If she could dissect the Lunar-

"Do not kill it," X warns. If it were anyone else, it would sound like a plea but this was X. It was a demand. And when he demands, it becomes an order.

She pouts, "Why!? Here I was going to love you forever and now you're telling me not to touch it?"

His mismatch eyes harden. His face showed no emotion.

She sighs, "Alright. Fine. But let me at least examine it."

He made no motion or comment that he heard or cared for what she said. Which meant she had better do as she was told.

A/N: Hmm...I decided to try a bit of third person POV while Kae's (finally) out. This is actually my normal writing style but for some reason I'm prefering to write in first person.

Ahem. Thank you everyone who has been reading thus far :)

Chapter Sixteen: Call me a Liar

Chapter Sixteen: Call me a Liar

His fingers trace along the black tattoo-like marking on the right side of the boy's face. He traces it down to his neck, stopping where the thin blanket covered the rest of his lithe body, and back up again to the bruising and cuts that were a mix of red, blue and purple. It was almost as if X was in a fixated trance, fulfilling the need to permanently embed the boy's sleeping features into his memory.

His fingers linger on a tiny scar that just clipped the left eyebrow. It was older than many of the other scars that painted his body and almost faded completely. As X's fingers shift some of his hair, dampened by sweat out of his eyes, the boy moves slightly in his sleep. He looked as though this was the first time in a long time since he had any proper sleep.

X could feel the presence of everyone within this clinic without much effort and knew that he was being watched, not that he particularly minded or cared. He slightly shifts his gaze in the general direction of the opened door that let in the only source of light to this dark room. The youngest of the group, Mist, was staring in from the side of the ajar door, appearing as though she hoped that she was hiding, though even without his enhanced senses, her shadow draped in and fully gave her away.

Mist then jumps at a voice behind her, "How's he doing?" Hanna smiles.

X looks up, unsurprised to see her there. His interest was lacking in her presence and he went back to look at the boy, not caring to answer or acknowledge her any further. He had no reason to respond.

Hanna did not seem to mind as she steps closes to him, Mist shadowing behind her. "His vitals are strong, despite what he's been though." She tapped a holographic screen that suddenly appeared beside her, dousing the room in a soft blue glow. Her fingers tapping away.

See. No reason to answer such a question that she herself knew the answer to or could acquire such knowledge without his verbal input. X could feel and hear the heartbeats of those around him. Hanna, steady and sure, her excitement was sated. For now. Mist, quicker because she was caught and a natural nervousness that she has.

"This boy has no registration, so he is definitely from the outside, not of the city." Ah he could feel the excitement bubbling up in Hanna once again. Precarious curiosity this woman has.

Registration. Such an irritating concept. Those who were inside the Fences were all digitally registered and genetically marked like pets. All their data, right down to their sleeping patterns were monitored constantly. X naturally wasn't. Who would acknowledge that a monster existed inside the walls? Especially one they created? No one. No one wants to admit their dirty little secrets. Certainly not one this dirty.

"Oh I do hope he wakes up. Imagine the information I could record. Living outside to the constant exposure of Lunar Radiation...fascinating!"

X could see Mist frown just a little, "But what if he wakes up all...you know..."her voice a whisper.

"Crazy?" Hanna asks lightly. "It would be unfortunate but no sample is unwanted to me. Any and all information is invaluable. No matter what form it takes."

"You should be putting him down, not extending his miserable existence." Fenir's voice bounces around the dark room, his shadow taking up most of the limited light. Rain, not far behind him.

Hanna snorts, "If I wanted your opinion, I'd ask." She then flicks the holographic screen and it disappear into thin air. She then brings up another two and taps away again, her eyes shifting between them rapidly, not missing a beat.

"This is not about your wishes, Doc. This is about you risking our lives."

"Oh piss on that solider-boy."

"You said that he was bitten."

"Yes, the shards are consistent with that of an Alpha." She motions with a finger at the boy's shoulder with the puncture wounds lining it.

"So there is no way he isn't infected."

"...That is still hard to determine."

"What do you mean by that?"

Hanna sighs, "There haven't been any progressive changes since he's been here."

"And what do you call that?" He points towards the marking lining the side of his face that traveled down the side of his neck and below the blanket. But Hanna knew what he was really referring to.

"Unknown."

Fenir growls at her.

"Easy, tiger. I still haven't been able to figure it out yet and I'm not about to make assumptions. Who knows what happens to those on the Outside.

"You confirmed he was bitten by a Hexer."

"Yes. I did. What of it?"

"Then he will be wolfing-out, foaming at the mouth and killing all of us in sight."

"We have X for that," she looks up at X with a big wolfish grin. "Don't we, X?"

X just stares at her.

Hanna was used to his clear lack of responses. Her humor was lost a little as she continues, "But it's this that has me concerned." She flicks a holographic screen around to face Fenir. The graphs and data lost on him. But the bullet wound magnified was clear on the screen.

"What about it?"

"...It's consistent with the ReX markers...however-"

"What? If anything he should be more than well on his way to being a Black Beast or Hexer or whatever, what else is there to know? We should just put him down now. It'll save us a hassle and put him out of his misery. He'll thank you for it."

"Would you shut up for five seconds? This is why I hate you military-types. Always going by your 'gut instincts' before actually understanding any-thing and then go 'whoops' when it blows up in your face.-"

"That 'gut instinct' has saved your ass more than once. Don't come looking for me again when you're stuck." Fenir glances at the kid, "I feel sorry for him. I do. But he will be in pain. Not to mention he's far from human anymore. There is a high chance that when he wakes, it's not going to be some lost little puppy. It'll be a monster that will kill every single one of us. I'd rather kill it before it kills us." He begins moving for a weapon in his jacket.

Hanna's slams down her fist beside the unconscious teenager, causing the monitors to flicker red in alarm and the lights to switch on in the room. She was not going to have this discussion again, "I'm still in-charge ex-solider boy. I say 'jump', you are to respond 'how high?' Got it? What I say goes. My word is law. If you don't like that then you are welcome to exit the room. I don't need your input at this point in time. Go shoot something if you're bored."

Fenir stares her down but she no sign of backing off meekly. Eventually he blinks, turning away and removed himself from the room growling, "Then at least have him restrained."

"Good boy," Hanna muttered under her breath, going back to the monitors. The room revealed to be simple and blandish white with a white table-like contraption in the centre that the human subject was rested upon. This was what was referred to as a Station. Simply lying on it can determine ones physical status and could administer basic aid when required. This included clotting blood and sealing wounds without the need for bandages.

Rain looks back at Hanna after Fenir was long gone, "As you were saying?"

"Oh hmm?"

"The bullet wound? He was in the middle of a war, you'd expect a few holes. He's got burns, grazes and whatever else. One wound shouldn't matter."

Hanna shoves a piece of loose blonde hair back behind her ear, unable to look him in the eye directly, "ReX."

Rain remains silent.

"It...was what they were concocting when this mess started."

"You mean..."

Everyone glances at X for a moment.

"Similar situation but completely different strain and structure. ReX causes the body to rapidly take to the changes in structure that form the crystalline fragmentation of the DNA. That splintering overturns into a cancerous state."

"And eventually makes a Queen." Mist's voice was quiet.

"You mean...those things aren't..." Rain blinks, unable to believe them.

"There was more than one research group playing around, you know. Or rather, still at play, I should say," Hanna states matter-of-fact.

"So...he's turning into a Queen?" Rain frowns.

"That's just it. The wound is identical to the pattern displayed when the ReX bullets are used but...there is no bullet to speak of."

"How...?"

"Could his body have absorbed the ReX strain then?" Mist tries to wrap her head around it.

"No...the pure strain of ReX isn't in his system. Same with the fragments embedded in his shoulder from the Alpha. His body hasn't absorbed or adapted to it at all, like it's rejecting it to the point of ignoring it completely," Hanna explains.

"That's-"

"Unheard of. I know," Hanna goes back to looking at the screen.

"Then where's the bullet?" Rain asks.

"No way to know," Hanna shakes her head.

"...And the markings?"

"I'm still waiting on the results. At most all I can do is keep him alive. It's already taken a while to read the ReX markers. I have to be absolutely sure."

Chapter Seventeen: Fragmented Dreamscape

Chapter Seventeen: Fragmented Dreamscape

The alarms sound out in distinct screams. White walls now drenched in flashing red of the warning sirens, singing their song of alarm.

Rain looks up at Mist, who in turn looked back just as confused as he felt. They stood from the table, leaving their meals and conversation behind, completely abandoned as the noise drowned it. They both knew that the siren could only be coming from one area. The boy.

Rain frowns, grabbing his weapon by the door. He knew the Doc didn't want harm to come to this new 'plaything' of hers but their safety still came first. X may be able to destroy it in a second, but you never know and Rain would never forgive himself if anything ever happened to Mist.

As they come down the passageway, leading into the actual clinic where they housed the boy, Rain saw the Doc quickly streaming down from another hallway, meeting up with them instantly.

"What's happening?" Rain asks.

"I think he's awake. Isn't it exciting!?"

The worst thing is, that was a serious question.

As they come closer to the room, Rain notices the sudden drop in temperature. Their breaths now visible as clouds, mingling with the air.

"Stay back," Hanna barks at them before continuing down the hall.

"What's going on?" Mist shivers behind Rain.

"...Don't know." Rain's his eyes were fixated on the glass in front of him that was now completely covered in ice and beginning to fracture. The sirens suddenly cut off, like someone had pulled a switch.

Hanna stands in front of the door, frozen to the spot, her eyes wide.

Rain touches Mist's wrist, telling her to stay back. Mist nods, shivering completely now as the temperature still lowers.

He comes forward, to check on the doctor but as he does, he looks in to see the room completely transformed. The air was deadly still. Clear fragments that look like glass was suspended, floating in the air slowly as if in a dreamy sleep. The clear bright ice flicked out around the room, suspend in a ripple that clung to the walls. All glass was fracturing, crying out in small shrieks of dismay as the fractures slowly climbed higher but never actually shattering.

In the middle of all this was X. He stood with his back to them, blocking them from seeing the room properly. But as Rain stepped closer, Hanna's arm snaps out, stopping him from stepping into the room. "Not yet," she whispers.

Rain looks at her for a moment, then back at X. Whatever was happening in there...he didn't know. All he knew was that something happened and it didn't sound good. ...Maybe Fenir was right. They should have put that boy out of his misery.

Rain slightly shift, seeing that X was reaching out towards something. Was it the kid?

Mist comes up beside him, letting out a squeak of surprise. He looks at her then at what she was looking at. The kid was up, sitting bolt straight up on the Station. His eyes held no life in them. But that wasn't what shocked Mist. The markings had grown, like a living thing. Thicker, darker and more vine like marks growing over his right side. The right eye was also completely inked in black, save for the glowing yellow iris staring dead ahead.

This kid wasn't human.

<><><><><><><><><><><><><>

I shouldn't be here.

Why shouldn't I be here?

A massive expanse of white was spilled out around me like a barren tundra wasteland. The sky and earth was hard to distinguish was both were pale white shades of bone and ash. Light snow slowly fell around me, enhancing the quiet.

A single, snow-covered tree was in the distance, marring the perfect white with its contrasting black body. But I liked it. I remember this place. It was...Where am I?

I frown. I've been here before. Anne was just born. I remember that. Where is she? At the house with Mum. We came here for a holiday one year. Cody was off with Dad, learning how the ski. I wondered off from the holiday house, looking for them and found this lonely tree.

But the tree shouldn't be here.

I don't understand.

It isn't this tree. This tree shouldn't be here.

Then which tree should be here?

Not this one.

...very helpful. Almost as bad as...who...?

Where is Cody? ...Why isn't Markus here? Markus wasn't born yet. But he should be here now.

Something rose up in in front of my eyes, making me jump back in surprise. Our house was now gone. The fires and screams echo around me in a vacuum. Blood splattered over me, drenching the snow is pristine red.

What?

I look down at my hands. Thick trickles of blood stained them. Looking up, I see someone shouting out at me but I couldn't make out their face or what they were telling me.

This isn't real.

No. It was real.

But it's messed up.

Dreams are always messed up.

Is this a dream?

Silence.

Where are Markus, Anne and Cody?

The air around me shifts and the world suddenly dropped from under my feet and I fell into a world coated in dejected darkness. The air squeezes from my lungs, making me collapse to my knees, struggling for breath. It felt like tar. It closed in over my windpipe.

Gone was the fire and snow. Now was total darkness and pure pain running thorough my brain, splitting it in half. I cling to my head. This...isn't me. I shouldn't be here. Something pricks into me. Flashes of white cloth. Pain. Blood. Longing for death. I was in a lab. I was hooked up to something. Wires...computer...flashes of coloured lines flick across my vision. Urgh I don't know this place. I don't know these images. But they are scary and make me feel so small and helpless. Why aren't I dead? Why aren't I dead? Why am I still...

These aren't all my thoughts...they are getting weaker.

"You shouldn't linger here."

That voice...I don't know it.

Something's touching my face. It's soft and warm. Familiar. Safe. Longing.

Is not safe. Not for Dreamer to be. Not Dreamer's dream.

Mr Tiger...

Suddenly it hit me. Like a bullet to the brain. Markus is gone. Anne and Cody are missing. I have to find them.

"It isn't real," the voice is now more intense, drowning out this horrible world I accidently fell into.

I blink and suddenly everything disappeared. Then in front of me, his thumb stroking my cheek as if to soothe me, was X. His bright intense mismatched eyes, falling on me completely.

I blink again. What the hell? I don't remember this place. Why is there ice everywhere?

His fingers touching my face felt like electricity, moving under my skin, searing it to the point that my bones ached. What the hell is that? I jolt from his touch, flying backwards off of some table I was apparently on, and came crashing to the floor in shock. I smacked my head pretty hard. I look up at him, seeing him staring fixedly at his fingers that were only just touching me a moment ago. I thought that I might have hurt his feelings as I had retreated from his touch. But instead, he was...fascinated by something.

Hearing someone laugh from the doorway distracted me from that weird feeling and why X was even here in the first place. Looking over there I see this blonde lady looking at me rather amused. With a boy staring pointedly at me and a girl beside him was hiding her face, blushing.

I look down at myself and realise I'm naked.

Quickly locating a blanket, I rapidly wrap it around myself, really wanting to disappear right now. I just flashed everyone. Great. Way to leave a lasting impression. 'Hi. I'm just your friendly neighbourhood flasher'. Shit.

The blonde lady suddenly comes closer and I move backwards, as far from her reach as possible. But I suddenly hit a wall of ice with nowhere to go.

"Oh come now. I'm not gonna bite you," she grins, still amused with the way I'm acting. "I might nibble though."

So not making me feel at ease here.

"Ok. Ok. Let's start with the basics. I'm Hanna. This bundle of sunshine is X. Those two twins at the door are Rain and Mist...and the cranky one behind them is Fenir. Don't mind him, He just forgets to eat his greens."

I wasn't the only one who was surprised to see that big bulky man behind Rain and Mist as the pair jump into the room. Fenir also has a gun pointed directly at me.

"Put that away," Hanna manages to growl rather scarily at Fenir without looking away or losing that smile on her face.

"He's a threat to all of us."

"Ignore him, please." She smiles sickly sweet at me still.

I'm really uncomfortable here...

Then a thought hit me. "Where is the tiger?" I quickly ask, my voice was raspy and it hurt my throat, like I've been screaming at the top of my lungs for a few hours.

Hanna looks at me like I was a plant that could suddenly talk. "Oh wow," then she was on me with a touch and pulling at my face and jaw, ignoring my personal-space rights. "All his signs are normal. Blood pressure and heart rate are normal. Oh fascinating! There is no sign of the cancerous splintering in his system at all. The Lunar radiation doesn't seem to affect him whatsoever."

"Ra-radiation? Get that out of my face-Ow! Waaah! Crazy lady! Wait-" I try to move away from the overly-touchy-grabby lady. "Can you stop for a second!? Hang on!" I pull away from her, putting my hands up and realise that my right arm for the first time.

My right arm is black and smooth, like onyx. A few scales illuminated against the pale light. My nails have become thick talon-like pieces of darkness, the very tips a milky white (like some weird ass version of a French-tip. Shut up, I know what they are because Anne forced me to paint her nails once.). I shakily touch the skin. It was soft but the random scales were hard and smooth. My palm still felt like my hand but it was still foreign to touch. What is this? The dark scaled arm ended just at my elbow, fading back to my original pale skin but thick tattoo like vine markings ran up my arm and along my shoulder until I could see where it ended. I...What am I? What is this?

This isn't my arm.

Chapter Eighteen: Hello Kitty

A /N: Hey-o

So I managed to pump this chapter out...sorry for the long wait. My life is in turmoil right now, so I'm gonna warn everyone now, I do not know when I'm going to be able to update anything for another few months. I may have a sporadic update here or there but I will mostly be unable to do any of it until i get this mofo of a degree finished. I am in the home stretch! FINALLY!!!! so my proper updates may not happen again until...maybe December...ish

Hopefully by then, I have enough breathing space to look at my other poor works that i still have yet to continue...or start... (□(□)□)

ahem, anyway thank you for all the support! and I do hope that i can continue to amuse you with my works

----

Chapter Eighteen: Hello Kitty

The bowl of...orange stuff sat in front of me as I stare at it without being able to work up my salivating reflex. To be honest, it isn't really appealing, especially with that big grumpy guy glaring at me through the window to my 'cell'.

If looks could kill...

I switch my gaze back to the slop in front of me. Crazy lady said that I had to finish it before I could even considering see Mr Tiger ever again. So she's playing the 'blackmail game'. I glare at the spoon beside the bowl, going to pick it up with my left hand, a little awkward as I'm right-handed. But I don't want to even look at that right appendage at the moment. I was allowed to dress (finally) after much grumbling about only having a sheet to cover myself. That crazy doctor finally gave in after laughing so hard at my dismay. So I was given a shirt, hoodie and some track pants that I assumed originally belonged to the boy called Rain. He didn't seem to like me much either.

I look up to make sure the grumpy old man was still trying to gain the ability to incinerate me with a look. And sure enough I met his dark eyes...when was the last time he blinked? Does he even have eyelids?

I see his jaw twitch a little and take it as a cue to stop looking. I look around the room instead. It was removed anything warm or of substance, expect for that table thing (Doc called it a Station) and the most cold seat and desk that I am currently sitting at right now. And it was all devoid of colour. Just white. I was forced in here a few days ago. The other room I woke up in was still that weird ice thing. I don't really know what was happening and when I ask the crazy blonde doctor she just shrugs at me and says that it was me. How...?

I shake myself of the thought. I didn't get anywhere trying to think about it for the past few days. Why would I now? No...the only thing I can do is eat this...whatever it is- and see if the tiger is still in one piece after crazy blonde lady has been alone with him since I've been knocked out.

It's been trying, to say the least. Every single bone and muscle hurts when I move. Just thinking about picking up the spoon makes my muscles twinge in pain. Sucking it up, I move the spoon into the thick...creamy...? Substance and awkwardly raise the spoon to my mouth...it tasted strange. Like fake pumpkin and powder-it was awful. I drop the spoon back down, while trying to swallow. I pull a face staring at the bowl, how is she expecting me to finish this?

"Heya, Big Guy!"

I jump as the door opens and blonde doctor was suddenly there. She walks up smoothly to the table, "How's it going? Eating?"

"It's awful," I mutter.

She chuckles, "Yep, it's not really made for taste. Rather it's easy on the stomach and high in nutrients that you seriously need. You've lost a tonne and a half of blood and bruised from head to toe. I'd give you a streak burger with extra-large fries and onion rings but we are low on real food I'm afraid." Then she added as an afterthought, "That and your body wouldn't be able to handle anything intense until we get you hydrated again. Small steps. I can see in your overall health check that you do not eat regularly anyway, so even if you weren't thrown around like a rag-doll in that battlefield, you would still be in the position you're in now. Minus the rainbow colours your body has taken."

"Oh wonderful."

She pats me on the back, "So, finish this bowl and we can go see your little friend."

I glower at her and the bowl.

"Hey, I could have given you a proper potion of this. You only have another two spoonful's to go. Or do you want me to spoon-feed you? You made the deal with me. A litre of water and three spoons of this for you to meet your tiger."

I glared at the bowl and try again. The sooner I get this over with, the better.

"Didn't expect you to be a picky eater."

I mumble, "Me neither." But there was just something about this fake food that rubs me the wrong way completely.

She must have noticed at how awkward I was holding the spoon, "You're right-handed aren't you?"

I ignore her as I lift the spoon to my mouth. Urgh it's not even in my mouth yet and I can already taste it again.

As I'm about to put the damn spoon in my mouth, a presence suddenly appeared near us and I jump, looking up at the mismatch eyes that seem. ..almost dead as they regard the scene in front of him.

The Doc chuckles, "You would be awesome in a jump-scare video."

"Jump-scare...?" what kinda thing is that?

But she ignored my ignorance, "Hello X. What brings you up here today?"

X continues to stare at me and then looks over at the Doc. And as usual, says nothing.

Doc shrugs, before looking back at me, "Come on, trooper. Two more mouthfuls and you're gold."

I wanted to mutter something unintelligible under my breath, but with the way that big all guy...Fenir, was staring at me still, I thought better of it.

Finally taking my last awkward mouthful of orange crap, I put the spoon back down while swallowing.

"The look on your face..." Hanna looked as though she was on the verge of cry-laughing. "Ah, I want a camera."

I feel rather miffed. Instead, I make sure that the hood was firmly over my head and the sleeve was covering the thing I have to call my right-arm.

"Alrighty, as promised, we'll go meet your little kitty-cat. Let's see you standing." She motions with her arms. As I stood, she nods in approval, "Good, you're still a little wobbly but you are a bit steadier on your feet."

I couldn't meet anyone's eyes, staring at the floor.

"Ok, let's hustle!"

Ok. Is it just me or is this doctor waaay too enthusiastic.

She basically marches up to the door, where Fenir was now in the way.

"Move yo-ass," Doc shoves a pointed finger at his chest.

His arms are extremely burly. Like they're about to burst out of the sleeves at any moment as he crosses them over his chest. "I am not permitting this."

"Move it, Boulder."

"Please, Hanna," his voice is sounding kinda desperate there.

"No. Move it." She protest and he eventually exhales, moving to the side. She looked back at him, "Look, if you're that untrusting of him, you can come along and bring the tranqs." She then continued on down the hallway, not waiting for his response.

I glare at her back. Since when have I been downgraded to a psyco badger with rabies?

Just as I was about to follower out of the room, I hear something that makes me stop.

"Denying what is a part of you, will be denying what is all of you."

"Huh?" I stare at X, who was gazing at the wall.

His eyes slid over to me before walking passed, as if dismissing the entire conversation that we weren't even having.

That guy is so confusing. I shake my head and follow after him. And of course, the moment I took one step out of the room, Burly Big-Arms took a steo in behind me, with a gun at the ready to shoot me in the back of the head. And I do not think they were tranq bullet either. I look up at the ceiling, half praying that he wasn't trigger-happy. But, I think he was looking for me to give him any excuse to end me.

But strangley, I don't hate him for it. Scared half to death, yes...but nothing else.

"I've put the tiger subject down in the stroage," Hanna calls over her shoulder before coming up to a big metal door that looked like it'd take three people to lift the bar that went across it that secured it in place.

"Why on Earth did you go and do that?' Fenir asks, a little annoyed.

"Because I got sick of the claw marks all over the walls. At least, in here the walls are reinforced. Help me open it, would you kind sir?"

Fenir grumbles before walking up to the door and opened the hinge-lock by twisting the handle of the bar one way before I hear and audible click and he then pushed the bar up with relative ease. As it opens, I hear the Tiger making almost coughing noises.

"Go on in," Hanna made a rolling motion with her wrist.

I step up to the doorway.

"Are you sure this is a good idea?" Fenir mutters, I hear the gun click, ready to shoot me in the back.

"Nope," Hanna replies cheerily. "But I wanna see what happens. I've never heard of a Miasmic Beast being with a human...ever."

It was just above a whisper but I heard Fenir mutter, "That kid ain't human."

It stung a little. But, I still manage to go through the doorway to see that every single thing in the room had been knocked over. Cabinets, paper, medicine bottles...it was a mess.

Dreamer!

"Look out!" Fenir shouts, changing the gun's direction, to something that almost bowls me over but instead a giant black paw curls around my side as a giant head buries itself into my side.

"Ok...that seriously hurts."

Danger. Bad. Hatred. Fear. Smell of death

The tiger's head turns to Fenir, baring its teeth at him. Get away!

It's ok...I pat it's head. I've missed you, Mr Tiger.

"Oh, I haven't seen her so lively."

"Her?" I look up at Hanna.

"Yeah."

Mrs Tiger!? "A girl...?"

"Yes...you didn't know?"

"Um, sorry, I didn't have time ask while I was being shot at and big giant crystal zombies were trying to eat me. Also...there are no words in my head."

By the look on Hanna's face, I really shouldn't have said that. "Sorry, please repeat that...?"

"Uuuuh...I can sort of listen to her in my head...? But it's really just emotion and colours and sensations and sometimes images...there aren't 'words'...I can't describe this..."

"Metal linking, is not an uncommon occurrence with developed abilities," X interrupts.

Hanna looked thoughtful, "That is quite true. I just never really thought it to happen with something who wasn't another subject with abilities...but then again there was a subject who was very attached to a cocker spaniel puppy. Hmm...interesting. I would like to take a brain scan of this while you talk with the cat."

"Um. Pass." I say while the tiger goes back to rubbing her head all over my stomach. "Ok that seriously hurts."

Smell wrong. Get smell back.

Oh. Um, well please stop, it seriously hurts.

She immediately stops but then bring her head up to my face and brushes her head against my cheek.

Well this is cute.

Hanna stares at me, as I try to stop the tiger by pushing against her face.

"Do you mind if we begin asking you questions?" Hanna's voice was so serious, that I almost froze. "We need to start getting serious answers from you."

I glare back at her, "You need to do something for me as well."

Chapter Nineteen: Deal

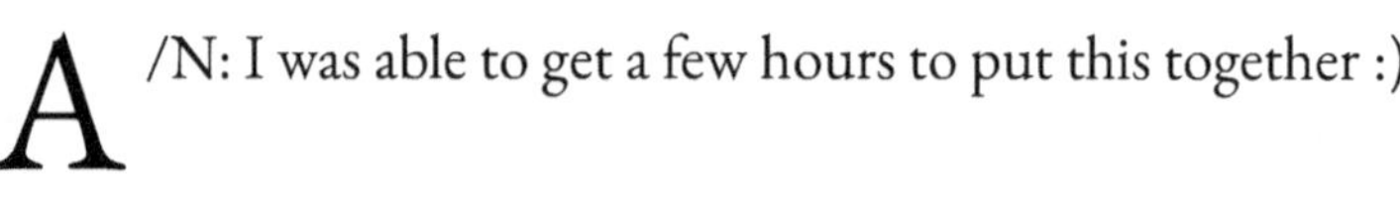

A/N: I was able to get a few hours to put this together :)

Chapter Nineteen: Deal

"Interesting. Hmm...alright, but shouldn't we move somewhere a little more comfortable?" Doc grins at me.

"You what-? How can you just go along with it without knowing what he wants?" Fenir scoffs at both of us.

"'Nothing's for free', isn't that what you always say," she says simply before leading me back out. "I'll let your Lady come along. I don't think she'll detach herself anytime soon."

I look down and remember the paw still pulling on me. I untangle myself but keep a hand in her fur and move after Doc.

I was forced back into that white room, this time an entire entourage filled that cube room. The tiger sat herself around my chair as I sat at the desk, waiting for the Spanish Inquisition to start. This time Fenir was inside the room, glaring at me, next to the door. Like I'm going to make a run for it.

Where would I go? X settle on the wall to my left, opposite to the Station, staring into space.

Doc had found herself a chair and sat directly in front of me...it feels like one of those bad cop shows. I sigh, looking down at the tiger before shifting my gaze back up at the Doc. "You can ask whatever. But..." I bite my lip, I am hesitant at the idea of asking this but what else could I do? "My sister and brother are missing." I had no idea who took them. Were they taken separately? Where they dead? I have no clues. No leads. No power. Nothing. Nothing at all. What other choice do I have here?

"Siblings!?" Doc's spine stands straight.

I nod, glancing over at X, unsure if he remembers that time in the woods, a little over a month ago. "I want to find them."

"How are they missing? Who took them?" Doc was leaning towards me. ...She is waaay too intrigued by everything.

"...I don't know. My sister..." I frown, my memories were a mess. "I..." I wasn't able to finish, so I try again. "My brother Cody was taken away in a van...my sister...Anne...Anne was...helicopter..?" I remember the sound revibrating like a heartbeat was the blades as they went round and round. "Anne was taken by a helicopter. When Cody was taken he was injected by the same stuff I was when X," I look up over at him but he was looking somewhere else.

"Ah...so it is possible that they were taken separately..."she sounded like this was going to be troublesome. She then took in my accusing look, "Tranqs are a common commodity between groups in the business of capturing Outsiders, and there are unfortunately a lot. Armies, mercenaries, researchers and a combination or 'em are always looking for subjects."

That makes us sound like animals. Something slowly burns inside me, the old frustrating anger that I have been keeping buried for the last ten years was reigniting. "You included?' I ask bitterly.

"Me included. But I'm more interested in the Miasma to be honest," her eyes shifted over to the tiger. "It's something that's been the root of a lot of problems but it seems everyone is more interested in the effects rather than the cause lately." She looked a little upset at that. "But, that being said, you are very interesting to say the least."

"I'll let you do whatever you want to me. You can dissect me, kill me, whatever you want. But I want to find them and I want them safe. I don't want them tested on or used or whatever it is that you do to us on the Outside."

Fenir snorts at my demands.

Doc raises her hands up, "Oi oi, don't paint me as the crazy scientist that'll dissect everything in sight."

"You do dissect everything in sight," Fenir quickly retorts.

"Shut up. Furniture doesn't talk." She then turns back to me, "Are your sister and brother like you?"

"...like me...?"

"Cursed."

I scoff, looking down at my arm. How ironic that question was. I wanted to laugh and cry at the same time but try to hold it in, my left hand squeezing this wretched right arm.

"What's so funny?" Doc asks. The tone wasn't offended, just her usual curiosity.

"I..." I didn't even know what to say. But instead try to answer the original question, "My brothers and sister are what you all categorise as 'Cursed'. Cody," the dumbfuck, "had developed strength, also some accelerated healing. Anne's abilities are...unstable and she could do so much. She can read minds, talk with my brothers in their minds...she could create electricity for old household appliances...heat and freeze water...psychokinesis as you would call it. She also a bit psychic. She can predict Miasma storms and is hyper aware of her surroundings."

Doc's eyes widen, "That...we've never come across someone that was psychic."

I harden my gaze as I continue. This exactly why why I never wanted my family discovered, "She's twelve. My brother, Cody, is twenty. I'm the second eldest."

A half smile entertained Doc's lips, "And you're extremely protective of them."

Until I fuck it up.

"You said 'brothers'." Fenir notes.

I sniff, the fresh wound that I barely held together as it is, threatened to leak open and drown me in blood.

Pain? Where is the pain? The tiger sniffs at me, her big yellow eyes wide with concern.

I think she's misinterpreting my physical and emotional pain.

"Yes." I manage to say..."Markus. He's my baby brother. He was also Cursed and...died when all the fighting started," I say bitterly, biting my lip as I feel myself wanting to sob my heart out at all the frustration that was building up. Cody. Anne. Markus. I want them all back.

"Ok. I won't push you," Doc replies with a soft smile. "Then, can I ask how you met little Lady here? Have you always been with her?"

I look at the tiger, unable to stop myself from reaching out to stroke her head, "No. She's as recent as this," I slightly shift my right shoulder, motioning towards the claw. I quickly retell what happened when Cody and Anne were taken then onto what happened after. I left out the unmanly details but when I got to the Keystone, she shot to her feet, knocking over the chair on the way up. Making me jump a little in surprise.

"Let me get this straight," she puts a hand up as if to stop me. "You can get close to one of the Keystones?"

"...That was the first time I was near one." I then quickly explained how I got stuck in the room with a boy. "Next thing I notice, X lands through the roof...then I woke up here with this thing as my arm. Am I some sort of half-formed Hexer? I was bitten..." I remember that much at least. That ugly helmet Hexer is going to be nightmare material for the rest of my life.

She picks up the chair and flops down, she seems a little rattled. "...I still need to do tests but for all intents and purposes, you are not a Hexer. But you are very interesting. Not only were you able to get close to one but destroy it as well!? And still mentally intact? That's...well...very interesting."

I look at her strongly, I am too desperate to get her to help and I feel like she was getting off track, "I'll say this one more time. I'll let you do whatever you want to me but I need to find my brother and sister."

She takes some time to respond but then nods, "Agreed."

"Say what?" Fenir interrupts.

"Shut up, Fenir. This is something that even I can't ignore. If his sister is as powerful as he says she is, no one is going to leave her alone. We might have another Syndrome R on our hands."

"... Syndrome R?" I ask, a little disturbed at the way Fenir's features shift slightly.

Doc glances at me, a soft laugh, "You know human nature. Once we find something new and interesting, we pick at it and warp it to suit our needs. Long story short, someone played with energy radiation of one of the greater Miasma storms and injected the raw form into unwilling subjects and boom! The very first, of many, unstable bioweapons. X here, is another. So are the Keystones."

"...you mean Keystones and Hexers aren't made by the Miasma...?"

"Nope. Humans did that. They even still use it as a way to undermine a city. How do you think this City," she opens her arms up to the room, "Went down?"

"I didn't even realise it was a Nest until I wondered in," I say quietly, not wanting to revisit recent memories. "There was a build-up of an army around it. Then everyone started fighting over it. We were caught in the middle...it was how I lost everyone."

She nods, "Someone was after something in here. Another City didn't like the idea of opening this tin can after what had been done to it about six months ago. It's a small City...they didn't have a chance to contain the spread. I was surprised that the Tower still functions. Lucky for you. You'd be dead if it wasn't."

"The Tower...?"

"It's the power source for everything, including the force-field that surrounds a City. Without it...well we'd be living like you have been for the last decade."

I stare at her. The big gold crystal thing in the middle of this place... "I saw the Tower. The Miasma crystal warped around it, like it was repelled."

"Towers are a mystery, even I don't know much about them. All I know it's what saved a lot of places from that Miasma Disaster."

It's also what's caused this entire mess.

"I can see by the look on your face, you disagree."

I stay silent. I was only seven when all that shit happened. I don't remember much except we were on the wrong side when those giant walls went up. I don't even remember when they went up, now that I think about it. I instead get back on topic, "What happens now?"

"Well, since you seem stable enough to move about, I need to report back to HQ. From there we'll see-" she must have seen the look of protest on my face as she holds her hand up before I could even open my mouth, "-I will also inquire about your brother and sister. Then we'll see what happens."

Chapter Twenty: Rupture Reality

A /N: The song is Garden of Imperfections (ft. Q'Aila) by Miro

I quite like the song...and i guess it sort of fits...?

Anywho, I'm still drowning in assignments but i had a moment of 'must need to write this before i forget it' and yeah completely ignore the impending due dates like always...which i'm going to regret later but I'm not going to regret writing, it's who I am at the end of the day XD

Chapter Twenty: Rupture Reality

The water cascades down my back as I stare at the tiles in front of me. It felt so good to have a proper shower since forever. But my mind was unable to focus properly. It felt almost like grasping for air.

I was told to clean myself up soon after Doc said that she wanted to contact someone. Then Fenir forces me down towards the showers and shut me in this bathroom. With the orders 'don't do anything funny. Go straight back to my cell, ah blah blah blah'. I think he's slowly starting to warm up to me. He's letting my bathe by myself.

It was only now that my curiosity finally kicked into gear. Who was she going to contact? Were they Suppressors? I mean I saw X with some before. But did that matter anymore? No, it didn't. I had to find them. I had to find Cody and Anne and take them somewhere safe. No matter what it takes. No matter what happens to me.

Where will it be safe?

That inward question stopped my thought process. Where was it 'safe' anymore?

I don't know. What if they're dead? A bloody image flashes in my vision-

I gasp, shaking my head to stop myself from going any deeper.

No. They're fine. I have to get them back. That's it. I'll sort out what happens after when I have them both back. Take a page from Cody's book for once and deal with it when it is the crisis not a possibility of one.

I reach for the touchpad on the wall to stop the water (it took me five minutes to figure out that everything is digitised) with this new conviction. But it's really hard to think that way...My thoughts almost immediately paints the worst possible scenarios. I sigh, looking for the towel while stepping out of the cubicle that was the shower. Finding it on the sink, next to my new clean clothes, I take it to dry my hair. As I pull it down, I came face to face with my reflection and stop.

Even through all the bruises and cuts, I could see my right side covered in black markings. Even the side of my face. I turn my head slightly while leaning in. It cut down my face, across my cheek and even down over my jaw. It travelled along my neck, shoulder and finally to that demonic arm below. I look down at my own hands, instead of my reflection's. The contrast of the flesh on my left and right arms was lost on me. My right arm...

Bile rose to my tongue. It was befitting, a demon's claw. I curl it into a fist. As it did, it convinced me more and more that it was real.

It killed someone. This...was the hand that killed the boy. Everything else paled to that vivid memory. That boy was a weapon. His body was stolen from him and used against his will and I killed him. Instead of finding some way to help him. Cody's words jarred my thoughts 'You're useless'. He was right. I have never been of any help to anyone. I had to rely on Cody, Anne and even Markus. I was never of any help. I was never strong enough to protect my family. At most I could only chase after them. And that wasn't good enough. Not now. Not ever.

I look back up at the me -the pathetic, useless me that stares back with dark brown eyes reflecting my inward emptiness. Bitter anger build up and I didn't stop myself from punching the mirror with as much force as I could muster. The fragmentation cracks across the surface in a spider's web. But I still saw the distorted reflection. I hated myself so much. I could feel the burning tears building up.

I bite my lip, suppressing the sob cracking in my throat. I can't do this now. I'm losing time feeling sorry for myself.

I quickly dry and dress myself while beating down my rage, trying to paint the mask of calmness back on my face before I go back out. I can't crumble now. I can't show it. I forcefully pull the hoodie's long sleeve to hide the right arm and the hood over my head.

As I open the door out to the hallway, I jump as a body was standing in front of me. Looking up, I see X staring directly at me. I couldn't say anything as words died before they could reach my throat. I couldn't stop myself from looking away from him. It was uncomfortable, stifling even.

Feeling like we were in a standstill, I couldn't handle the silence much longer so I summon the courage to look up at him and say quietly, "Is something wrong?"

All he did was blink. I wonder if I could get around him, looking to see if there was any room and knew that I was stuck here. I look back up at him. He was silent, looking slightly to the side, as if he was hearing something else before his eyes dart back to me, a strange mix of emotion flicker through his eyes as they fall down to my side.

I was slightly confused as he reaches forward. I flinch back but he didn't hesitate to take my right hand and pull it forward between us. I notice the small drops of red staining my sleeve as he pulls on it, revealing the hateful hand. It took me a moment to see the cuts on the back of my hand, wet with dark red blood. I didn't even realise I had cut my hand or even felt the pain until it was in front of me. My knuckles were spilt and oozing blood. It stings like fire with an ebbed pulse. But the contact of his slender fingers burned so much more, numbing my brain.

I wasn't sure what he was going to do or say until I feel the sting of his thumb gliding over an open wound on the back of my hand. I pull back and he let me go as I cradle it to myself, "That hurts!" I protest at him.

And with his usual response, that being nothing, he stares at his hand that was now painted in the dark red of my blood before he reaches for me again. And for some reason, I let him. Not sure what he was doing, he brought my knuckles to his lips. I freeze in place as his soft wet warm tongue glides over my knuckle, burning me as he tastes the blood and I winced at the pressure and pain mixes. But those aren't the only things I'm feeling and it confused me even more. Liquid heat fizzed down my spine, leaving a tingling sensation right through to my toes. A soft intake of breath left me in my surprise.

Perplexed with myself and what he's doing, he on the other hand went from my next knuckle, lapping at it in just the same way. I-why aren't I stopping him? I continue to stare as he goes for the long cut that split the top of the back of my right hand. I could feel an electrical undercurrent but I was fighting myself from being submerged. I couldn't understand where this feeling was coming from and why it wouldn't stop. I was fighting myself from wanting to be consumed. What was this feeling? I wanted to let go. Mentally wrestling with my conflicting and confusing emotions, I could only continue to watch. It almost felt like I couldn't disturb him.

Hearing footsteps brought me back to reality. What is he doing? I pull away, stepping back and he let me go. -What was I doing!?

"There you are!" I recognise the girl's voice as she quickly approaches us. Her bright pale bottle-green eyes took us in rapidly. X, who looked like nothing happened and me; blushing from top to toe. "...Um...Hanna..."s he seems a little nervous as she addresses me. Well I did flash her...it was a lasting first impression. It made my blushing turn a shade darker as I remember. "She says that Lady is getting kinda upset and that I should look for you."

"...Lady...?"

"Um you're tiger-friend."

Doc's gone and named the tiger.

I guess it suited her. I want to get away from the unsettling feeling I get whenever I'm near X while he looks calm like nothing ever happened. I was about to tell Mist that I'll go back-

"Mist! Don't get so close." The boy charges soon after her, pulling her back behind him as he glares at me like I was about to eat her, his arm outstretched in front of his twin protectively. "Get back to your cell. Now."

I blink at the harshness of his actions and words, it wasn't like my jaw was wide open ready to swallow her whole, here, "I'm not going to hurt anyone."

"How can I trust what you say?"

I guess he has a point. But the way he and Fenir glare at me still hurt.

It was amazing how the contrast of their same coloured eyes looked. Mist, who was a little mortified and nervous and Rain's were dripping in hostility and threat.

I couldn't stop the grim smile. "You're right. You don't need to trust me. I'm going back." I shift my eyes to Mist, "Thank you for telling me." I felt the sting. Not from Rain probably hating my guts but because they still had each other. That Rain could still protect his sister. That Mist still had her overprotective brother.

Going back to my little prison, I see Lady pacing it.

She stops and looks at me through the glass. I guess when I told her that I was coming back, I took too long by her standards as a mixture of bright colours of relief and impatience flood my mind.

Dreamer! She leaps onto the glass, her big paws and face pressing against it. I let a small sigh escape and smile a little. At least someone's happy to see me. I willingly go back into the prison with my big, bouncy cellmate and await my fate.

Chapter Twenty-One: Kite Flying

- -

Chapter Twenty-One: Kite Flying

I was dosing off, leaning against Lady on the floor, when the next thing I notice I'm roughly being pulled to my feet, half dragging as Hanna pulls me along.

"Our ride's here," She grins at me, as I stumble after her, Lady not far behind.

What ride? I shift to pull back from Doc but she had me in a vice grip. "What's going on?"

"We're going to HQ directly. They were so interested in you that they are even willing to pick us up."

"What happens if I go?"

She shrugs, "It beats staying here, doesn't it? 'Sides, I think you'll enjoy this!"

Enjoy what?

She pulls me along the corridors to a heavy steel door and opens it to the outside. Something that I haven't seen in a while as the sun practically blinds me.

Squinting as my eyes try to adjust, I came face to face with something that belonged in a sci-fi movie. "Is that-?"

"-An airship, yes."

I'm probably ogling so much that I'm expecting my eyeballs to roll out any minute. It was black and sleek with electric blue along the wings. It took up the helipad in its entirety, that it somehow landed on without me even hearing the damn thing.

"Ok, let's get that tongue back into your mouth and you onto the ship," Hanna pats me on the back as the hatch on the airship drops down like a ramp and someone comes half-way down the giant thing that looked like it could take a tank or two aboard. "Yo, Hanna. I was told you needed a lift?"

He looked like a pirate. Even had the eyepatch to match. Though instead of a wooden pipe, he was smoking a cigarette, little disappointed to be honest.

Fenir picks that moment to come up behind me, "Took you long enough."

The pirate chuckles, breathing in deeply before letting it out as a cloud, "Hey, you could always walk. Where's the van?"

"Round front, Rain will drive it in."

"Eh? You letting the pipsqueak drive it? Last time I tried, you chewed me out. Talk about favouritism..." Pirate-man must have spotted me, as he flicks the cigarette butt to the side, he skips down from the airship's ramp and comes face to face with me, the weird ornaments that hung from his belt clink together like bells as he did, "This the kid? And his pet?"

I look up at the tanned pirate, expecting to see a parrot on his shoulder.

He grins at me and I notice a few interesting tribal tattoos along his arms that went under his shirt, "I like those eyes, boy. A little defiance never hurts eh?" He then thought on something, "Where are my manners? Lieutenant Vincent Osiris Black, at your service. Call me-"

"Oz, less talking, more 'getting on the ship and getting ready for taking off'." Fenir snaps, "You can talk the boy to death when we're in the air."

"Aye-aye, capi-tan. Just being polite." Oz pulls back from me, "Well, welcome aboard the Hollow Kite." He motions with his wrist while bowing towards me before standing straight and getting aboard himself.

"Come on, champ," Hanna, taps my shoulder as she walks towards the giant-ass sci-fi airship. This was more what I was expecting to find. But this city didn't show any indication it housed anything like this.

I stop at the foot of the ramps, looking beyond the airship, I could see the ruined city, still paralysed by the standstill of time after the Hexers had taken over. The Fence, still standing in some places where everywhere else was skewered by the long black crystal obelisks. But beyond the fence...was Anne and Cody. Somewhere. And Markus.

I hesitated. Markus was still here. But if I say anything about him, would they try and dig him up? I wouldn't put it passed Hanna. I mean how many times do you come across a boy who turned himself into a tree? They wouldn't leave him in peace.

"What's the hold up?" Hanna turns back. "Did we forget something?"

I look towards the gate, with a silent promise and resolve to come back to him, "No." When I have both Anne and Cody...could we reverse what he's done?

'Feels wrong!'

The mental protest grinds me to a halt and to turn back to see Lady who was hesitating to put her front paw onto the ramp. I go back down to her and hold my hand out to her face and she nuzzles against it.

I try to convey to her, 'You don't have to come with me...you can stay here if you want to.' I had no right to ask her to come with me.

'Dreamer is going!' She bares her teeth, almost like she was pouting and I had to smile, despite myself.

'I want you to come with me.' I really do.

'Then I go with Dreamer!'

'But you need to get onto the airship. We are going somewhere that looks like it will be too far to travel on foot.'

She makes a soft whiny noise but then puts her foot on the ramp, then the next, unsure as if she wanted to bolt in the other direction.

'I'll be with you' I try to reassure her, my hand never leaving her head as I walk backwards up the ramp.

I felt someone behind me and turn to see the mismatch eyes that look down to stare into mine. I feel myself blush remembering what he did and quickly turn back to face Lady. That was when I felt a slight touch on the hair on the back of my neck. I whir around, my hand slapping to my neck, only to see his back to me as he walks up the ramp. Was that my imagination?

It took a bit to get Lady up the ramp and onto the ship, which stuns me. The interior was all space-tech corridors, doors and ramps. The area that I was standing in was large and open. Obviously the storage/deployment of anything (and anyone) that they were carrying.

"This way, starry-eyes," Hanna calls from atop of a flight of metal stairs.

I look down to Lady and back up to her, unsure if I should push Lady any more than I'm already doing.

'Want to go further?' Lady asks, but I could sense her anxiety. 'Can go a little further.'

I bite my lip but lead her to the stairs anyway. As we go up, I see the coloured glass that let us see the sky and a little ways down, it eventually becomes a viewing platform for the pilot at the very front and in the middle with all the flying gadgets that I wouldn't have a clue how to use. A number of buckled passenger seats with their own board of buttons and screens lines either side of the main seat.

Pirate-man presses a few buttons as he lounges over his seat, "Everyone buckling in?"

I sit down in the seat three chairs behind him on his left, the furthest point from anyone. Lady sits beside me, her eyes wide and shifting around, her emotions are still anxious but there is a little wonder and curiosity as she looks out the blue-tinted glass that swallowed the entire ceiling and walls of the platform. I saw X was sitting in the front left seat, silently looking ahead.

Hanna took to the closest seat at the front, to Oz's right, picking away at the buttons and touchscreens like she knew what she was doing.

"Stop doing that!" Oz moves her hands from the controls.

"What?" She smacks his hands back.

"When I'm in the big shiny driver's seat, I'm in control, woman!"

"Say that to my face!"

"With pleasure. Don't touch anything!"

"Whatever, mum."

"Oz. I've given you instructions and coordinates, why aren't we moving?' Fenir plonks into the seat opposite from me.

"Yes, yes, right away, as soon as Doc stops touching everything."

"Oh shut up Pansy!" Hanna snorts.

"Hey, not everyone here likes the air-con set to something suited for polar bears!"

"Well I do and I get what I want."

"Not on my ship. I'm King and my baby is my domain!"

"You. Wish."

"Oz! Today would be nice." Fenir growls again.

"...Right away, sir." And with that I could hear the build-up on some kind of engine. Next we smoothly leave the ground, hovering for a second.

"Unnatural. Birds only. Not me.' Lady shivers and I reach out a hand to pat her.

"I'm sorry to do this to you.'

'I go where Dreamer goes,' her yellow-black eyes focus on my for a second before she jolts as the ship turns to a different direction and lands on what I can imagine to be the street below where Rain was waiting with the truck.

Within a few minutes of awkward silence, Rain soon appears and while completely ignoring me, buckles himself into the chair in front of me. Mist soon appears and sits in the chair in front of Fenir, "Everything is secure. Awaiting further instruction."

"Good. Oz, you know where to go." ...was Fenir sharp with everyone?

"That I do." Oz didn't seem to notice and before long we were in the air and I found myself practically glued to the window. The clouds and sky flying passed at impossible speeds. I haven't been on any sort of plane since I was six...and I can barely even remember that...other than Cody hated every minute of it. But this was...amazing? Aweinspiring? I dunno but it was freakin cool!

"By the by, crazy boy with the pet tiger, I didn't catch your name."

I frown but couldn't help but mutter, "Kae."

"Oh really!?" Hanna twists in her seat to look back at me.

Oz scoffs, "You never thought to ask him his name?"

"Nope."

"Stupid scientist. He isn't an 'it'. Also, he's old enough to be around before all this shit," he motions around him. "He's bound to have a name. Ain't I right, Kae?"

I was silent and saw that Mist was looking a little ashamed at me but when I turn my full attention to her, she quickly looks away.

"We should reach HQ in an hour...they're being a bit anal about letting aircraft through...after y'know...well you saw what happened in Bellasera ..."Oz grabs my attention again.

"Bellasera?" I couldn't stop myself from asking.

"That was the city we were just in, mate."

"...Are ships like this one common?"

Oz looks back at me for a moment, "Only in the last three years...and only in the big cities...and of course only those who can afford or know how to make one. –Hanna! Would you just stop? Otherwise I will eject seat you outta here and you can walk the rest of the way!"

"You're music selection sucks big time!" She was back at the buttons agai n...

"You don't hear me complain about the crap you listen to."

"That's because I use earphones and don't force anyone to listen to the shit you listen to, like any courteous human being."

"You? Courteous? Did hell freeze over when I wasn't looking?"

"Of course it did. I rule, remember?"

"Explains a lot. All hail Satan!"

"Would you two just shut up and drive?" Rain snaps.

"Oh how I missed the Grouchy Pipsqueak backseat driving!" Oz's sarcasm could be felt this far back.

"What did you just say?"

"Enough!" Fenir roars. "There will be no music. There will be silence so that I don't miss anything on the airways."

"Party pooper," both Hanna and Oz mutter in sync.

"Jinx!"

"-Jinx again!"

I could hear both Mist and Fenir sigh.

I guess this happens a lot.

Chapter Twenty-Two:
Bolin

A /N: I've finished for the year! and hopefully forever. I'm sick of uni and no money :/

But anywho, I can now focus a bit more on my writing for a bit. I will be on holidays for 2 weeks at the start of december, so I should be putting out updates between then and now. Afterwards, I will be looking at the other works that have been lacking in updates for...over a year...oops.

Chapter Twenty-Two: Bolin

The first thing I notice in the distance was the pale blue orb of another Fence after flying along an endless expanse of ocean for the last fifty minutes. This one is massive. It felt like it took up most of the sky, like an impending tsunami wave building in the distance. It looked so alive, as the blue energy pulses and swirls. In the very centre of all the high rise buildings and skyscrapers was a twisted black tower that just screams 'Eye of Sauron' and it almost touched the highest point of the Fence.

"Welcome to Bolin." Oz chuckles when he saw my face. "One of the Five."

"What are the 'Five'?" I look back towards the city that was approaching us and just keeps getting bigger.

"Just the biggest of the cities that became prosperous and breathing down the necks of all the other city-states. There's two in America... two in Asia including this one, and one in Europe. But it's not like we go by those names anymore."

"Why not?"

I see his shoulders shrug, "I ain't the one who made the decision, kid. I just follow like everyone else, like the sheep that I am. There's nothing but grave dust of the Old World. Funny how fast it turns around. I don't think we even use 'continents' or even 'nationality' anymore. Just the city-states...a nd Outsiders."

I stare back out the window, feeling a little heavy. There's no way we can go back to how it all was, can we? I look back to Lady, who was starting to calm down. There isn't any way back. This is my reality. I lean back and shut my eyes, letting out a breath.

As we came into the airspace above the Fence, Fenir flicked a switch and began talking, "This is Hollow Kite returning from a ground run. Permission to enter?"

There was silence until a strange automated female voice comes over a speaker, "Permission granted. Welcome back."

As soon as the voice finishes, a hole expands in the orb energy directly below us and the ship descends into it, down into the city airspace below. I watch through the ceiling as we clear the orb that it closes back up above us, making me feel slightly claustrophobic.

I look at the skyscrapers all around us like mirrored monoliths. It gave that extra surreality as everything is high-tech and futuristic. Everything was piled on top of one another. Shops, houses....living spaces all cramped into the streets and buildings as a somewhat functioning and organised chaos. Neon lines ran along the buildings' sides, advertisements on projections along the buildings...as well as 3D holograms. Even some airships like they were in traffic like the vehicles clogging up the streets below. This is insane.

But it felt wrong. Like life was being choked from it.

'No forest. Only jungle of stone and smoke. Death and suffocating.' Lady presses onto my thoughts.

She was right. As opposed to Bellasera, there weren't any gardens or parks with trees. There was nothing green and it was suffocating. The air almost felt tragic. I frown at this feeling. I didn't experience this in the other city. Sure it was desolate and destroyed but the air, though stagnate, didn't feel like this.

"Are you ok?"

I look up to see Mist staring at me.

I swallow, pushing the oppressive feeling down, "I'm fine. I've just never thought I'd ever see something like this."

"Being an Outsider, this probably looks really weird." Oz chuckles.

'Weird' doesn't even cover it.

As we come to a building with an almost detached helipad attached to its side, Oz moves the airship so that it smoothly lands onto it. "Ride's over, kiddies."

Hanna stands and comes over to me, "All ready?"

I nod and stand to follow her. I pull the hood over my head, it's becoming an automatic reaction now. As we come down to the platform, the hot air and smells knock me stupid. Fuel, humidity, death, waste, cheap perfume and rot. How could anyone stand this?

"Oh my God, why is it so hot!?" Hanna complains. "Come on, the sooner we're inside, the sooner we get out of this."

I follow her as she heads for the door.

Just as she reaches for the door, it swings open and a group of mismatched people who I could only assume to be some type of soldiers surround us and even had matching black guns pointed directly at me. Wonderful.

"This is the subject in question?" The man closest to Hanna asks, his eyes never leaving my face, he looked barely old enough to even join an army.

"Yes, Mike. Now would you put those away? He came here of his own free will. Why do you think he isn't in restraints? I'm gonna get mad in a minute if you all don't stand down."

"Sorry, ma'am. Orders."

"Orders," she scoffs, "I'll tell you where you can shove-"

"We are to escort him directly to the chief."

"Then do it nicely and without pointing those at him." She pushes his gun up. "I'm sorry about all this, Kae."

What was I gonna expect? A marching band and streamers?

She glares at this 'Mike' until he says, "Weapons disengaged."

The others followed suit in pointing the guns away from me but their eyes still look rather hostile. Great more Fenir's and Rain's. Just what I always wanted.

"What of the Miasmic-Beast?" The man asks at Hanna.

"She's fine. As long as you stop pointing things at his chest, she won't attack."

As if to illustrate the point, Lady puts herself between me and them like a shield, as she encircles her body around me as best she can.

"Now that we have that nasty business out of the way, let's go see the idiot." Hanna walks through the door and expect us to follow suit.

I quickly do exactly that, with everyone glaring holes into the back of my head as I pass them. I held in a sigh. I'm defenceless and I'm the suspicious one?

Walking inside, it was thick grey and white hallways with metal doors that I presume slide open. Why doesn't anyone like handles in this place? There were black touchpads with red lights that I guess would switch to green if you're allowed through...and scream at you if you're not. Escaping is going to be interesting.

As we walk passed any idle bystander, they quickly got out of the way of Hanna and glare/stare at me as I walk passed. What the fuck did I do to them? Did Fenir forward a message to the entire lot of them? 'Please stare angrily at the boy with the tiger. Can't miss them'.

"Not understanding leads to fear. Leads to anger when blame can then be placed," X whispers beside me.

I jump. When the fuck did he get there? I hiss at him, "Would you cut that out?"

He looks down at me, his facial expressions blank as if he didn't understand what I was getting at. Probably didn't.

I sigh, rallying myself for whoever this 'Chief' is.

Hanna comes to a door and presses a hand to it and it slides open with a 'hiss'. "After you," she motions to me.

I go in to see a simple enough office room that I would expect to see in any business space. A green spider orchid sat in a black pot on the polished black desk, contrasting in colour. The wide tinted windows looked out over the city streets below. It was big and open without much else in here.

"Hanna. How many times have I told you 'knock' first?" A thickly accented voice came from a doorway that I don't remember being there, behind a practically empty bookshelf on my left.

"Whatever. You had to be rude first." Hanna glares at the man coming towards us. He looked a lot like her. Same long blonde hair and blue eyes. It would be safe to assume they are related in some way.

"I have to be safe. Especially when you drag things home." This damn Viking was annoying me already as he motions towards me when he said 'things'.

"Oh shut it Siem. You wanted to look at him."

"That I did," he steps closer, his eyes peering right at me. "You were able to get close to and destroy a Queen, weren't you?"

I felt my voice die in my throat as he stands in front of me, his heavy gaze bearing on me like a weight I didn't want to deal with. Two metes of intimidating muscle is hard to stare at.

"Is he mute?" He asks Hanna.

"No. But the way you're glaring at him would make anyone want to jump out a window."

"I'm not glaring. I'm just looking."

She sighs, "Kae, don't worry, my brother is a teddy bear. He just forgets to put the teeth and claws away. His name is Siem. Siem, this is Kae. And yes, he appears to have been able to destroy a Queen and no, he isn't a Hexer,

I've run every single test against his DNA and none come back with any indication that he's a Hexer."

"But he is something."

"...Yes."

Siem rubs his chin, while thinking. "You said you had something to show me as well."

"And I think Kae will need to see it as well."

"I'll look at that in a second." He then dismisses the conversation entirely. "Fenir, thank you as always in assisting my sister. You four can hit the showers and get some food and rest. I won't require you guys again until tomorrow."

"As always, sir," Fenir slightly bows his head and turned to leave, his eyes fell on me and the glint in them scream 'try anything funny and I'll kill you'. Rain soon follows in behind him, not even looking at me.

"What is it Mist?" Siem asks as she was still rooted to the spot.

"I want to stay. Kae seems to be a bit unsteady since he entered the city's airspace."

"...As you wish. Everyone else who doesn't need to be here can leave."

"Is that wise?" Mike asks, completely suspicious of me.

Siem chuckles, "You doubt my abilities?"

Mike looks taken aback, "Never sir."

"It's ok. If something happens, I'll let you know. Stay outside the door if you really want to."

I'm getting offended here.

As everyone but Siem, Hanna and Mist left, Siem's eyes fell on me again and it made me squirm. "Now. Let's get down to business."

Chapter Twenty-Three: Simon Says 'Jump'

Chapter Twenty-Three: Simon Says 'Jump'

"Kae," Siem made me feel very small. "I will make things very clear. I will not hesitate to kill you if you do anything that threatens my people. It has taken over a decade for us to build what we have and anything that jeopardises it I will deal with it without any reservations. And I won't lose sleep over it either."

He really makes me feel right at home. "I got it," I mutter. What else could I do?

I see a smirk form on his lips, "On the flip side, I will protect you as best I can. Now," that smirk disappears as his eyes linger on my fingers that I wasn't able to fully hide, "show me." He holds out his hands and I make no move towards him. He must have realised how threatened I felt as the sharpness in his eyes soften. "I promise not to hurt you as long as you cooperate."

I felt like growling, my lip twitches as I hold out my arm.

His hand is rough and big as he takes my hand while the other forces the sleeve up.

I hear Mist's sudden intake of breath and I look away as the onyx-scales are exposed.

"Hanna has explained to me that you said that you did not gain this arm or..." he pulls on my hood to expose my face, "appearance until you made contact with the Queen."

I look back at him in the eye, unable to completely hide the bitterness from my face.

"So you know what they really are," he muses, letting go of my arm.

I take a step back, pulling the sleeve and hood back to hide myself.

"I'll agree to your terms...but you have to follow mine. Are we clear?"

I feel like someone pulled a rug from underneath me. "Huh?"

"You are looking for your siblings and require our assistance. In exchange, you'll give yourself up...to me. Well, to our cause more specifically. It'll be interesting, I have to admit. Especially with your cat-friend. It is rare to find a Miasmic-Beast not trying to maul us to death. For you to have tamed one...perhaps that shows promise that we may yet be forgiven."

"Forgiven?" I frown.

"Yes," and he doesn't bother elaborating. "Now then, Hanna. You said that there was something interesting you wanted me to see."

"Yep. A recording." Hanna grins, going over to his desk and fiddles with something that brings up a weird holographic screen in the centre of the room, making me jump back from the carpet. "It's only about ten seconds long...it's been damaged rather strangely."

As she hits a button, the blue screen becomes a weird colour before it flickers over to what looks like the room they had me cooped up in when they first caught me. ...And there I was on that table thing, laying down like a corpse....is that seriously what I look like? I look like someone decided to drag me through hell -ass first- and my hair was a birds nest. I couldn't stop myself from reaching for my hair...yep still sort of a mess...Did my bones really stick out like that?

Suddenly, the 'me' on the holographic screen had the eyes wide open and sitting bolt up. I notice the markings moved and pulsed along my body like a snake and actually seep into the eye as it blackened and the iris became yellow and snake-like itself. Where that 'me' sat, ice began to crackle along the ground, growing with the groaning snap of deep-water ice. Then that 'me's eyes flick to what I imagine to be the camera as the yellow eye pierces through my bones before the video suddenly stops with a snap.

"The recording ends here and there has been no way to put it back online since. I was barely able to save even this much of the data." Hanna reverses the recording and freezes it on the 'me' that's staring directly at the came ra...and it's really spooky.

I look at the three pairs of eyes now staring at me. The silence is killing me.

'Two Dreamers. One scary and harsh but gentle and sad. Me like the waking Dreamer. Not as scary...but still gentle...still sad. Why do two appear?' Lady's question makes me look over at her.

'That was a picture that shows the past...but I do not know this 'other me'.' Lady's inner thoughts were still confused but she accepted my explanation anyway. I guess whatever I try to say, it does sort of transmit my meaning as it is raw thought and emotion.

"Start talking," Siem's voice felt really loud in the still, tense air.

"He has no recollection of this. This was in an unconscious state. His mind felt a threat and responded." Hanna walks over to the hologram.

"What was the threat?" Siem asks.

"...At a best guess, it was a dream."

This just sounds stupid. "I've never been able to do anything like this before."

"That is most likely because your mental state has never been this unstable before." Hanna looks at me keenly. "Whatever interactions you've had in the hours after you had lost your siblings may have triggered all your dormant abilities for survival. Before such a time, there hasn't been a proper opportunity for your abilities to manifest. Triggers are required for the accelerated adaption to occur. Before this, I believe you had your eldest brother and younger siblings manifest their abilities and yours, strangely, remained dormant."

Well ain't that a kick to the gut. Don't even know half of what she's saying. But everyone else here seemed to understand just fine and I felt a bit too hesitant to raise my hand and ask questions in the class.

But I understood this much, "So I can freeze things." I don't particularly like the cold...and now I'm stuck making ice-cubes. Excuse me while I'm not exactly thrilled here. Cody can at least 'hulk-smash' his way through things.

"No. That isn't what you have done."

"Then what's all the ice?"

"You manipulated the state of the elements that make up the atmosphere. You caused them to take solid form."

Isn't that ice? I may not be a chemistry expert but nitrogen and oxygen need extremely low temperatures to be solids.

"Reality manipulation," Siem whispers, I think he was talking to himself. His eyes then fell on me. "You are certainly something." I think I'd rather go back to being the 'Oddball' right now...

"It's not like I can do it right now," I protest back at him. I don't even know what the hell's going on. I apparently wasn't even conscious when it happened.

He lets out an amused breath, "And I'm grateful for that. Though I have to wonder what you can do. You're probably almost as bad as X."

Was that a backhanded compliment or a complete insult?

I must have made a face as he grins at me, "Ah, you're right Hanna, he is a character. Tell me...what was it that calmed that state down?"

"Curiously, X seemed to have been able to drag him out of that state. However, I haven't been able to work out the mechanics of it." Hanna continues.

"Not everything needs to be figured out, Hanna. If X can potentially calm any triggers that may occur within Kae, leave it at that."

"The reverse may also be true," Hanna states quietly.

"...Even more curious..." He then step back up his desk and shuts the hologram off. "Kae. I will help you find your siblings. But you are going to help me."

"And what exactly am I helping with?"

He grins, "World peace."

I just give him a deadpanned look.

A chuckle escapes from him, "Well, sort of. We are a sort of secret police and I'm going to need your help with certain cases. Can I trust you?"

I glance at Mist who was quiet the entire time. "...Do I have a choice?"

"You always have a choice."

"But not if I want to find my brother and sister." And if I wanna come out of this room still breathing.

"...No."

"Alright. Fine. But as long as you help me find them."

"Of course. Now, since we've got that out of the way-"

"Sorry Chief, this is urgent!" Someone in a mask and gloves came racing into the room, making us also stand there in shock. "I heard that Hanna is here- There you are! It's an emergency. The procedure isn't going well-"

Hanna's eyes harden and she nods, "Tell me the details on the way." She immediately rushes for the door, following the medic person.

"Do not think I'm done with you, Hanna." Siem growls. "You're going to explain exactly what you've been up to and why I shouldn't lock you up in your lab for good this time."

"Sorry. I'll come back to hear you whinge, later." With that, she disappears out the door in a rush.

Siem sighs, "She's going to run herself into the ground one of these days."

I look back at him. But whatever he was thinking, it disappeared from his face as something flickered on a smaller hologram that appears on his desk. "And so it continues," he mutters. "It seems duty calls. Mist please show the new addition and his pet around would you?"

Mist slightly bows, "Yes sir."

"Oh and Kae?" The way he calls my name made me pause. "Be careful not to wonder out into the city."

Like I could go anywhere anyway! I follow after Mist and just as Lady's tail makes it out, the metal door slides over and the light on the touchpad changes to a yellow.

"Must be serious," Mike states as I find him sitting on the floor.

I look between him and Mist, "The touchpad turns yellow when it's 'serious'?"

"It's a type of lockdown. Yellow means that he's placed the room on sound-proof and disabled sound in the camera recordings. There is also no way for us to get in unless we use the emergency codes," Mist explains quietly.

After some silence, Mike gets to his feet, "You're gonna show it around now?"

"Don't be mean, Mike," Mist's voice is actually a little harsh.

"Yeah-yeah-yeah, whatever." He then points his fingers at me, almost ready to strike my eye, "I'm watching you, Outsider. Any funny business and I'll kill you." With that, he turns his back on us and struts down a corridor. Lady growls after him but he completely ignores her.

Well, isn't he charming?

"I'm sorry...Kae," Mist apologies meekly, she even hesitated to use my name. She is really skittish isn't she? "Please don't take it personally..."

"It's probably the same for us," I put my hands into the front pocket of the hoodie. "The hatred my family has felt towards those who made it inside the Fence's in time."

She looks up rather shocked. "Oh-um...of-of course...sorry."

I couldn't stop my head from tilting slightly, taking in the apology but then let out a breath and smile, "Let's take the tour. There's nothing better to do, right?"

Chapter Twenty-Four: Cats in Elevators

Chapter Twenty-Four: Cats in Elevators

"Um..I don't know where to start." Mist looks away nervously.

I shrug, "What's this floor then? Starting here is as good as anywhere else right?"

She nods before heading away from Siem's door. "So this floor is basically where we hold any briefs for missions or meetings...otherwise it's mainly just Siem's floor." Mist moves through the deserted hallways as our shoes and footpads were the only indication that we were the only ones around.

'What is Dreamer doing?' Lady wonders a little behind me, sniffing every now and then. The weird clinical scents were even making my nose itchy.

'Looking around a new territory.' I try to think of it as she might see it.

'...Is it Dreamer's? There is no scent that it is.'

'Not mine. Rather it is the man that we just saw,' the image of Siem flickered through my thoughts, 'Yep. Him. It's his and everyone around here.'

'...Then is not good. Territory is not owned.'

'It's ok. We are here as guests. Part of a pack.' For now.

'Not right...but will follow.'

Sorry, Lady.

"...Kae?"

"Hmm?" I snap out of the emotions that Lady was pulverising me with.

"Are you ok? You were really out of it just then," Mist peers up into my face, stopping me in my tracks.

"Ah, sorry. Lady was asking me something and it gets...a bit distracting."

"How cool," she grins offhandedly, taking me by surprise.

"Cool?"

"How many people do you meet are able to talk with a giant tiger as you do?"

"Normally those who are taken away in straight-jackets," I mutter.

She shakes her head, "I still think it's cool. Well, um. Anyway, we're at the lift."

She presses the button indicating that she wanted to go down that was on the wall in front of us. I'm not sure if Lady's going to agree to this, I couldn't help but look up at her as she lazily licks her chops.

"We could take the stairs if you'd prefer," Mist must have caught on. She indicated to the door beside the life, just as the door open.

'Can you ride it?' I indicate to Lady, the box-like room that just opened. This just screams claustrophobia.

She looked at it and I feel her mental shrugging at me before she puts herself (somehow) into the box. There was enough room for Mist and myself.

"She seems ok with it," I shrug, getting on.

'It's small.'

Spoke too soon.

But other than that, she didn't move away from the lift.

"It's a good thing that we have reinforced elevators installed," Mist states absentmindedly while pressing on a button that was floor '5', "We made it so that twenty people can get on in a hurry."

I noticed that floor 5 was the lowest floor besides ground or basement. "I'm guessing there's no one through four on this?" And I swear there were more floor above us.

"What? Oh? We only own floors five through to ten. The rest of the building is owned by other occupants...it helps when we technically don't exist."

"Secret police thing?"

She nods.

"You guys are not Suppressors?" I ask.

She turns to me fully with a shocked look on her face just as the doors open to a rather noisy floor. "No. Nothing to do with them." She said 'them' rather acidly.

Ok. Not a subject to bring up. But it makes me wonder why X was with a few of them just a month ago...

Mist's voice goes back to being light, "This is one of the personal floors...but it is also the most popular as it's also the diner. We have a really good team that handles the menus."

I look up to see some people talking amongst themselves and immediately go quiet they see Lady...and by extension me.

Mist still walks on, the place at least seemed a little less clinical. The floor was covered in short navy blue carpet and the walls had more of a house like feel to them (like actual creamy-painted walls). But it still felt like dark tunnels and still had the sci-fi metal 'whoosh' doors with the touchpads. I slowly walk passed a few people, following closely behind Mist as she nonchalantly goes right to an open doorway and walks in. Coming inside it was a café styled dining area with large glass wall tinted windows that looked outside, at much the same landscape that Siem's office did. I frown, looking out the window. I felt that if I was left undistracted my attention comes back to the hollow tragic air that this entire city held. A sudden shudder ripped through my spinal cord, like someone just perked up to stare at me. Clear, empty eyes as if disturbed from an eternal dream.

"...- normally have set meal plans but we're allowed to order what we want in the mornings. That's if we're not off on a mission somewhere else of course." Mist continues on, dragging me away from that sudden chill.

I shake myself of the feeling, like a snap from a frozen dream.

"Are you ok?" Mist repeats the question from only a few minutes ago.

"Yeah...I'm ok. Just a little tired I guess."

"Yeah...you have been through a lot. I keep forgetting that...not much a medic am I?"

"Medic?"

She nods, "That's what I'm training for anyway...I like to be as good as Hanna one day."

"She's really that good?"

Her nodding became stronger, "One of the best you could ever meet."

"How old are you, Mist?"

"I'm eighteen."

"And you're out here doing secret police work?"

"I'm not the youngest. Most of us have nowhere to go and are too...different to successfully assimilate ourselves into society or have the capacity to function...so we all wound up following Siem and with that we've been able to survive and help...even though society might view it as unorthodox."

Indeed. Who else would let a boy with an arm that looks like he traded it in for a demon's and his oversized cat that glows in the dark?

"X is practically the poster child of this place," she smiles up at me.

"Why is his name 'X'?" I ask before I could stop myself.

"That's-"

"His actual reference is Subject 10 but it's with roman numerals, so 'X'." Rain grumbles as he stood from a white round table just in front of us.

Dammit I didn't see the bastard. The other three people sitting with him all mirrored his haughty expression...well this is going to be fun.

And here I was hoping I wouldn't see him again for at least a few hours. Yay me. Well at least he's talking...silver-linings where you can take them.

"Mist. Why are you getting more involved than necessary? We've done our job. It's best to steer clear of this."

Mist shakes her head, "That isn't fair, Rain. He isn't a bad person."

"That's not the point. Any moment he could lose it," he's now turned into a full blown snarl...silencing the entire cafeteria and all eyes on us.

I take it back, I rather the silence treatment.

"Hanna said that he isn't a Hexer!"

"That doesn't mean anything in this case. He could flip and just start killing everyone. You remember what Hanna said. He's mentally unstable."

Gee thanks.

"It's not fair to judge him like this. He hasn't done anything to us. And Hanna only said that when we first found him! He's gone through more shit than most of us here. Besides, Siem's accepted him, so shouldn't you?"

"I won't. Not after what happened to Reed. Never again."

Mist at first went wide eyed in shock before turning into a glare, angry tears building as she tries to control the reaction, "Don't bring that up. You swore never to bring that up again."

Well ain't this awkward. I look around the room, everyone looked like they were told to swallow razor blades. Whoever this 'Reed' was...they must have left a bad taste.

"Mist..." Rain began, his irritation fell. Obviously step on a landmine.

She sniffs and pulls on my arm, "Come on Kae. I'll show you more of the place. I shouldn't have taken you here. I'm sorry."

"It's ok," I could only manage that much, still a little shocked. I wanted to ask but with the way she was trying to compose herself back together told me to keep quiet.

'Blood and death.' Lady murmurs in the back of my mind.

I look up to see X coming out of a lift that we were heading towards. He stops and holds the door open for us and we all managed to fit on in awkward silence. X effortlessly presses the seventh floor button. "Siem has forwarded that he's to retire to the seventh floor."

I look over at him as he stares at the numbers.

"Oh. Um well I haven't finished showing him around though..."

He looks over at her in silence.

"I can show you around later, when you've rested a bit more I guess," Mist says quietly. "Come on. I'll show you how to get into your room." She hurries out the elevator's doors once they opened and sprang down one of the hallways that looked exactly like the one that had the dining area just moments ago. I feel like we're in a labyrinthine hotel.

She comes to a door on our left. "I think it is this one." She looks up to X (who decided to follow us) who nods once as confirmation.

"Ok, I'll just let you in." She presses her hand against the glass surface of the touchpad that immediately flicks green and the door opens.

Peeking inside, I see that it looked rather posh with timber floors and a fluffy white rug that immediately greets your feet at the door. On the right was a modern glass desk with shiny screens and a black bookshelf beside it. On the other side was three pairs of doors. One went into a white bathroom and the other two were for a built in wardrobe. At the far end it stepped down into a space for a bed that was pristinely made with blue sheets and a thick inner-spring mattress and of course a pillow. Behind that was the wall-window that was blocked by a dark navy blue blinds.

It was a freaking massive room.

"Will Lady be ok in here?" I ask, looking around. I mean she can easily fit in here but she's still a wild animal. Lady finds her way in and goes to check out the bathroom.

"This will probably be temporary," Mist smiles, watching me as I investigate the room. "This is a spare room. I guess I'll leave you to it...Um, I'm sure we can continue the tour a bit later. Good night anyway...sorry about everything."

I nod, "Sure. Thank you, Mist."

She nods and scurries off, leaving X in the doorway. I stare back at him as he watches me. Erm...

"You can hear it," he whispers.

"What?"

"The cry."

I frown, even more confused.

"Do not let their lies come in," he reaches forward, pointed directly to my chest. "I...can promise. Promises to protect from those lies. But do not let them in."

"Who?"

His fingers were just barely touching me. "Those who will lie to come in."

So not making sense. "X-"

His attention is suddenly drawn to behind him and he retreats from me. And with that I was left alone and locked in here confused as hell, while Lady just found the shower's 'on' button.

Chapter Twenty-Five: First Job

A /N: Hey...so I haven't been able to update as much as I wanted to...something happened in my personal life that's just made me feel really lousy and it's made want to just sit in a corner and cry out of frustration and hurt and anxiety...it's just overwhelming. But I didn't want it to affect me so much that I just shut down completely so I hope to have at least one or two more chapters up before I'm forced onto a 10 day family trip to see relatives in a few days. I'd rather not, but I have to :/

Chapter Twenty-Five: First Job

My eyes snap open from a shallow sleep as the doors automatically open (and I checked, I was locked in here without a key and the touchpad goes 'access denied' so I gave up, sat on the floor and fell asleep) to see a dark blob in the doorway and painful bright light as the backdrop. At first I thought that someone was going to kill me but my body was slow from exhaustion and the battering and the bruising, so moving wasn't a liable option. Plus Lady is using me as her pillow again with her head on my stomach as she continued to sleep.

As the shadow came closer, their features became a bit clearer. "Chief wants you." It's that brat Mike. "Get up already."

I wanted to say something sarcastic but he had a big shiny gun in his hands and it looked like he was twitching to point it at me and blow my brains out. Instead, I push on Lady's head and she immediately awoke. Confusion smacked my brain first as she looked around, obviously forgetting where we were. As she tries to find herself, I painfully get up, my bones even crack as I make the ascent.

I stumble after Mike as he glares over his shoulder at me when we come to the lift.

"Am I going to be told what's happening or are we keeping it a surprise?" I try to ask anyway.

Mike chose to ignore me. Yep. Surprise. I just love those!

We hope onto the lift in silence. My eyes feel scratchy as I try to rouse myself from this bone-weary exhaustion that I don't remember having. Maybe I was on pain-meds and I didn't even realise it and now they've worn off cos I can so feel every freaking muscle burning and the shoulder ached with a vengeance. I could go back to sleep just standing here, despite this. I am that tired.

"You were sleeping on the floor." Mike murmurs and I almost lost the words.

"...I didn't even realise I went to sleep." That much was true. After looking around the room and trying to get Lady out of the shower and found that like her regular cousins; she really loves water. I sat on the fluffy rug and the next thing I knew it, I was out.

"Outsiders..."he mutters under-breath.

My eyes slide over to him, "You have a problem with me being from the outside?"

He went back to ignoring me. I felt my anger bristle at this hostile welcome I've been getting since I first met Fenir. I shut my eyes and exhale, there isn't any point in getting upset. Like with Fenir and Rain, I was just going to have to get over this. My memory flashes back to the last fight I had with Cody. It felt like a lifetime ago. Calling me what these people are, 'Civs'. I look to the side, suppressing the mix of dejection and futility that's bubbling up my throat again. All I wanted to do was break down and howl out my lungs.

The painful silence broke when the doors finally opened to the floor I was sort of familiar with. There were way more people clustering together in the halls this time around. The air was much colder and still then I remembered. It's night. I don't know how I knew that but I just did. The air felt too quiet. I frown at the feeling of how different the air felt between my fingers.

"Get moving," Mike prompts with the jut of his chin.

I frown as I get off, Lady not far behind me as I try my best to look like I was ignoring the billions of eyes now turned in my direction as I head for Siem's room.

The door slides open without anyone needing to open it.

I see Siem hunched over his desk, staring down at the screen.

Before I could even open my mouth to ask just what was going on he spoke, "I would like your help."

I frown, "With what?" Last time I checked, I'm probably the most useless person here.

"We're low on people at the moment. That last operation was not...as successful as I had hoped. It's left us in a spot but I can't call this off either."

"And that is...?"

"There has been reports of a Keystone spotted in the city-"

"And because I've come back not wanting to gnaw on your bones, you thought of me." How sweet.

He gives me a grim smile, "Exactly. I simply need you to confirm whether or not it does exist and what developmental stage it may be at."

Then Hanna decides to grace me with a jump scare as she starts talking from behind my ear, "Any saturation in a surrounding area of a Queen above 36 percent will start causing 'infestation zones'. But because no one is overtly turning into zombies, the nest, if there is one, is still young. The Queen may still be in its juvenile state, depending on what strain of Hexer it may be. And you're the only one so far who hasn't come back crazy. Even X can't handle anything above 40 percent. Everyone else starts feeling the effects at about 20 percent satuaration." ...There are strains...? What nightmare did I walk into?

"Just what are Queens?" I glare at them. They're referring to these unwilling victims as 'it'.

Hanna looks away from me bitterly, "It's a bioweapon-type infectious disease that is produced by a host that someone started developing about thirty years ago. It's only become a 'popular' way to cripple a city recently when someone found a way to accelerate the process."

"Why?" Why do this to anyone?

"If there was a way to take down your enemy from the inside by one single tiny seed with no consequence, what would you do?" Hanna proposes to me.

"But these are people!" The image of the kid that I had destroyed painfully flashed through me.

She shows me a sad smile, her voice only a whisper, "...I know."

Siem comes over to me, "Can I ask this of you? If what I've been told is true, you may be able to decrease the risks that we face."

Why was he asking? It's not like I have an option. "I'm 'yours', right?"

He let out a breath, ignoring my comment. "X, Rain and Seth will be accompanying you."

Say what? "...You do realise that Rain hasn't exactly put me on his 'favourite person's' list, right?" In fact I think I'm so far away from that list that it's a spec on the horizon at this point.

"Not many of us are," Siem chuckles. Well that's given me hope. "Give him time. Seth is another matter."

"And Seth is...?" I do not need any more people hating my guts. But then again ninety-nine percent of people in this establishment have so far hated me, so he's probably in that area.

"Interesting. Hopefully you'll find him helpful –depending on his mood. He will be my direct communicator. All you need to do is look around and see if you can find anything. And I expect all four of you back at dawn. Don't attract attention. You aren't registered and if they find that you're an Outsider, that arm of yours is the least of your problems."

Not like it isn't much of one now. "Won't it be more obvious with a glow-in-the-dark tiger?" I motion towards Lady.

"You will have to leave Lady here."

Say what? "I can't."

"I promise that Hanna-"

"Hey!' Hanna glares over at him.

"-won't touch her. But you need to look at this from my perspective. She is a Miasmic Beast. If she's seen around the streets, it'll cause a panic. Miasma Storms are fairly uncommon in Bolin but they are intense when they occur. I don't need to add 'panicked crowd control' to my list. She will be fine here. I promise."

I look between him and Lady. The Viking all serious and Lady staring at me with her big innocent eyes.

'Why does Dreamer look upset?' She blinks.

'I need to go somewhere...and you can't come along...apparently.'

The look in her eyes and body language drops into distress, 'Why?'

'...To keep you safe.'

'What about Dreamer? Dreamer safe?'

'...I-" I can't promise that I would be safe. How would I know? I don't even know what I'm about to get myself into. She also has a direct link to my thoughts, so she can read my hesitation and doubt quite easily. This is as annoying as Anne in my head.

Anne...

I harden my heart. I need to do this. I need to play along. 'I need to go. I need you to be safe.' If brining Lady along increases the chance of her being killed because of what she is...and what I am. I'd rather fall alone. She doesn't deserve this.

'Don't want to.' Lady replies feebly. She could gather from what I was thinking that she couldn't come. That it would put her in danger...and in turn puts us both at a higher risk of exposure.

'Neither do I...but I need to do this...'

She stares at me for a moment before one solid thought forms, 'Understood.'

"I'm guessing you've reached an agreement." Hanna's voice pulls me from the lurid, calm colours, tinged with worry; of Lady's mind.

"Yes. What do I need to do?"

Siem watches me for a moment before he continues, "Hanna will need to do a check-up on your condition. From there, grab something to eat and X will collect you." ...I feel like I'm going to be continually 'baby-sat' for the rest of my life.

"So, let's get this over with!' Hanna practically drags me by the arm, out of Siem's office without so much as a second glance at her brother. Lady quickly pads after me, towards the lift again. This time, Hanna pushed for a floor down.

"I'm guessing Mist wasn't able to take you here yesterday," she states as the lift opens onto a bright white clinical hallway that smelt strongly of metal and bleach.

My hand almost twitches to cover my nose. The chemical smell is almost burning me. That metal was tinged with the rust of blood and death. Sick and dying.

"This floor and the one below is our 'hospital'," Hanna reaches for the closest door and opens it with a finger to the touchpad. "Lay down on the Station." She motions for me to walk in and I saw one of those stupid table-things. This time with a desk and chair near it with a computer screen and a plant on the desk, bring some colour into the bright bleached white.

"How's the pain?" She asks just as I hop up onto the damned thing.

I give her a look.

"That bad, huh?"

Lady sneezes.

"I'm guessing she's not liking the smells in here. Ok, lie down on your back."

"I can barely manage either," I mutter as I do as I'm told.

I stare up at the ceiling, a circular light blinding my eyes as I wait for whatever she was doing.

She sits down and a holographic screen appears in front of her. "Ok, nothing abnormal is coming up. Your temperature is slightly feverish but that's to be expected...other than that...you're good to go. I'll just give you another dose of the pain-meds –non-drowsy- of course with something to help the fever that may build in a couple of hours."

"What time is it anyway?" I had to wonder. The window in Siem's office was pitch-black now that I thought about it.

"Three 'o' nine." She saw the disgusted look on my face, "Sorry, Siem likes to start early when it comes to these sorts of cases, when the city is practically asleep so we can move about a bit faster without running into so many casualties. Normally I'd tell him to hold off for a few days...but he can't afford to wait if there is so much as a hint of a rumour of a Hexer population in the city...especially for one as large as Bolin." She then moves to take a closer look at me, "I'm going to give you something light and you're going to eat at least half of it, ok."

She only took a couple of minutes before returning with a bowl of cooked apple and I shovel it down my throat without tasting it. It went down easier than that orange sludge she fed me last time. With that, she handed me a few pills that I looked suspiciously at, but my sore muscles and bones won the argument in the end.

Just as I was downing the last gulp of water, X appears in the doorway.

Chapter Twenty-Six: City Sights

A /N: I'll be away for a week and a bit...wish me luck...i'm seriously going to need it :/

After I come back, I should be able to look at my other neglected works...if anyone has a preference as to which one i should update first, please tell me :)

Also, I have edited a bit of chapter 25. Nothing major...it just felt off tempo for me

----

Chapter Twenty-Six: City Sights

We headed down the in the basement level of the building on the elevator in dead silence. Gauging X's moods is really impossible. At the moment it seemed that he didn't want to acknowledge my existence. As the doors open I was hit with a wall of humidity that sucked the cool air from my lungs, leaving me breathless. Coughing while looking out into the stark darkness, I realise that we were in a dimly lit carpark and it brought back the fresh memories from Bellasera harsher than the air.

Am I going to have to do that again? The look on the nameless boy's face as he disappeared pulled apart my heart and I was unable to stop my right hand from clenching on the fabric in front of my chest.

I felt someone's gaze on me and I look up, realising that I had stopped and X was the one looking back at me. I look away from his gaze and tried to get out of his line of sight. A little ways passed a number of thick round columns I could see Siem, an extremely unhappy Rain and a new guy who could have only been Seth as he leans against a wall, smoking on a cigarette absentmindedly. He was of mixed Caucasian and Asian heritage.

Siem looks over at X and I felt there was a hidden message in their eyes, before Siem's slide over to me, "Kae. You know Rain," he motions to Rain who just glares at me before turning away, "and this is Seth."

Seth looked about X's age but his dark eyes held something else in them as he measures me with an appraising look. I surprisingly didn't feel any hostility from him...or anything at all. Which had my guard completely up. It was the same feeling I got from X. They could kill without emotion. Death without reason wasn't a foreign concept for either of them.

"They will be your protectors-"

"You mean babysitters," Rain growls.

I'm never going to make his Christmas card list.

Siem did nothing to combat his words. "Seth will directly receive orders from me. Need or see anything, tell him directly." He then addresses Seth, "Don't be out in the open passed dawn."

"Understood," Seth slightly moves his head in acknowledgment. He drops the cigarette butt and smashes it under his boot.

"Kae. You should know that all three have orders to take you down immediately if they suspect any of your movements."

Just sign my death warrant why don't you? Rain will probably wait until Siem's back's turned and pop bullets into my chest.

"Hold your end of the bargain," I growl at him. I've just about ran out of patience with these people.

Siem's eyebrow slightly twitches. "Indeed. Normally, I wouldn't send someone of questionable ability and...origins out into the open like this. But if a tool presents itself as a better option than sacrificing my men, I will exploit it."

Knows how to make me feel all special. "I got it." I got it the first time round when he fucking wakes me up at three in the morning.

"Good. Seth, it's all on you."

Seth straightens from the wall and heads over to a streamline shiny black thing that looked like a sports car at first but then it had similar parts of the aircraft and no wheels...it's a flying car...holy fuck. "I'm taking this." Why is everything black?

"Oz won't be happy," Rain states but still moves to get into it. Does Oz like black?

"Don't care." Seth opens the driver's side and turns back to me, "Get in."

I look back over to Siem.

He saw the look in my eye and lets out a breath, "I will promise a further discussion on finding your family when you return. This takes priority."

More like 'if' with Rain's attitude. But I nod anyway and turn back to Lady. 'I've got to go.'

I feel her accept what I say and I reach out to pat her head. 'Until dawn. I will be back.'

'Wait for sunrise?'

I nod and pull back from her and she didn't follow and despite knowing her for only a week it was killing me to leave her behind.

I get into the backseat of the car-thing as it has four doors just like a car and the interior was similar to what I remember from a time when none of this was real. The faded memories had the similar texture and smell. Two seats at the front and the three seats in the back. Mum and Dad in the front. Cody on the left side. I was on the right and baby Anne was in the middle. The same. The memories almost overlap and I shake myself of it when X opens the other passenger door.

I look out the window to shut these memories off.

"Everyone strapped in?" I see Seth eyes flick to mine in the rear vision mirror and I quickly look for the seatbelt. It was over the right shoulder, just like any car and buckled in.

The engine vibrated through me as it came alive. The energy was alive. Similar to how the Fence's electrical orb felt. The pulse I remember feeling when I touched the door sends a shudder done my spine as the energy builds and the car lifts from the ground and shoots up the ramp without hesitation into the dark cityscape of an alien world I was never part of.

In the darkness, I couldn't see the streets save for the lights from buildings and other cars. Lights from stop lights and signs. It was all overwhelmingly nostalgic, tainted with a futuristic utopia of flying cars and airships. I look up to see that the Fence reflected the dark starry sky, invisible to us form the inside as if it wished to peer at the far lights without interruption of pure light pollution that I would have expected from a city of this size.

"This isn't a joy ride," Rain growls at me, snapping me from my amazement.

I look back over at him for a moment, "I'm only looking." How often does he think I get to be in a flying car, inside a city...no a 'city-state'?

He completely turned around to look at me, despite the lack of light in the car, "I didn't have a choice and I didn't want to do this but I'll be clear. Give me a reason and I'll kill you. I dare you."

What has his frilly panties in a twist?

"Chill, Rain," Seth's voice was a spectacular baritone, almost as alluring as X's. "There is no reason to work yourself up so quickly."

Rain goes back to looking out the front, "Just get this night over with," he mutters.

"Mist's still angry at you, isn't she?"

Rain meets him with silence and I swear he's pouting.

"...Where are we going?" I openly ask.

"What the point in telling you, Outsider." Rain snips.

I hold back a sigh.

"...To the lower sections. It's a lower economic zone." Seth instead indulges me with the answer but his tone was chilling to the bone when he addresses me. I knew then that he had no judgement towards me. Nothing that would make him hesitate from burying a blade into my chest.

"It's where the poor gather. The homeless, drug-addicts, gangs fight turf wars...it's typically a very violent, very dirty business." He continues.

So it's the underbelly and black market. Wonderful. They couldn't pick rainbow unicorn land where clouds were made of cotton-candy?

"Where the wound has already festered, who would notice another adding to the rot?" X says absent-mindedly.

Is it just me or is he starting to make sense? Who would notice Hexers rising in population in the city's underside before it's too late? I frown at the thought. Was that how Bellasera was taken down> The area was almost completely construction, no one would be allowed near that area until the developments were completed.

"Awfully talkative tonight aren't you," Seth speaks quietly. "...Your name is Kae?"

"Yes..."

"And an Outsider?"

"Yes."

"Can you actually get closer to a Keystone?"

"...So far." What was he getting at?

The car suddenly drops from its height and skims over the lower area and even in the car, I could feel the air shift. It was humid and choked with smoke. The forgotten and desperate emotions clung to the air like slime in a bog. It was making me sick and I shut my eyes as I feel a headache beginning to throb softly behind my eyes as we get further down.

"We're almost there," Seth's voice cuts into my brain and I open my eyes and looked out the window, almost shocked at the difference in atmosphere.

From what I felt in the air, reflected in the streets. The lights were bright and chaotic. The streets and buildings were made of old, cheap, flaking and crumbling materials.

A thought struck me, "This is the original city." Before the city went up. The infrastructure of the old world left abandoned and filled with those thrown out with it.

"Good eye," Seth agrees and it was almost praise. "This is one of the furthest areas from the Tower. The further from the Tower you are, the high the poverty."

That means we're close to the Fence's wall.

Seth pulls the car up and lands it inside an old broken and abandoned warehouse filled with empty shipping containers and trash. "We're going to wonder around for a bit. Kae, X, if you sense anything, tell me immediately and from there we'll wait for Siem's instruction. Avoid going into the main streets." He states all of this while turning off the engine and unbuckling himself.

As I get my own seat-belt off and open the door, I immediately wanted to close the door again. The air was more putrid than what I was expecting. Even in the backstreets here where there was little life, it hit me like a steel-wall. The heat mixes with a sickening sweetness and acid...bile, piss and shit. Stagnant water mixing with salt and toxic breeze. It was an onslaught of taste and smell. I wanted to gag. There was an undercurrent of rage, despair and desperation hitting my every cell, telling me that death wanted nothing more than to choke every last life in this place. The city has abandoned this place and everyone living in it. I hold it together as I step out of the warehouse and into an abandoned street filled with more litter, hearing a calls from prostitutes in a street over, begging for business and becoming sassy when they were ignored.

I look over at the others who simply ignored the city's stigma and walked into the darkness towards what looked like a pier.

Pity and sorrow plagued this place as much as the rage, violence and hatred. There was nothing to be done except cling to life or accept death. No one would notice.

This was going to be a long night and I don't think Hanna gave me strong enough medication for this shit.

Chapter Twenty-Seven: In the Dark

- -

A /N: Heyo

So went on holiday...met relatives who i haven't seen in 18 years... remember the reason why...got sunburnt to a crisp...now i'm tanned with snow white legs (sexy!)

and just to add to the tension, i had to still deal with the aftermath of the issue i had with a (now ex-) friend (the bitch) and a lecturer (old hag) who were out to make my life a living hell. (both can go take a long walk off a short pier for all i care :))

But now that's over with, here's an update!

- -

Chapter Twenty-Seven: In the Dark

We walk passed a series of abandoned shipping containers lining the cemented docking area along the waterfront. I've almost tripped over a number of indescribable (yet heavy) objects, probably calling for attention from whatever lies in the dark from all the racket I was potentially creating. From that I've earned Rain grumbling about me calling down the neighbourhood and hoping it'd get me killed. I'm just going to make him background noise now. Before his short fuse makes me crazy.

I stop and look out at the dark waters, still as a mirror as it reflects the bright lights in the distance of a world away to those who had to call this decaying disremembered place 'home'. But what stood out the most was the Tower. It was darker than the sky and the illumination surrounding made it that much more out of place that space and dark-matter were nothing but shades of white compared to it. It was that detached from reality, it held no capacity to reflect the lights surrounding it.

I walk out along the pier, my feet carrying me to the very edge as if to get closer to that surreality. It was a pretty picture, I had to admit, even with the distasteful décor on this side of the water. I wonder if people on this side stare at it with a 'one I'll be over there' thought.

"Keep moving," the grouch calls at me like I was some dog on a leash. Kinda am...well now I'm sad...and probably going through an identity crisis.

Sighing, I turn back around to face them, only to have that god damn giant-ass wall looming over the horizon and blocking out some of the sky with grungy, hollow buildings sticking up and hiding at least some of it. Some even had dim light poking out the tattered holes that would have once been mirrored-glass windows. Below that I see at least the grouch and Seth waiting on the boardwalk; Seth smoking and Ebenezer Scrooge (as usual) glaring at me impatiently. I quickly scan up ahead to see X, completely in his own world.

Just what are we looking for exactly? A neon arrow that screams 'this way!'? The Keystone I stumbled across wasn't exactly out in the open and I had to fall through about three storeys of a parking lot first. I'm just that lucky.

Keeping in line in front of bad cop and apathetic cop -I try to ignore the feeling that my spinal column is in jeopardy- I find my gaze always returning to the bright lights of the city (and creepy tower) far away over the putrid water that strangely smelt of a dirty fish-tank and a dish-cloth that been used for six months. I feel a slight wave of hot air pick up slightly and was a little relieved as it carried away some of the smell and sort of felt nice against my exposed left hand-

I collide with a wall and realise that it's X standing in front of me, looking at a bridge just in front of us. At first I wondered if he had a problem with old wooden, half rotten bridges but then followed his line of sight and saw a storm drain outlet. Oh don't tell me-

He moves towards it, jumping like a freaking cat from the bridge and on top of the metal and concrete thing without a care and simple swings down into the open mouth that has little more than a trickle of water coming out of it.

No.

Just no.

Seth on the other hand, kneels down on the bridge, looking down at X "You sense something down there?"

I look down to see X's eyes on my face as he slowly nods once. Great.

Seth then turns to me, flicking his cigarette away, "It's worth a shot."

I ain't going down there.

Two seconds later, Seth jumps down and swings of the rim into the outlet, leaving me up here with grouchy.

...Ok, fine. I'll go. But how am I supposed to get down there? I ain't no parkour acrobat. At best, I can hobble across a flat surface and maybe trip once.

X points to the top of the damn circular thing and I kinda got what he was getting at, he wants me to do what he did. I judge the distance from the bridge to it, it wasn't that far...I can probably jump that make it...

I gear myself to land on it and as I do, I almost slip but manage to gain my balance to look at stage two of the problem. Getting down. As my body is literally the colours of a rainbow at the moment and hurts to move more than walking, I force myself down the front on my stomach, my legs...then torso...then everything else, hanging over the edge. I feel someone grab me and pull me under. As my feet found the slimy and wet hard ground (good thing I was given boots), I came face to face with X...who still had his arms around me. Well ain't this awkward.

He lets go and steps back, pulling me to the side in time for Rain to swing down and land as graceful as the rest of them.

"You're way too skinny," Seth's voice is tinted with amusement.

I had no comeback except for a, "Shut up."

He shrugs and pulls out a light source, a small torch that only illuminated to show more black/dark in here. Oh and the fact that most of this tube is lined with black slime. We trudge (well I do) our way down into the deep dark, the entrance was eventually gone behind a number of turns and it made the claustrophobia start to rise in my stomach. And I'm stuck in here with these three.

X has taken the lead once again, his back illuminated by Seth's torch. The only sounds I hear in here is my breath and the water as we disturb it, walking in opposite direction of its flow. My sense of time I beginning to be disoriented in this dark pipe. How long have we been down here?

Just as I was thinking this, the pipe opens up into a wide open area that took five seconds to get the distorted shapes. It was like a sort of catchment area for the different drains to run into at once into one column, only for it to divide again into different tunnels, one of which we just crawled out of. The water in the big main one, I think was a sort of 'storage' like a tank, only with rainwater. There were several pump lines entering it, to funnel the water wherever but I don't think they've been in use for a long time...especially when I look over to a wall and find the wiring cut.

As I step onto the pavement surrounding the pipes and catchment, I have sudden fear of never being able to escape if I happen to fall into the mass of black water that just barely touches the sides of its container.

"What is this place?" My voice echoes harshly in my ears after the million year of silence we just did.

"...Some sort of old water catchment system? An underground aqueduct? I dunno." Seth again shrugs as he walks over to another tunnel, looking up into the darkness as only a slight trickle came from it. "Point is, it's the exact sort of clichéd thing someone would think of using to dump a baby Queen." He then looks over to Rain, "Hanna's given you the equipment to track the saturation levels. Probably should start checking which of these," he indicates the four large pipes that were dumping water into the catchment pool," tunnels has the highest."

Rain walks passed me muttering, "Some help you've been."

I would take offense, but he was right. I have no idea what Siem was expecting from me.

As Rain mucks about with a weird-ass thing that looks like it belongs to a ghost hunter, I look closely at the four tunnels. Two on the left have a softer flow of water...the one on the centre-right had nothing. But it was the far right one that had my attention for some reason. It has the stronger flow of the four. I step up to walk into it, only to have X grab my wrist to stop me.

I felt like he had one of those toy electric buzzers in his hand as I jolt awake.

"Don't listen," I could still distinguish his gold and silver eyes even in this limited light as he stares right at me.

I frown, not understanding what he's getting at. I can't hear anything. Only the water flowing. I turn back towards the tunnel, "Is it in there?"

He doesn't respond, only lessening his grip on my wrist, but not fully letting go.

Seth walks over to us, just as Rain starts pointing the thing into the furthest tunnel from us and slowly proceeding down the line. "We're going to have to go back in an hour before dawn breaks on the horizon. Will you have enough time to check, if the radiation is low enough?"

X looks to be considering the question, his eyes flickering on me for a moment. "Unknown. The radiation is unstable if we are dealing with a juvenile Queen. There is a possibility that they are still 'conscious'."

"..I didn't think of that," Seth eyes then slid over to me. "Siem wanted me to bring you in case the saturation can become higher than what X can handle. With a Queen...or Keystone as you Outsiders call them- that may still has a 'consciousness' the saturation fluctuates unstably." He's talking like I should understand.

X lets go of my hand gently...I'm beginning to think that he was making sure I'm not going prancing off. "When a Queen is still 'conscious' the disease is fighting between dormancy and activity. The saturation bounces between the two states until the 'consciousness' ceases," and he decides to speak whole sentences to me.

"It's too unstable to produce Hexers but can drive people insane with mood swings and unpredictability. A clear indication can be that suicide rates suddenly jumping or the murders become more gruesome, that sort of thing," Seth continues the lesson.

"That's what happening around here, isn't it?" My eyes narrow in realisation.

"Thirty-nine incidences of suicide in the last six hours alone. Like Siem said, he doesn't want to leave this to chance. A lot of the population is congested in these areas. Hexers will spawn like wildfire."

I really don't want to ask this...but "...What do you mean by 'conscious'?"

"When the Queen is still 'human' during the transformation."

Chapter Twenty-Eight: Banshee

Chapter Twenty-Eight: Banshee

I mentally went back to the nameless boy, the pain he experienced until he forgot himself, begging for it to stop. The memories scraped against the glass that was keeping it from spilling forth and drowning my own thoughts. Screaming out into the dark wishing for an end...an end that I gave.

Isn't there another way? "Can't we reverse it?" I ask. What would happen if this person was exactly like before?

Seth mulls over my question but as the frown didn't shift from his face, I expected his answer, "There isn't one. Only death."

"They aren't willing victims!" I snap. Who in their right mind would agree to turn into a black sticky mess that make people insane?

"...the way it affects a person is like frying an egg. The cells are too dena-tured that it can't be undone. It's not just the physical characteristics that are changed...DNA structure, brainwaves right done to the molecules... Hanna has looked into this for years, the change is too great."

I look down the tunnel, unable to process anything anymore.

Rain came by and checked the tunnel that we were in front of and turns to face Seth, "The first two tunnels have a stable saturation of about twenty to twenty-six percent but it seems to be climbing...As for these two," he motions to the two closest to us, "They are a bit more erratic, bouncing between twenty-eight and eighty percent. It looks like the pipes come from the same source."

"X?" Seth sighs.

X looks down the tunnel, almost as if he could see down there perfectly. "I can risk it."

"...Alright. But you are only going down there to check. Do not engage." Seth's eyes then wondered to me, "That goes double for you. Especially if X cannot handle the fluctuations. You're only getting a visual. I don't want to have to explain to Siem that I got Hanna's toy killed."

Aaaannnd identity crisis. "Wait. You aren't coming?"

"Unlike you, we are normal human beings," Rain snips. "We do not have the heavy gear with us to walk on in there. So we're stuck with you."

Then why didn't you bring the 'heavy gear', you ass? I wanted to growl at him but kept my mouth shut. He has a gun and was still looking for an excuse to use it. But I couldn't completely keep the glare out of my gaze and he returns it like a laser beam was going to shoot out of his eyes any minute and I would melt into a puddle of sludge on the floor. Quite frankly, I would welcome it.

"Okay, kiddies. That's enough," Seth pulls up his hand between us to break our eye-locked battle. "As Rain states, even though we're trained to take on this sort of shit, it's the unstable fluctuations that will get us long before it will affect X. And I for one do not want to experience the idea of cleaning up the aftermath if that happens. Siem would have a fit at the damage."

"Clean up?" my frowning became a little less irritated.

"It would be easier to put me out of my misery," Seth states his demise like he was commenting on how dark it was in here, without batting an eyelid. "Believe me."

I did...there was something about him...how he moves was similar to X. ..something 'broken' inside him. I was starting to put the pieces together and became suspicious that Seth and many of Siem's 'secret police' didn't properly fit the mould that these 'Cities' had and what exactly that might mean, as Mist had said...but I didn't really think about it until I was standing in front of Seth and receiving so much animosity from Rain.

Actually that makes me wonder about how little I knew about what happens inside the walls...at how much Cody resented...was it worth it? Was it worth all of those years of anger and envy, gazing at these blue snow-globes from a distance?

I let out a breath, these thoughts were barbed and circular. No answer, just irritating. And good at fucking with my head.

X suddenly steps into the wide mouthed tunnel, waiting for me to follow.

"...Be careful," Seth adds as he reaches into his pocket for another smoke.

Simply nodding, I quickly fall in line behind X, realising that neither of us have a torch and begin to panic as the darkness feels like it's pressing in on the walls as the opening disappears behind us. I don't want to stumble in the dark...and it's wet, I can tell that it's rushing by my ankles.

X stops, causing me to collide into his back, wondering what's going on. Just as I was about to protest that if he was going to go breaking my nose, he could have at least warned me, I feel his fingers slide something into my palm. It was a cylinder. I knew it was a torch and straight away twist the top to let the tiny light break the dark and a little relief comes along with it.

I notice his fingers linger a little on my wrist before turning back to the front and continue on, without a word between us. Was he...trying to reassure me? Even though he let go, I can still feel the liquid burn tingling on my wrist...bizarrely.

He is seriously one of the most awkward, frustratingly confusing people I have ever met.

As we silently wade our way down the tunnel, I begin to hear something in the distance. At first I couldn't distinguish it as anything more than a vibration in the air, softly cutting into the sound of the water trickling through the hollow tunnel. But as I concentrate, I come to realise that it was someone screaming. Screaming and screaming out into the dark, ricocheting off the thick walls, bouncing until it hits my core and fills me with dread. The screams were of pain and insanity, continually calling out, echoing on and on until it barely resembled a human's voice.

I really, really want to go home.

The soul-wrenching wails continue out like a call. I stop, frozen at the thought. The person was calling out, the sound was piercing and frightening that had a strange mix of allure and repulsion. I wanted to bolt in the other direction but at the same time to come closer. ...I would really suck in a horror movie. I feel my teeth grinding together as I clenched them hard, trying not to think too much, trying to ignore it...I begin to wonder if I need to get rid of the torch so that the thing can't see it.

A sudden gasp of hard breathing draws my attention to X. I quickly flick the light so that I could see him fully and notice the pain etching its way through his body. "Are you ok?" Stupid question; but I tend to do that on impulse.

His stares dead ahead as he tries to control his breathing, "Getting too close," he murmurs, shutting his eyes slowly and opening them again. "Too many voices. Round and round. Death. Joyful. Sweet songs...Can't listen...Round and round. ...Bright red. The taste...pure red of blood...It makes me thirsty." His eyes shut again. "Don't listen."

...I'm going to go out on a limb here and guess that the 'suicide or gruesome killing' effects options that this 'baby' Queen has on X, I'm going to go with the 'brutally murdering everything in sight' one. I look at him fully, wondering what I should do. I'll admit I'm just a little scared of the idea of going on ahead by myself and facing whatever this thing is.

Wait. It's really quiet all of a sudden isn't it?

It's stopped screaming.

The deafening quiet was making my ears ring.

What does it mean if it's stopped screaming!?

"Run."

I look up at X as his eyes suddenly snap open and his body moves at lightning speed to push me to the side and I trip, dropping the torch as I felt something rush passed. Something cold collided with X as he grunts and both he and the thing disappear in the dark, leaving me to fumble for the torch.

Grabbing it, I flicker it in both directions and notice that I'm completely alone...and drenched.

I get to my feet and make the stupid decision of going after them. What's happened to X?

I frantically power walk, heading further down the damned tunnel than I was comfortable with. I was crushing my molars, swallowing back the impulse to scream out X's name and flail my arms everywhere. My breath is shuddering as it escapes, the panic was beginning to set in as I feel like I've gone on for hours but still haven't found any sight of him.

Sounds of screeching and water splashing draws my attention up ahead and I half let out a breath in relief that I at least found something. But that gets sucked out of me as I realise that there was light further ahead. It was synthetic. Pale orange from dull lights.

As I step into it, I see that it was a replica of the weird capture-chamber that we left Rain and Seth behind in. This time, the water was higher and looked like it was covered in black oil that barely seeps out from the big capture camber. Around the edges I saw veins growing out of the water along the cement walkways but have yet to reach the walls or the tunnels. I see that the high ceiling had the old lights baring down on us below, revealing a set of stairs that lead to a sealed in metal door.

Looking down at my feet, I realise the black slime that has been lining the drains...all the way to the start.

A screech draws my attention completely as I see X struggling against something...'monstrous' didn't even begin to describe it. Crystal spikes jutted out of its back, much like a Hexer but the front was different. It was like two bodies were stuck on top of one another...The 'human' part was this naked girl's torso hanging off the neck, chest and stomach of a bigger, black slime and crystal monster. The girl's eyes were covered by black slime slashed across them like a blindfold that melded in with the flesh of the beast's neck. Her hair drapes down to her chest, barely covering her breasts on her sickeningly white skin. Her arms and legs disappeared into the monster, swallowing her forearms, hands and legs from the knees down. Her body slouches forward as the beast swerves to take a swing at X. It looked almost like a lizard...but without eyes or a mouth, just a general shape of a head and most of its body was a strange combination of mush and crystal and only had two front legs. The back end ended as a strange formless tail that melded in with the oil slick of the water and the slime that covers all the tunnels.

I'm utterly speechless.

This was a 'juvenile' Queen!? I am so fucked. At least in Bellasera it was immobile.

I must have let out a breath as the girl, who looked like a lifeless hood ornament, shifts slightly, sniffing the air and her head turns in my direction and opens her mouth, letting out another one of those strange off-human wails that leaves my ears ringing again.

Yep.

Fucked.

Chapter Twenty-Nine: Bloody Mary

A /N: well this chapter was a pain to write...i have scrapped and re-written it like three times...and i'm not sure if i'm happy with it but i know if i dwell on it, i won't be able to continue.

Happy new year's :)

Chapter Twenty-Nine: Bloody Mary

Abandoning X, the two-legged thing lumbers towards me without pause and I'm standing here like an idiot. This time, Cody isn't here to save me. I dodge passed her outstretched knife-like fingers as she pounces like a cat -and I'm the mouse. She probably didn't expect me to move as she crashes into the side of the tunnel, rolling down a little. Getting back up again, she lets out another banshee screech, making me cringe and my vision shaky. So her goddamned voice can mess with my head...yay...

She comes for me again and I dive to the side in time for her to rush passed, but swerves around mid-stride and bounces back in my direction. I don't think I can keep playing dodgeball with the lizard much longer. This time as she runs her scream takes on a new pitch that muddles my brain-leg connection and she almost had me, clipping my left side and sending me into a nearby wall, hitting my head with a loud thud. My vision went black as I crumble to the ground. Wanting nothing more than to let that dark abyss take me out of this nightmarish, humid and wet situation. But instead, I try to open my eyes and roll onto my ass, hunched over hoping the world stops spinning.

Shaking my head, I try to get some focus back into eyes as my brain swims about my skull. I'm also wondering why she hasn't ended me yet as I'm basically a stuffed pig -apple in mouth- waiting for it. But as my mind clears a little, I see X is preoccupying her. He darts around, flipping and spinning, dodging her attacks while striking with his own hands (that I swear are now clawed). I could watch forever, entranced by the grace of this weird death dance. But I could see the pain contorting his face and I felt something lurking behind his eyes, growing stronger as his rationality ebbs away and his attacks are slowly transcending into something more bestial, lost sanity.

I get back to my feet, ears still ringing while the world goes through vertigo and I try to hold down the baby-food I was force fed at three in the morning...why am I here again? I could hear something, almost coherent words, as the Queen screams out in frustration. It almost sounds like 'Help me'.

I keep myself up by leaning a hand on the wall, my entire body feels like it was set on fire while someone was beating the shit out of me. ...I think that the medication is wearing off. Wonderful. A particular burning sensation across my shoulder stood out more than the rest of my body. When I looked at it I realised that the long pointy witch fingers of bloody Queen Mary over there had nicked me across the shoulder, ripping right through the fabric and it felt like she hit bone but I couldn't be sure in this light. But what hurt the most is that through all the bleeding and stinging pain;

I could feeling something like acid bubbling in my veins and made me hiss as I try to compress my shoulder to slow some of the bleeding. I really can't come out of any of this shit unscathed, can I?

I watch as X sinks a hand into the side of the Queen but the muck just absorbs his hand, pouring over his fist as if to take him with it. He pulls back to strike again, this time directly at the torso of the human but she seems to notice this and screams out and he retreats in what I describe as pain, only for the giant claws to come out swinging once again.

Was there anything to hit her with? I look around, only seeing the stairs and the giant pool of black sludge. Then from the corner of my eye, I notice on the wall that was part of the dreary staircase, I see there was some miscellaneous bare iron pipes. It's something at least.

Limping over to it, I notice the Queen losing interest in X once again, sniffing the air slowly, her jaw hanging open when she picks up whatever it was she found and pushes X away. She then turns around and the human head cranes out at me as I grab the pipe strongly in both hands, the metal completely giving me away as it lets out a soft ring as it scrapes the floor and wall.

She obviously didn't like the fact that I was up and about as her human head became...less human as her mouth deforms, leaving only this lipless hole framed with spikes and the jaw opens further than humanly possible. Ok. Nightmare level acquired. Perfect. Great...fuck. I want to run now.

But instead I wield the thick iron pipe like a bat, wanting to at least get her in the face before she kills me, (as at this point, I really don't see the point in running) and managed to time it perfectly to clips her in the arm as she brings it down to slash me, knocking it out its path and smacking into the floor with a thud. She looked up surprised at what I just did and I could even see her frown at the anguished noise that the iron pipe had made when it connected with her arm. Her hit was heavy and if I had taken the blow instead of redirecting it just then, I think it would have broken my arms instead of just making them really numb. ...I don't think I could do that again. As she bears down at me, and I knew she was going to strike-

The pipe disappears from my hands and I felt naked for a second as my eyes went wide at the loss, only for X to come up and wield it, and connects a shot to the up-side of her face forcing it to awkwardly turn. The surprise attack got her off-balance and she tips into the water tank with a great splash and bubbles. My eyebrows probably went through the roof as I stare at X and the bent iron pipe that he just used as he breathes hard with sweat dripping off his face...and I don't think it was because he was out of breath.

He drops the iron pipe as it clangs to the floor, stepping back a little until he hits the wall, slouching over, trying to control his breathing as he stares at the floor.

"X?" I whisper, about to reach out to him.

He looks up at me before I touch him and I almost flinch at the ferocity that reflects in his eyes. They soften when he realises that it's me but then takes in my shredded shoulder. He reaches out and touches some of the fabric around it, his fingers coming away darkened by the blood and look up at me again with anguish reflecting in them that almost made me cringe. I could almost feel something from him, like an apology.

I take in his stare. "I'm ok," I'm half lying but it didn't really matter. Staring into his mismatched eyes, I see that the irises were thin slits like a cat fuelled with pure excitement before a hunt.

But we weren't allowed much of a respite as I was about to ask him what we should do next (my vote was run) as he pushes me to the side, his eyes going feral again as he hisses, "Get away, it's-"

A black mass strikes us from behind and because of X moving me to the side, it grazes passed, skidding to a stop on top of the water before turning into goo and dissolving into the black goo all over the fucking place. Wonderful. I touch the side of my face and notice warm sticky blood pouring form my cheek when she had got me.

"She can fucking materialise!?" I yell at him, unable to suppress some of that panic that was just building up now.

His attention though was on the water at the moment so no remark back. Not like he hands those out anyway. She manages to attack again, this time from the middle, driving me and X further apart and I feel like that was her plan. This happens another few times as she bounces between us until we were on opposite ends of the hall, with X closest to the stairs now. He grabs another two iron pipes, ready for her in a sword stance. Would be feeling the awesomeness of that but right now, a little preoccupied. She lunges at me like a freaking shark but I still managed to stumble from her grasp by landing on my ass. Backwards crawling away from her, I hit a wall to see her disappear and rematerialize in front of X, her wails now a lot harsher and I think were accelerating their effect on X, wearing him down until he was almost kneeling and covered in his own blood. He lost one of the iron pipes, holding onto the side of his head while barely managing to hold onto the other. It was like someone was trying to bind him with ropes, forcing him into submission and he was tolerating it. But he's now on the verge of wanting to burst out.

When she had him on his back, she didn't take the final blow, instead it was more of a 'don't get in my way' kinda thing as she races after me again. I see my doom about to come crashing down, her mouth wide open as the sound penetrates my mind. I roll up into a ball, hands over my ears, desperate for some sort of buffer against that horrible sound. She raises up, reaching out in a pounce.

I don't want to die.

I can't die.

I haven't found them yet.

The Queen bounds headlong, her long talons outstretched.

Not now.

Not yet.

Not you.

It won't be you.

Fuck! Stop it right now!

Something snaps in my head as the sound of metal sings out, lashing forward from behind me. I stare in shock as the Queen stops in midstride, her hands stopping just short of my face. Spears of solid metal had lashed out, puncturing her hand and grazing her sides. Some even pierced through the beast's shoulder and right through where the mouth and brain would have been but the 'human' torso was practically unharmed. Looking closer at the spear I could see glowing crystal blue veins cracked along the metal that shone like a polished blade. ...It was ice and I think glass?

She shrills at the new unfamiliar predicament, jumping back with out of the blades like a fucking ghost going through a wall. But I had hurt it. It was dripping with thick black liquid dripping off its hand where I had gotten it.

'I had gotten it'? Did I do that?

Not able to contemplate on that, she decided to go after X and he was just...sitting there, looking at the ground in subdued silence. His hands were slack but...not in an 'I've given up' way but false; waiting...and I felt something in me break, I couldn't let them attack each other anymore. My instincts were screaming alarm bells at me to stop it.

So my body gets up and I make a strange motion with my hands, almost like I was pushing something out of my way. This made the water stir from the floor tank, shooting out as ice from underneath the Queen in spikes, creating a makeshift wall between them. This stuns the Queen and she looks at me (...not an appropriate time but can she even see?) and growls, only to finally comes at me again and for some reason, I let her. I let her grab me like a doll in one taloned hand, pressing me up against the wall, my feet just dangling from the ground and I just look at her, her giant hand swallowed up my entire torso. The girl's screams out, her voice echoing in my mind. But...I could see something coming from under the bandage across her eyes...tears...?

She brings her face closer and I couldn't stop myself from reaching out to touch the side of her face and everything went black before my eyes, as I feel myself drop into limbo.

Chapter Thirty: Broken Reflections

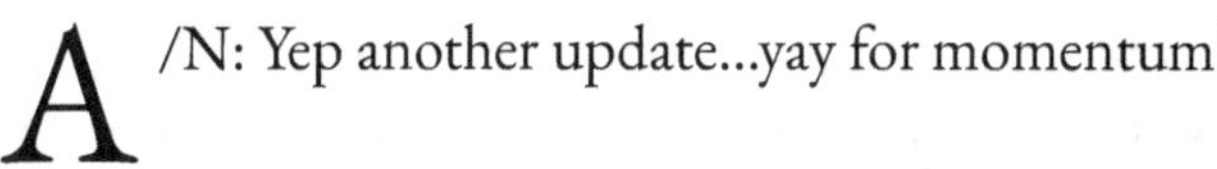

A /N: Yep another update...yay for momentum!

Chapter Thirty: Broken Reflections

My eyes open onto a world that was a vast and empty dark space, like a desert on the verge of twilight and complete night. Only, there were no stars or moon or anything, except a low halo of dull light running the horizon, it felt like the death of light.

As I hesitantly take the first step, I notice that the ground giving off a pale light, illuminating a small halo ring around me, giving me enough sight for a few steps in any direction around myself and it followed underneath me like a shadow. Half wanting to run around like a headless chicken to see if it would follow me, a glowing of blue light slowly dances passed me, leaving an ethereal trail of purple. Watching it, I see another one joining it, travelling further away from me, a soft ghostly chime escapes from them as they move.

Feeling the need to follow them, I quickly walk in their general direction. As I did, I see outlines of charred black tree skeletons but there were only a sparse few. A few more of the wisps sprang up, moving in the same direction I was but in slower speeds, bobbing up and down, like they weren't in a rush. One runs passed my side only to turn into black smoke and dissipates into nothing. Feeling a bit curious at that I keep looking ahead, peering at the trees more closely and saw that a few were crumbling, branches falling off into smoke and disappearing into thin air. This world was dying. And a feeling of déjà vu mixes in with the unfamiliarity of this place. ...Like I had been here before but it's been twisted by this person's reality.

I can't ponder on this. I need to find this girl...I think? Is that where I am again? Whatever it is, I know that is what I needed to do.

Walking passed another tree, I notice that its colouration was split down the middle. On the side that I'm coming from, it was still dark, dead and crispy looking while the other side had brilliant blood red foliage and a dark brown trunk. I stare up at it and a wisp goes through the branches, but as it does, some of the foliage crumbles into the all too familiar darkness, along with the wisp choking into smoke. I recoil back a step.

I walk further along my path and notice the difference as I head further in, the dead wasteland was turning into an autumn forest, sickening from the black rot slowly taken over the trees. The corrosion was obvious, the woodland will soon look like the rest of this place; there was no time left. I bite my lip, not liking where my thoughts were heading.

As I walk under another tree, this time with minimal black rot, I began to hear someone screaming out in distress, echoing from the depths of this place. I try my best to stop my knees from shaking, preparing to meet whatever it is in here. Will it be the Queen? Ready and waiting to rip out my throat? What difference does that make now? Either in here or out there, it's the same. Death.

Rounding a tree, I try to piece together the scene before me.

Between a few trees was a bedroom; two walls strung up like I was looking in on a set on a show. The wall colour was a strong fuchsia pink with a full bookshelf and an unmade bed beside it and on the other end was a small build in wardrobe. On the floor was a thick round pale grey rug that I had a strong urge to roll on; it looked fluffy. There was even a decorative orange and black glass ceiling light dangling from an outstretched branch, creating a false sense of a 'room'. On the floor was a girl who was about my age, looking into a rustic gold oval mirror that was on the bottom of the wall adjacent from me. The girl was smashing her fists against the mirror, sobbing and calling her heart out.

"Stop! Please, stop it! Why aren't you moving? Please! Please! Stop me! Please!"

She continues on and on, her fists thudding on the smooth glass but the mirror doesn't break.

A dreaded feeling rises up in my chest as I suspect who this girl is. What should I do? "Hello," the word awkwardly fell from my mouth before I could tape it shut. Ok, a nice friendly greeting. That'll work...

She yelps in surprise then whirrs her head back at me, then back at the mirror's reflection then back at me –then back at the mirror. Her eyes wide open as she gets onto her feet and backs up to the corner of this 'bedroom', right in front of her bookshelf. She then went back to looking at me then the mirror.

Yep totally going well...

"You-you-you," she points to me then the mirror. "That's you."

I look at the mirror from here, it was only a shiny silver surface to me; it didn't reflect anything and I couldn't help frowning in confusion.

"You're in here but you're supposed to be out there! This is-this- who are you? How did you get in here? It has you...oh my god, don't tell me I sucked you out of your body! It's about to rip out your throat and now you have to sit here and watch it. What'll happen? Will you disappear? I'm am so sorry. So sorry....I didn't want to but I can't stop..." she collapses to her knees, her face in her hands as she starts crying her heart out.

I bite my lip again, trying hard to think as she sniffs. I step onto the creamy pink carpet (nice change from the dead cracked ground) and then the rug, kneeling down to her level, trying not to look stupid (as I'm feeling really awkward). "I'm Kae."

After another sniff and rubbing her nose across the back of her sleeve, she looks up at me, "Kae?"

I nod, staring into her bloodshot soft brown eyes, she is pretty even as a hot mess.

She almost smiles at me, "It's nice to meet you, Kae." She then extend her hand out between us, the one that she didn't use to wipe her face, "I'm Zoe."

I take her offer at a handshake, feeling incredibly shy as I've never really done one of them in about a decade. Even then it was sloppy and awkward but I don't think she cared. She grabs a pastel blue cushion from her bed, hugging it as she curls up, almost relaxing. I take in what she was wearing, I think it's a school uniform. A dark green jumped and a check-pattern tri-coloured skirt with black shoes and white socks that went to just under her knees.

Her eyes flicker to the mirror, "Why aren't they moving? I mean you...and," she hesitates to say, "'me'. Out there. In the real world."

"...I don't really know...but I guess thoughts are instantaneous sometime s...and really I don't think that when you 'dream' that you take notice of the time."

"I guess...I'm sorry for what I've done to you out there...it looked like it hurt...your shoulder I mean. And...your friend..."

"It's ok. He's made of stronger stuff than me."

She shook her head, "You were able to move around even after all that screaming...I saw..."she hesitates to say the next bit and only murmurs it softly, "When someone wondered in before you and your friend, I saw what the voice could do. I-I ripped them to shreds while they just stood there...it was horrible."

"I'm sorry for what you've been made to go through...been made to do..." I feel so much guilt for what this girl has been forced into becoming.

An awkward silence settles between us before she clears her throat and asks, obviously trying to keep the conversation going "So, how did you get in here?"

I shrug, "I can't really explain it...this is the second time I've done this...s orry...I'm not really helpful, am I?"

She gives me a soft smile, "That's ok. How old are you anyway? You look so young."

I sit down on the floor, "Sixteen...Seventeen...? I'm not really sure."

"Younger than me either way. I'm eighteen."

This must be what it'd feel like if I had been on the other side of the Fence...or if this world never existed. I'd be at school...have friends, just random everyday shit. But that isn't the case...I was watching my fingers as I drew them through the plush rug. I needed to distract myself, "...this 'forest' I walked through...and leads to this bed..."

"It's my favourite place...I think I read it in a book once and I've always wanted to go to a maple forest in the middle of autumn and I've always imagined it like this...well...mostly," she paused. She knew about the sickening darkness consuming it, "and this is my room."

Her security and paradise meld together into one another. Dreams never really made sense I guess. I look at the mirror, "Is that how you see what's going on?"

She nods, "...Ever since I can't get out of here, my mirror became a tv," she laughs nervously.

"Can't get out?"

"Yeah. Before I was still out there, I would lapse into here until one day I couldn't get back but I was able to yell at the mirror and it used to listen to me but now it's almost impossible...I've lost all control of my body" her eyes suddenly widen, "...and it's naked, isn't it!?"

"Um...yeah..."

"Oh my God!" she wails into her pillow.

Feeling the awkwardness level rising, I quickly look away and around the room, my eyes landing on an elegant red dress hanging on the door of her wardrobe and I get up to look at it. "This is nice."

She looks up at it and a sad smile glances across her lips, "I was going to where it to prom." She stands up, abandoning the pillow and looks at it lovingly, "It was so hard to find one and then I just saw it one day and...yeah...I saved up for it for months, made the shop owner promise to hold onto it for me and then..." She glances back at the mirror for a second, "But that doesn't matter anymore. I'm in here...this isn't even real and everything is...gone."

I felt only desolate helplessness and wanted to cry for her, my eyes were feeling itchy. "You could still wear it," my voice was barely a whisper.

"How? This isn't real-"

"This is your world. You can decide what's real or not," I urge a bit more strongly.

She looks at me in the face, taking in what I just said and then looked back at the dress, "Turn around."

I did as she asks and turn back out to the forest...and my eyes widen at the sight; the forest this deep had started showing signs of the darkness creeping up and corrupting everything. Shutting my eyes I try to block out the sudden rise of impatience; we were running out of time. Zoe is running out of time.

I let out a breath to try and calm myself, what could I do? ...I knew the eventual answer to that question but not yet. Please just wait a little longer.

"Ok, you can look now."

I turn around and see her standing there rather shyly, waiting for my judgement.

The dress suited her perfectly. It showed her curves without having to dangle out the cleavage much. I might not know much of about fashion or dresses but she really shines, standing there in her red dress. She even managed to apply the right amount of makeup and had her hair in an up-do and dark thick tendrils escaped. She was picture perfect.

She took in my stare and touches her head, "I thought that since you were right, I could imagine my hair the way I wanted it to be and it went like this instantaneously...that's a time saver," she nervously laughs again but then looks at me earnestly, "...is it ok?"

I nod like an idiot, "It's perfect. You're perfect."

She giggles, holding both her hands out for mine, "Then...can I have this dance?"

Chapter Thirty-One: Save the Last Dance

Chapter Thirty-One: Save the Last Dance

"I...can't dance." I want to bolt in the other direction right now. There's an opening right there-

She smiles as she takes my hands, paralysing me, "That's ok, I'm not expecting the samba, just put your arms around my waist."

I've never danced with anyone before in my life. Fuck. I think I'm redder than her dress as I do as I'm told, she's really soft...and warm. She's the same height as me. Her arms go around my neck, "Just follow my lead." And we just sway to an unheard rhythm.

As the seconds tick by in silence I realise that she was drawing me in closer so that she could rest her head on my shoulder and her hold become more of a hug. "You know, I was going to confess my feelings to my crush at the prom," she mumbles into my shoulder. "I was going to ask him to be my date."

"I read in books that it's supposed to be the guy who asks..." I would find the prospect terrifying.

I could feel her grin, "Probably, but I didn't want to risk waiting. I wanted to jump in first and snatch him before anyone else...I'd probably be turned down though."

"I don't see why."

"Thank you. What about you?"

"Me?" I decided to tell her the truth, "I'm an Outsider. I haven't been near any proper civilisation until a week ago. So...no school...no dating...no dancing..."

"Ah, well...you're doing fine."

"Am I?"

She nods, "Yep, just fine."

I asked the question that made my soul go cold. "Can I ask you how you came to be like this, Zoe?"

"I was walking home from work, late at night then I felt like I was shot in the back...and I woke up in that place." Her memories saturated my mind. It was a dark night and she was walking alone back to her house. She checked her phone for a message only for something to puncture her chest through her back, blood pooling from her chest. She didn't feel pain, just collapsed forward onto the walkway and the world darkened into black. She woke up in the catchment area, to watch the door at the top of the stairs shut with a heavy thud, leaving her alone and scared in the darkened tunnels. Her ankles were broken. She could only crawl to the stairs by her hands. The pain was indescribable as she tried to reach the door and bang on it over and over until her hands bruised and bloody. She began coughing up black goo and her arms darkened. Things grew from her back, wracking her in pain-

"You don't have to keep seeing, I can feel it hurting you," she whispers, drawing me out of the memories.

I shudder and swallow the bile rising, "...Did you see who did it?" I realise that we've stopped moving and that she was holding onto me tightly.

"I can only make out dark outlines of people wearing army gear. Even if I did, my memories are starting to go fuzzy..."

The desert and dying trees...the wisps decaying into smoke were fragments that made up 'Zoe' were all disappearing. She wasn't going to graduate from school. She wasn't going to go onto collage. Get a job...get married. ..have a family...grow old...she was in a permanent standstill. Permanently eighteen, waiting to go to prom.

"What about your family?" I had to ask. Was someone missing her? Was someone looking?

"...I was in an institution. My parent were killed in the Disaster."

An orphan to top things off. She had no family. She was probably one of many orphaned children. One that no one would immediately notice disappearing.

"You're right about that," she chuckles, "I often skipped class when I could."

A perfect target.

"Yep."

She then takes her head from my shoulder with a slow exhale and strong determination in her eyes as she whispers into my ear, "It's ok now."

I pull back, still holding onto her, a mixture of confusion and anguish wreck my body.

"..It's ok." I could almost feel her say 'I know why you're really here'. "I'm ok."

I stare at her, blank faced. "Wh-wh-"

"I'm glad I got to be your first dance," she could smile. She could actually smile at me. "I always wanted to be a professional dancing instructor, you know."

I did know. Why do I know? I knew she liked cats. Had a strange fascination for bonsai but her matron never let her keep them in her room. She used to feed a stray dog on her way home every day. Every day without fail.

I look around and see that it's gone awfully dark. Her room was the only thing left that was visible. The trees and the forest were gone. Everything's gone.

"I-" I was speechless. I don't want to.

She hugs me properly, "It's ok." I realise that my right arm had moved back, my fingers straight and ready for a strike. No-

My hand moves before I could stop it. My arm sinks into her stomach without any resistance, right through to the other side. "I'm-I'm," hot tears spill down my cheek from the shock of what I just did. "I'm sorry." I'm so sorry. What-How? What have I done?

She still has her smile as she hugs me closely, "You saved me."

"This isn't saving!" I scream out, a breath shudders in my chest. "That boy said that too. How is this saving anyone? I haven't saved anyone!" I hug her back as tightly as I could with one arm. "Saving you means you get to go home. You get to ask that guy out in this dress and you get-"

"Sssh," she covers my mouth with her hand. "You stopped me. You stopped me before I did something terrible. You saved me from that."

I sniff, looking out into the darkness.

"I got to meet you, Kae. I think that makes me lucky." I don't see how. I think that if anyone sees me they should run and hide before I get them killed. "I hope you find your brother and sister..."

I don't remember saying anything about them. I look up to see her gazing up at what should be the sky...or at least the ceiling, "I always wanted to see the real sky one more time. The one without the Fence in the way."

She then looks back down at me, "I'm so sorry that you are the one who has to do this, it really isn't fair on you to carry this much weight for us," she kisses me on the cheek, "but I'm also happy that it is you," and pulls back, revealing that half her face was the one from the 'real' her; freakishly grey skin, a slime band covering her right eye and the lipless hole with spikes, but I couldn't pull away.

She shuts her remaining eye as her body starts to turn to dust. "It was nice to finally meet you, Kae."

And with that she disintegrated before my eyes.

"It was nice to meet you too, Zoe," I say to the empty air. A single wisp sings out as it darts passed my face and turns into smoke. Her room was gone. Everything that was 'Zoe' is no longer here.

Something snaps in my brain and I'm pulled back to this fucking reality. I stare at the monster that was once Zoe, I had almost mirrored what I had done to her in her mind. I had somehow gotten free of her hold and my own claw was buried into the chest cavity of the 'human' torso. The Queen lets out an odd creaking sound before snapping apart entirely, crackling as the skin starts to darken and peel away like ash in a fire. I pull back from her as she crumbles to dust, feeling dead inside as I look at my hands as they took up my view. Both mirrored each other. They were dark as midnight, the white tips nails gone and only left long pointed black talons. I'm turning into a monster. It suddenly became hard to breathe, my lungs no longer wanting to cooperate. It hurts.

Collapsing to my knees, I beg for someone to end me. It hurts so much. End me before I do something else. My breath is painfully laboured, my vision spiked at the edges as a headache spears through my skull. My body wouldn't move as I sat there, sagging with my claws on either side, looking into nothing. The room was too bright for my eyes but I didn't care. Someone please kill me. The slime around the room started to harden and crack, flaking just as the Queen did. I look at the pile of mush in front of me. She was gone. I knew that her clothes had sunk to the bottom of the tank I don't know how I knew that. What does it matter anyway? Why am I alive?

"Kae! Kae! Look at me!" Someone had grabbed onto my face, forcing me to look at them. "Look at me!"

I see the mismatched eyes, still slit like a cat's, staring straight at me.

"What you can't accept, you can give it to me," he whispers gently, caressing my face. It was comfortable...soothing. I felt a weariness sink into my body. My bones and muscles ached so much. My shoulder felt like acid fire. But the touch of X's skin seems to be dulling everything. He slowly presses his forehead to mine, "Until you can, I'll be the one to do it."

I look down at my hands with blurred vision, I couldn't stop myself from crying. I see that my left hand had gone back to looking human and my right back to the weird-ass scaly/smooth, French-tipped claw that it was before.

"How many more will I have to do?" I'm not sure if I was asking X or just the empty space. I don't know how much more of this I can take. I was ripping someone apart from the inside out. I destroyed them completely.

"I don't know," X murmurs to me. "But don't keep it to yourself like this again. It will cause only you pain and destruction."

"I don't know what to do," I sniff, looking at him in the eye. I don't even know what he's talking about.

"Just let go of everything," and I feel his arms encircle my body completely, his cheek resting on top of my head. "For now, you don't need to do anything. Just let go."

My body went stiff in surprise at the contact. His warmth seeped into me and I couldn't stop myself from clutching onto the front of his coat, pressing my head into his chest and closing my eyes and poured my broken heart out, probably smearing snot all over his front. I've lost my family. I've destroyed a boy who doesn't remember his name. I killed Zoe before she could go to prom...I was beyond broken and yet...I've never felt this comfortable before. This...completeness was disturbing and it scared me but I couldn't move. I don't understand this feeling and it was scary but, I wanted it.

Chapter Thirty-Two: Tiger Pillow

A /N:

It's been a while

I apologise immensely for those who have been extremely patient...i just started a new job and it's really full on at the moment and it will take a while for me to get into the swing of things.

I can't promise regular updates but I will update at least once a month until maybe Easter holidays

That being said, I am looking at updating both Hollow Moon and Only Sky in the next month along with Vivid...depending on how everything pans out.

Chapter Thirty-Two: Tiger Pillow

My eyes felt like I had rubbed them with sandpaper as I open them from a drugged sleep, looking around a dim room. I could barely move a muscle as it felt like I was trying to lift an elephant off my chest. I lift my chin to stare into the eyes of Lady leaning her giant head on me, staring back at me while I was sleeping...again. Is this a habit?

'Dreamer sleeps, watching is fascinating. Heartbeat...' her emotions take on a form that wasn't recognisable and she wasn't able to fully describe it. She then shifts onto a memory of a small bird singing high in a tree.

'Song?'

She stares at me a bit more intently, ' 'Song' '

'Music'.

' 'Music' ...heartbeat...'song' 'music'...soothing.' She seemed happy with the words. Closing her eyes she inhales deeply, 'Broke promise. Sun above the line for sunrise. But Dreamer is back.'

'Sorry...there were things...' I could barely remember anything after that. I only remember getting out of the car and fell into Hanna's clutches as she forces me back onto one of these table-things and then I blacked-out.

I go to push on Lady's head to let me up again, only for my body the scream at me in burning pain that I freeze in place for a moment. My body was covered in bandages. Again. I still had the bite and bullet wounds in my left side...and now to add to the collection was a black goo encrusted bandage where Zoe's Queen had scratched me. And it burned. Burned like I was flaying it with salt jammed into the flesh. I stare at it for a minute, the stains were faint but they still seeped through like puss. I was almost afraid to touch it but I still reach for it. This was probably the only reminder of 'Zoe' left in existence. Even if it was a bunch of festering scratches. I remember she had also gotten me on the check but I wasn't in reach of a mirror to be able to see if it's the same. But it didn't burn the way my shoulder did.

Exhaling through my nose, I move to sit up in the bed as I get my bearings. I see that I'm back in that room they shoved me in with everything on lockdown, a red light on the touchpad beside the door slowly pulsing as a constant reminder that I'm stuck in here. Lady has positioned herself on the floor with her head still resting on the bed now that I had moved her off my chest.

How long are they going to keep me locked up in here this time? I look to the window, completely blocked by the dark grey blind pulled tightly over it. I was alone with my thoughts. And they were dark and crushing. I wanted out. I want to run away from the memories surrounding me, choking me. The physical pain pulsed as a shadow compared to reliving the moments of killing Zoe and the nameless boy. The tortured helpless look on my brother's face as I failed to grasp his outstretched hand, the fear prominent on Anne's blurred face as she was taken away...Markus in pain right until the end...Why? Just...why? What have I done? Why am I still here?

'Dreamer...sad...not like.' Lady moves her head to nudge me in the shoulder, her eyes big and expecting like a puppy. I reach out to stroke her fur. It was soft like velvet and strangely relaxing to feel it running between my fingers.

'I feel so...' I sniff, turning my head away to hide the sudden build-up of emotion and tears. All I do these days is cry. Cry and hate myself over and over. A numb memory flashed in front of me as I remember clutching tightly onto X, smearing snot all over him...and the uncomfortable emotions attached to it. I could even feel my cheeks slightly heat at the thought. Was I so devoid of warmth and affection that I needed to latch onto the closest living body like a brat? And what I felt-

The door slides open to reveal a shadow stepping in...and a feeling of foreboding rises from my stomach as I notice its Hanna cheerily bouncing in.

"Morning sunshine, the monitors indicated you were awake, so I came to check. I would have left you in the clinic but thought it better to remove you from anything clinical and crowded. Lady was also very convincing," she grins at Lady who just stares back.

'Dreamer sleeps, taking others pain. Bad. Not wanted. Sleeps for them.' Lady's tail flicks, almost annoyed.

'What?' I frown, looking over at Lady.

'Dreamer needs to learn to stay away from bad things. Dreamer should dream his own dreams.'

With that she dismisses me with a turn of her head, like I had no say against her.

Hanna comes for me with a little torch, flashing it in my face and blinding me as she pulls and pushes on my eyelids.

"Would you cut that out?" I growl, swatting her hands away.

"Everything seems ok. But your fever is still climbing...how's the pain?"

"Like a flipping joy ride through candy-land."

"Hah, very good. I'll see about upping the dose."

Do whatever. I swallow down some spit, feeling like I was choking on knives.

"Hanna..." I start, I wanted to know what was going on.

"Hmm?"

"What-"

"Is Kae awake?" Mist's head pops in from the open doorway, accompanied by a sullen Mike and grumpy-pants. I guess Mist is talking to him again.

"Yep," Hanna pops the 'p' before sitting half on the bed beside my arm to look at the bandages, "It looks like the discharge is slowing now...let me have a look ok?" As soon as her fingers unwrap the soiled cloth, no matter how careful she was, my body stiffened and I hiss as the wound meets the open air. It was a new level of 'fucking Jesus Christ, why the fuck are you doing that!?' stinging. My reflexes made me jolt and move from her reach.

"So the mighty 'Queen Killer' isn't so immune to them after all," Mike's sarcasm felt like a slap in the face.

"I never said I was immune. I said that I don't know," my voice actually shakes as I glare at him and Rain, unable to supress any of my emotions in time. They weren't there. They didn't know how much that girl suffered till the very end. What I had done...

The guilt was overwhelming-

Lady's ears flatten as she bares her fangs at all of them, 'Get out.' I hid the little satisfaction I felt when I saw the shock and fear flicker across Mike's face.

Hanna backs away, her hands up in surrender, whispering out of the side of her mouth, "Run along you three." Before backing up to the door and sealing it shut with her still inside. "It's ok little Lady. I don't want to hurt him." She steps forward again, "I'll be done as quickly as I can."

I reach out with my good arm, 'Stop.'

Lady stops baring her fangs but her eyes follow Hanna as she approached the bed again. I stoke Lady's fur to take my mind off Hanna pulling out a test tube and a Q-tip, "I think the wound will close over pretty soon...but I'm not sure how fast it may heal."

I was pulling on Lady's fur, clenching it in my fist as the pain is excruciating and I felt my breath dwindle in my chest. I couldn't stop myself from looking at my arm. The gashes were thich with black goo and the flesh surrounding it was an angry red inflames and crusted with a mixture of puss and more of the black goo and blood. But it was the surrounding skin that had me almost horrified; pale and covered in crisscrossing black veins like a Hexer. Fuck. I turn my head away regretting that I just looked.

"Don't hold your breath," Hanna quickly puts the Q-tip into the tube and sealed it up before putting it into her pocket. "It isn't spreading and hasn't had any detrimental effects on your body so far," my arm feeling like you just slowly burned each skin layer off with a laser begs to differ, "...I think it's trying to expel the poison from the wound rather than take it through your system. It seems to affect neurological pathways, making you more susceptible to the 'song' the Queen produces and your body is avoiding that. OK, breathe slowly out for me."

I did as I was told, my arm throbbing like someone was knocking it with a mallet every fucking second.

"Now take a deep breath ...good and out again...good. Keeping going and focus on your breathing," she goes over to a sliding door and take out a first-aid kit, sitting on the bed again and began fiddling with the box and cleaned and redressed the wound.

"You are a wonder, Kae. If it weren't you, you'd be turning into an Alpha Hexer and quite possibly the second Queen."

"Second Queen?" I barely managed with the first.

Hanna nods, "The primary Alpha is an almost perfect transformation and are normally the first or second turned. The Queen was having a hard time picking between you and X. It wanted X as its second but was fascinated by you. When the hive is large enough, the primary Alpha has been shown to expand the nest further by establishing a second colony and becoming another Queen and I can make the assumption that if the original Queen is terminated that the first Alpha takes on that role."

I dared myself for the next sentence to fall out of my mouth, "...Is X ok?"

She slightly smiles, "X is fine. Like you, he does have some resistance to a Queen."

I was actually relieved and I think she noticed the change in my face but didn't say anything, instead she just finishes with my arm and pulls back. "All finished. Right, I'm going to go do my rounds and put this into testing...just in case," she pulls up the test-tube...the black goo stark against the once white cotton. "When I come back I'll have more painkillers."

"Is that ok?' I motion towards the test-tube. I mean I might be ok but what if it was poison to everyone else?

"It should be as long as it's in this. You aren't resonating the song so it's really a poison that paralyses and turns you compliant when it's by itself like this. Your body isn't turning into a Hexer, Kae, so it lacks the element for it to affect others in that way. Don't stress yourself about this. Let me worry for you, you have several days of sleeping to catch up on and I'm quite sure my brother has more in store for you when he hears you're already awake. Mike will make sure of that."

As if by magic, a holographic screen lights up on the desk near the door.

"See what I mean?" she grins as she walks over to it and presses a button, "What?"

"Bring him in to my office," Siem's voice sounded static and irritated.

Yay for me. Mike and Rain has probably said something along the lines of me setting Lady on them to eat them or something.

"No." Hanna simply snaps. "He's done enough. If you wish to speak with him, you can damn well move your ass from your perch and come and see him yourself."

"...This is important. I need to speak with him in private." His voice clicks off and the screen disappears.

Hanna clicks her tongue in annoyance and looks over at me, "I can tell him to shove it up his ass if you want me to."

I shake my head and pull down the sheets and move to the side my bed, gaining a dizzy headache smacking me in the temples. "I want to go." I want to know what's happened since I've been out. I want to know what they have done with Zoe. I want to know if he'll keep his end of the bargain. I want my family back and I damn well want Zoe to be treated right.

Chapter Thirty-Three: Not Quite Human

Chapter Thirty-Three: Not Quite Human

While heavily leaning on Lady, I managed to drag myself into the forsaken office.

X was quietly looking out the window, fixated on something probably far away from the reality he faced. Seth stood by the door, staring at the smoke leaving his lit cigarette. Rain had taken a position close to Siem, who was in his usual position leaning over his desk with his face drowned in blue of the screen on his desk. Mike was next to the door, glaring at me but retreated a little when Lady walks by. Mist was here for a few seconds but then Hana came up behind me and motioned for her to come over. Next thing I notice is her flitting down the hallway to the elevator.

Leaving us all in a thick, heavy silence.

As I stand here waiting, I can feel my body sway like I'm drunk.

"Get the boardroom open." Siem looks directly at Hanna as she finally walks in and the door shutting behind her.

She snorts, going over to a door on the right that I never noticed before. She presses a hand to the touchpad and it opens onto a brightly lit room with a table shaped like a ring and chairs lining the outside.

Without much resistance, I make my way towards the room like everyone else and plop down into the nearest chair. The room has three black walls and the wall of windows; similar to Siem's office. There was another door that probably lead outside into the hallway and the touchpad was blue.

Both Seth and X refused to sit down, leaning on the walls. X had taken a position near me looking out the window, his eyes were still focused on something distant. But when he feels my gaze on him, his gaze switches over to mine and I quickly look away. I could still feel the intensity on my face and try to distract myself by looking out the window.

The air was alive with flying cars, the traffic somehow managing to determine roads in the sky between the building and open space and each other. I would be amazed, watching it for hours but now I was more sloth than anything else. It was already a battle keeping my eyes open without my vision going blurry every five seconds.

Siem was the last to enter into the room with a round table with the giant hole in the middle. Once he did, the door shut and the touchpad turned blue. I suddenly felt extra claustrophobic but noticed that Mike didn't follow. Small miracles when you can count them.

Siem saw the confusion on my face, "All monitors have been switched off. There won't be any record of this conversation."

Well that's cleared everything up. And also just made me a little disturbed at how much is being 'monitored' and 'recorded' normally without the blue light. Especially in my 'room' when I'm asleep.

"I do not want any of the information to be over heard or leaked out to any of the higher ups of the city. Keeping your extended existence beyond being an Outsider is a priority."

For now, you mean. I kept that dangerous line of thought to myself.

"They do not know much beyond you being from the Outside and their interest is sated with that for now and I would prefer to keep it that way. For your sake as well as ours. You are the only one of your kind so far and we do not have the manpower or resources to utilise you to the extent they would want. Or worse, to look for more like you."

I stare at him as he makes his way around to the other side, directly opposite from me. "We need to get moving as fast as possible. If a Queen could have been planted so easily, I am beginning to question this city's future. Hanna, report."

Hanna steps forward and a holographic screen appears in front of her face and she simply flicks it out until it becomes a large 3d hologram that took up the empty space in the middle of the table. "Ok. From what has been recovered of the Queen and from reports prior to its termination," when Hanna stated this, I almost wince. "We can gather that the Queen's influence has only started within the last week."

"But how long has the Queen been down there?" Siem's voice was blunt.

"That's...hard to determine." The hologram in the centre that was stats of suicide and murders in the area drops and is replaced with images of black sludge on the ground of the water catchment area that I just knew that was left of Zoe. My jaw tightens at the images but I couldn't look away. "The cellular reconstruction I've attempted so far cannot cope further than the first stage of mitosis...it's impossible without the original body intact and alive-" her voice drowns out at the memories flooding my mind...the pain...loneliness...despair and fear. She was alone right until the end. Alone and confused and scared. So scared. In that confined darkness begging for an end. Calling out over and over.

"...only indication is the rags of clothing found at the bottom of the main catchment tank." Hana's voice float back in.

"We cannot identify it with only that," Siem states.

I frown at the way they speak of her. Like a thing.

"...Zoe," the word barely escapes as a whisper, no one heard it. They continued their discussion. Why am I here?

Something inside me begins to crack, the fracturing was almost audible in my head.

"Shouldn't you be relieved that it's dead?' Rain's voice. Empty of empathy.

"How can we understand something if we continue to destroy it first?" Hanna defends.

"What are its origins? The shirt looks like it belongs to a student," Seth's voice joins in.

"What of its registration?" Siem shoots back at Hanna.

"Are you an idiot? Of course they'd remove any Registration from the Queen before using it. There is a possibility that it could have been a failed experiment."

"She wasn't," why isn't anyone listening? It's breaking.

"The Keystone strain isn't something I'm familiar with. It could be a new strain altogether."

"Just what we needed," Rain said sarcastically. "Another Keystone type."

"Quit with the negativity. Kae got it in its early stages." With her voice, the hologram turns into a perfect miniature ghost replication of the watch catchment.

I snap.

Shooting from my seat, my hands slam onto the table with a loud thud, "Her name is Zoe!"

My blood boiled over, fizzing in my veins as my lip curls, "Her name is Zoe,"

"Kae!' Hanna and Siem call out my name in surprise but I was over it already.

"She isn't from Bolin. She was dumped here two weeks ago. They broke her anckles before literally chucking her in there to rot. She was an orphan. Jumped on her way home from work."

"Kae, you need to calm down," Hanna's voice niggled in the back of my mind but all I feel is a white hot rage. I can't stop.

Dreamer stop! Even Lady's voice was too far away.

"She didn't choose to become a Queen. No one ever choose this. Not her. Not that boy in Bellasera and certainly not my brothers or my sister who are still out there. Are they doing this to them? How many more?" My voice is strained it almost bleeds. "What right do any of you have to make any judgment on us? What right do you have to look down on any of us and play with us then toss anyone aside until they don't even know their names? Zoe was losing herself inside it all. The boy in Bellasera. No one cares!" Someone stop me. "How much longer am I going to have to play this game-"

Something pricks me in the neck and I immideately look over to Hanna who steps away with an empty syringe in her hand and a keen expression on her face. I shake my head at the sudden drowsiness and my vision goes dark. It was the same sinking darkness rising up to me as I crash down without feeling the ground, my voice barely making it, "How is any of this fair? ...I just..." I just want to stop...want to stop changing...stop before I turn into a monster. I want my family back. I want it all back.

Intense silence followed with Kae's decent. Stunned, save for X who had grabbed him at the last second before his head clipped the table, the others looked around the room. The hologram was fracturing into splinters of a jagged scene caught on a freeze skip like an old movie, white noise strips cutting into the image, destroying it completely. The walls and glass had cracks climbing from the ceiling down, almost touching the ground but stopped when Hanna took him out, the glass on the verge of shattering. But it wasn't the effects he had on the room that had them weary.

He was changing with the emotional rampage. The black marking climbed into his eyes, changing them to black and yellow. But his teeth and arms were showing more developmental change. Long black taloned claws and elongated canine teeth...he was turning. How far would it go? What would the change show?

But when Hana intervened, the changed reverted back like a wilted flower, pulling into itself until Kae, exhausted and drained, was back.

With a sigh Seth opens his mouth, "You can't keep turning to the Tranqs to calm him, he'll develop a resistance at this rate," while grabbing another cigarette from a hidden pocket in his coat, and lightning it. With a deep breath he takes in the imprinted memory from this morning. Metal, concrete, ice and diamond twisted into contorted forms, converging onto two different places. One was a series of spikes on an iron wrought fence, jutting up at awkward angles for a makeshift wall. The other was pure intent; forced forward into untainted violence with a kind of warped beauty.

That kid had done it. His eyes flick to the slumped form now in X's arms. Seth had seen him after X radioed them into the area; his eyes reflected nothing but there was something burning away within that dark emptiness. Was this how he looked the first time they found him? And his mental instability wasn't a joke if he could all this. No wonder Rain's so riled up.

His eyes slid over to Siem, "What were you hoping for by bringing him in? He was already exhausted and mentally shattered. We had given our reports without his input."

Siem frowns back, his eyes slide over to Kae's form, "We're running out of time and you were not there." His gaze flicks back, "I also gave you clear instruction not to pursue it." With that, he pulls back and touches the touchpad to his office and walks through it muttering, "That wasn't Hexer."

Chapter Thirty-Four: Grim Reaper

A /N: Hi :3

Sorry the chapter is a little short but I really wanted to post something up tonight. I'm still in the middle of writing up the other two works and I hope to have an update for one of them by next weekend.

If not, I will be on holidays for Easter in 2/3 weeks and will definitely be updating them :)

Till then, thank you for being so patient with me and I apologise immensely for the lag in everything. Work is extremely busy...and will be for a really really long time. Being paid helps though (just)

Chapter Thirty-Four: Grim Reaper

Letting out a breath, Seth waited for Siem's next move...and fix the lights/assess just how much damage Kae unleashed. He had recounted the events, as had X but Kae was, well, incapacitated at the moment. The gashes along his shoulder were festered and meant he wasn't completely immune to a Queen. They were shallow but they continued to seep black goo, even through the layers and layers of white bandages that are now wrapped around them. The boy's form was completely exposed without the hoodie. Seth had made the joke about his weight but in all seriousness, looking at him now, the kid was almost malnourished. Dark circles ringed his eyes and he looked like he was on the verge of slipping into a coma, even in his sleep. But despite all his 'human', his right arm completely subtracted from it, making almost everyone in the room warily glance at it every now and again...plus the giant glowing tiger sticking to his side probably didn't help. The tiger, Lady, stares into the boy's face, nudging him every now and then with her nose in distress.

Siem had sent out some of his men (and Hanna was chained to the floor to stop from joining them) to profile the 'Old World' rain and storm water system, collect the left over sludge that was once the Queen and the bits flaking away and washing into that goddamn lake. They had also collected the information for the holographic reconstruction of the area that Kae just destroyed and from the somewhat angry discussion Seth could overhear Siem having, Kae royally fucked almost all the data over.

They were stuck watching Siem relaying the orders back in his office through the door he left open and refusing to dismiss them just yet. Rain was in a corner as far removed from the kid as possible, busily glaring at the sod but at least was retaining the need to verbally contribute to the mess.

But X, as rare as it was, was holding onto Kae like he was something precious...a human emotion that Seth could bet was virtually foreign to a manufactured Death God.

X was far more in tune with that part of him that was created to be that perfect weapon on the battlefield than any other of his kind and probably ever will be. Seth could vividly recall such a time when X was an indestructible killing machine. In such a lop-sided battle, a single small form emerges from the bodies and fire. It had the form of a child, no more than fourteen, eyes reflecting the surroundings with perfect precision, never wavering, never shifting from the single goal; kill.

It darted around the battlefield like a ghost, tearing everything limb from limb without restraint or feeling.

Seth was another subject forced to undertake the experiments but he could never recreate the same results or beauty of death that, that X had. Because Oz and Siem saved him before he completely lost his humanity. Something he was quietly grateful for everyday.

X never had that luxury.

So it was surprising to all of them at just how...was the word 'obsessed'?- X was becoming with Kae. But then again no one has ever heard of a Miasmic Beast sitting in a room of humans without wanting to tear them to shreds. There was something...'special' or maybe 'off' about this Outsider.

Siem walks back into the room, his footsteps heavily clicking, "Kae has managed to affect systems on all floors. This includes the private property. It isn't too extensive beyond a blackout on the floors above and below here and that's what I am going with at this point. The backup power supply to the medic floors are currently running while we are trying to restore power. Structural damage hasn't extended beyond this room but it isn't anything too drastic beyond replacing the window. However, he's managed to affect all the files concerning this case...and anything on Bellasera."

Hanna lets out a breath, "Well, since he's going to be out for the next twelve hours, if not more, I believe it's time to leave him be. This time uninterrupted." Seth could tell that Hanna was trying to hide her annoyance at the hours and hours of research she has complied in her spare time just literally went up in smoke.

"...Fine."

"Good." She then mutters under her breath, "Why you needed the information out of him now is beyond-"

"Hanna. Did you just listen to a single word he just said?" Siem's voice became slow and controlled. "The subject that was used as the Queen's chrysalis was not from this city. They managed to slip through the security systems in place within the Fence and plant it without alerting any of the defences. They have managed to actually destroy the subject's registration without alerting any of the official authorities. Globally. This case is too strange. And I'm meeting with Yue in twenty-five minutes. I cannot present nothing when explaining why we were moving about old city infrastructure this morning without clearance."

"And what Kae's just done with in fact made it worse," Rain snapped.

Seth pulls away from the wall, "We wouldn't have known that the Queen was not a subject from Bolin. Worse, a targeted citizen. For them to use a 'normal' person..."

"But you have no liable evidence to prove this. It's an Outsider's word. How can anyone trust-"

"What reason would Kae lie, Rain? What could he gain?"

"That isn't the issue. Are we sure that...whatever drug-trip he went on was real? Can we be sure that Bolin's higher-ups will take what we say at face value?"

"Not like they have a choice-"

"Enough. Rain. That is my problem. Not yours. If you have no more to report, you are dismissed for the day." Siem's growl reverberates in the tense air. Waiting for him to leave, he turns to Hanna, "Get the techs onto this and see how much they will need to re-collect from the site. If we leave it too long, the city police will be starting to sniff about."

"Right. Well...X, we should move Kae to the medic ward."

"No." X moves towards the door, holding onto Kae gently in his arms. "Let him sleep somewhere away from the 'noise'. Let your patients heal on their own. He has done enough. Anymore and it will break him."

Hanna stares after him, "That wasn't what I meant, X."

"I know." But he still walked away, Lady not far behind him with a swish of her tail.

Hanna exhales, "Dammit. I only wanted to keep an eye on him in case something goes wrong. Kae's mental and physical health are too imbalanced."

Seth steps up to the door, "If there is nothing you need from me-"

"Seth Leonardo Black!" The minute he opened the door, Oz was right in front of him like a tall jingling shadow.

Seth mentally sighs.

"What right do you think you have to use my car without my permission?"

"Oh my god, someone's on fire!" Seth points behind Oz.

As soon as Oz took the bait, Seth pushes past him and makes his escape.

"Oi, you damned brat, get back here!" Oz charges after him.

Seth manages to slip into the elevator with X, just as the doors shut, leaving Oz angrily muffled shouting at the doors on the other side.

X watches Seth carefully, "You cannot outrun him forever, Seth."

"I can try." He could feel X still staring at him. "I'll deal with him later. How is the kid?"

X meets him with silence.

Seth could take that as a sign to stop asking. Instead he went with, "Where are you going to take him?"

"...Down. Away from all the noise."

"...Back where they've already placed him?"

"Too much noise," X shakes his head. "Too many know where that place is. Must be..." he slightly cocks his head to the side as if someone had just spoken to him. "...quiet and away from eyes."

"You aren't thinking the Abandoned Grounds?" Seth couldn't stop his brow from dipping.

X met him with more silence.

He couldn't supress the sigh. "It's up to you. But if Kae needs medical help, he'll be too far away."

"It would be better if he is as far away from Hanna as possible, for a while. Besides, I will be with him. It will be safe, away from everything and everyone. He won't need to fear what he is or what he can do."

Seth stares at Kae's slump form, "...If you think it's wise. But I don't think it's wise to put him somewhere where he could collapse the entire building from its foundations. But maybe it's a good idea. He will need to start training eventually. Understanding the training grounds would also be a good idea." The elevator stops on the dining floor and Seth jumps off. "X," he puts his hand up to stop the door from closing. "You need to be aware that the kid doesn't like himself. That he is petrified of what he is."

"...I know. You know as well."

"Yes. But unlike you or even me, he isn't going to cope by thinking it through. His thoughts will be too dark for him to process. He hasn't gone through the same experiences or training as us."

"I will be with him," X repeats, a frown forming on his face. A rare sighting to see any sort of emotion painting his features as the doors finally shut between them.

Chapter Thirty-Five: Safe.

/N: Hi :3

so, on holidays at the moment. so i'm hoping to get a few more chapters out over the next week :)

Chapter Thirty-Five: Safe.

I was under the same damn tree again. This time, there was no snow to dench the dead surroundings. The tree still looked barren and voided, stark black silhouette against the pale grey sky stuck in twilight. But the silence was still as ear piercing as before. The ground, dry and cracked seemed fragile under my feet like if I took a step it would crumble away.

This is wrong.

I shouldn't be here.

My dreams are bleeding into each other. This shouldn't be here. I shouldn't be here.

Soon there will be no difference.

Does that matter?

Yes. No...

Which is it?

What is and what was do not matter. What is reality...is only perception. Truth is false. Choice.

You are so helpful.

Sleep.

Isn't that why I'm back here again?

Silence again.

What is this place?

It's familiar but I shouldn't know this world.

But I do know it. Somehow.

The contradictions tighten in my chest with rising agitation, stopping me from taking a step closer to the dead tree.

It sleeps. Forgotten.

Whatever.

Safe.

From what?

Silence again.

"You're really pissing me off! Answer straight for fucking once!" My voice didn't echo on, like I'd expect it to in a wide open space. Instead it fell as mute noise like I was shouting at a TV screen.

This is bullshit.

No response.

Fucking typical.

Something runs passed me in my peripheral vision, I snap my gaze in the direction, only to see nothing.

I couldn't mistake her, even for a second. Anne.

Turning around full, I come face to face with a window, looking out onto the nightscape beyond. Blinking, I take a step back, seeing that I was in the living room of the holiday house in Switzerland. The warm glow from the big fireplace illuminated the room enough, giving the false feeling of warmth but I still felt nothing. Turning away from the window, I saw the stairs leading up to the bedrooms and the front door in front of it. But that was all. It felt like a dollhouse. Behind me opened up onto a familiar autumn forest, small blue wisps darting around and amongst the fire-coloured leaves. I turn back to the window. I won't go back there.

Not now.

Shut up.

Outside the window, I see Anne walking away from the house, out into the snow tainted silver by the moonlight. Gathering myself together, I run for the front door, bursting through in the hopes of catching up to her.

The door opens onto pitch darkness as I scream out her name. It was a darkened corridor.

Dreams are so fucked up.

Following the corridor blindly, I see the light at the end, with a wind picking up and snow seeping onto the floor. Like blood.

I look down. It's blood.

Taking a step back in fright, I look up and see Anne on her hands and knees, digging in the blood-tainted snow.

"Anne...?"

"...safe," her voice was softer than a whisper, I barely made out the word. She continues to dig in the snow, as if I don't exist.

I stand directly behind her, her dress in tatters and smeared in blood. I reach for her, my fingers actually shaking at the cruel fucked up joke my fucked up mind decided to pull on me. "Anne?" I repeat.

Just as I touch the fabric on her shoulder, her head unnaturally snaps up like a marionette on strings. What greeted me made me pull back in shock. A chunk of her face is missing. Her right eye-socket was completely gone. Only a jagged hole looking into a cavity of bone, flesh, blood and muscle. The top of her jaw peaked through torn flesh. Whole chunks missing along her cheeks, should more muscle and teeth.

"Safe." She muttered again, her exposed muscle moving in time with the words. "Too late," her fingers pull away from the bloodied snow and reaches for me. The skin was pale grey with black veins.

I pull back, the back of my head hitting something hard and I see stars with the throbbing pain. "No!"

Too late.

"Too late," I repeat, my voice coming out in sobs, unable to control the reaction, I look around the unfamiliar room. I'm tired of this. Where am I now? Where's Anne? I didn't mean it!

"Give back Anne!" I rasp, completely disoriented.

"Hey!" darkness grabs my arms, pulling me into disarrayed panic.

"No!" I scream at the dark. Stop it. I don't want anymore.

"Kae!"

"No! Give her back."

"Kae," X's face suddenly materialises in front me, the darkness around my shoulders became his hands. "You're ok."

I don't know if this was dream or reality. I can't tell the difference anymore but knowing he was in front of me, something solid gripping my shoulders made all the floodgates open. So I cry. Cry until my voice is hoarse and the words I mutter don't make sense, even to me. I keep on apologising. Over and over. Even in my dreams I'm too late to save anyone. But X stayed. He didn't turn into mist or runaway as my mind expected. Instead his warm form stayed wrapped around me until I sink back into a darkness without realising it.

My eyes open onto a darkened room that I've never seen before. It was small, only big enough to hold a bed within the walls. I realise that I was holding onto something tightly. Looking up, I see that it was wrapped in fabric. Sleeve. Of a coat? Arm. I was wrapped around someone's arm. Blinking, I barely register that it was X, sitting beside me on the bed. He must have noticed that I was half awake as he suddenly starts t stroke my head. Slowly, gently. Like he's trying to soothe me back to sleep. If I had the energy, I would be freaking out right about now. But the effort and the pain was too much to bare.

I notice that his fingers linger on my eyebrow.

...Ah that scar. I sleepily open my mouth, barely able to mumble through the sleep fog overcrowding my mind. "I got that when I was six. Cody went off to some skate-park and left me behind." I had to laugh at myself. "Even back then I was afraid that I was missing out on something...so I went after him. Didn't look at where I was going and collided with someone when I ran across the ramps and shit trying to get to him." I move to touch it myself. "Got blood everywhere and had a few stitches. Now that I think about it, it's the oldest scar...Kinda a reminder that there was such a world, once upon a time. Still, nothing's really changed. I'm still a cry-baby running after his brother."

"...Is that so bad?" X says after a time, his eyes focused elsewhere. "Your brother will always be looking over his shoulder to check if you're there. That will always be his constant... and will be something that he will always be expecting."

I half smile, "You have a strange way of looking at things, X."

"...Is it really so strange?" I felt his eyes on me, expecting. Almost a silent panic that he was afraid that I was rejecting him. Odd.

After a yawn, I find my voice, "Not really. You're you. I like it." I think I said something rather bold but I was too fucking tired to be bothered with it and felt my eyelids close again to sleep.

I wake again, this time looking at the ceiling. I shut my eyes in order to hold onto the image in my mind while searching for the quiet I should be hearing. And yet, underneath it, there was a strange thrum. Like a melancholic song playing so softly that you had to be concentrating specifically for it.

It pulses like a heartbeat. It was unnatural and was cruelly continuing to play, like a light that wished for nothing more than to be extinguished but was continually being drowned in fuel. But where was it coming from?

Two songs.

I open my eyes. There were two songs. Two rhythms. Both of death. One tragic. One suffocating. One wanting death of itself and one that wanting it of everything but itself.

"You're listening again..." X's voice almost felt like a shout and jolts me straight out of my skin. It was almost a scolding.

"Who...what?" I sit on the bed, twisted in the sheets.

"The calling."

"What are?"

He tilts his head to the side like a puppy. "Those who are calling out. Tragic screams. Over and over."

Why does he chose moments like this to talk in circles? I rub a hand over my face, looking around. "Where are we?"

"The Abandoned Grounds."

He moves over to a 'whoosh' door and it opens onto more blinding light. I blink at the painful onslaught, "I don't know what that is."

"...Training area and I guess you would call parts of the structure, 'ruins' ...or 'remnants' of an underground subway station from before...amongst other things."

"...Are you saying that your group are using some abandoned old world shit as your gym?"

He meets me with the silence as he walks out of the room completely.

I was about to mumble a number of profanities under my breath when he returns with two bottles. One's water and the other looked like orange juice. He passes them both to me before sitting down on the bed beside me.

I look around and notice that Lady was missing.

"She will return," X's voice was gentle. "She is exploring for herself."

I open the water bottle and take a few gulps down. The songs I was hearing..."There is something else out there isn't there?" I was at least sure that the song wasn't of a 'Queen'...I hope. But for some reason, it sounded similar...like they were almost the same kind of thing but ...not. Not like I'm having a hard time understanding anything already. Let's just add an extra dash of insanity shall we? Urgh this is giving me a headache.

"Yes." X says simply.

And he's turning it into a freaking migraine.

Chapter Thirty-Six: Threads

Chapter Thirty-Six: Threads

Letting out a sigh, I look around the empty, dark room. How long have I been down here? Who knows. The pain meds that X has been slipping me has made it impossible for me to track time...plus being underground kinda makes it hard to tell anyway. But thanks to the hours and hours of sleep, the level of pain was relatively reasonable. Minus the headache that is my life right now and the thousand plus scars, scratches and bruises adding to the tally I've acquired over the years of running and screaming.

But the dreams...they got so bad that the mix of dream and reality did my head in and I was a screaming mess for the most of it. From what I can remember (which isn't much if I'm honest) X stayed close, never complaining or getting upset with me...he just patiently calmed and reassured me over and over, much to my embarrassment.

But the memory of it stuck. Anne and that bloody tree. Some times when I was able to reach out to her, she literally turned to ash, scattered to the breeze, leaving me alone in the dark. Other times, my hand went straight through like I was a ghost and she continued to dig. My gaze fell to my hands. Still the same; the left is still normal and human, but my right... still looked like I lobbed it off Satan and stuck it on. Pulling it closer to my face, I notice that the weird vine tattoos above my elbow seemed to have changed. Do they change every time I go 'funny'?

Thinking back on it, I also get funky demon eyes...

What the fuck am I?

'Dreamer is Dreamer. Dreamer is kind and gentle.'

I look up to see Lady staring at me in the doorway. I know she is trying to help but it wasn't an answer that my spiteful side wanted.

Her ears slightly tip back, probably at all the negativity I was spewing out in the dark corner I've put myself in. But she still walked towards me, not backward on hopping onto the bed and circle around me like a big blanket. Surprisingly, the bed held both our weights without a groan.

I'm sorry,' I manage to say back to her as she runs her head on my shoulder.

'Not place for us. This human territory is wrong. Smell is wrong. Feel is wrong. Everything is wrong.'

'Hate to break it to you but I am...-mostly human...' I think.

'Dreamer is Dreamer,' she repeats, her raspy tongue glides over the back of my neck and head. I jump at the spiny rough texture of her tongue. She let out an amused noise. ...Is she giggling at me? I could feel her saliva wetting the back of my head and it sent goosebumps down my spine. I pull away only for her to use her paw to pull me back and continue to lick through the hair on the back of my head.

"Ew, I can feel it all sticking up," I complain out loud, almost ready to give up and be the ragdoll toy that I knew she could easily make out of me.

X picks that moment to show up with more bottled water and some more pain meds. There's barely any room left on the bed but he still managed to sit down in front of me, completely impartial to the fact that I was sporting a new hairstyle with tiger drool. He just holds the bottle and packets up until I take them from him.

"How long am I going to be down here?" I ask while opening the silver packet, not even caring what he was feeding me. And for some reason, I have never felt any doubt and took it without hesitation.

"...A little longer," X vaguely replies.

I glower at him but drink down the water anyway. I look at the door, I'm starting to get cabin fever here. As I finish the bottle of water, X stands again, taking the empty packet and bottle from me and going out of the door once again.

This time, I gathered myself to stand and follow him out the door. I only had about fifteen minutes before the pain meds kicked in and knock me out cold again. Not moving a muscle properly for god knows how long, has left me shaky in the legs and I wobble towards the door, leaning on the wall. The door led onto a simple, stark kitchen with standard bare-minimum kitchen things; benchtops, fridge, stove and chairs. But in the doorway of the next darkened room there was a window that looked out into the dark and empty subway platform.

One of the lights outside was flickering like in one of those horror films before a demon came out and threw you onto the subway tracks to get hit by a ghost train.

"This was a station attendant's room...Siem has refurbished most of the infrastructure of the subway for it to suit the idea of living underground, as well as for training." X answers the question before I could even ask.

I manage to hobble over to the stool in front of a breakfast bar as X was busy looking through the fridge. "X..." I start, but not sure what I was wanting.

He peaks up at me before coming over with another bottle of water and busing himself with a microwave. But I knew he was still waiting for the continuation.

"...do you have any other name than 'X'?"

"If I did, I can no longer remember it...I don't remember much outside the Institute...Memories are fragile when it is tampered with. Pain. False. Empty. Perhaps it is for the best that I cannot remember anything from before. Family. Friends. What they were...their colour no longer dyes the threads that were cut. Barren cut threads. Can longer taint if they no longer exist. New threads. New colour now dye memories and influences my being."

...As always speaking in riddles, but I picked on at least the first half of it. I do want to understand him as much as I can but I feel like I am limited to how much of 'X' will share of himself...especially when he talks so roundabout. "What is the Institute?"

"IRS. Institute of Research and Society. They were heavily involved in biotechnological research. Their focus was on Miasma application on living systems. It then extending to producing weapons...as most research does."

"So...there are ten of you wondering around?"

"No," His voice was sharp but then softened, "From what I know, I am the only ones left of IRS. There were three...but things were compromised."

"It doesn't have anything to do with this 'Reed' person?" The name pops into my head.

"Yes. She was...an 'unfortunate' case, I think the term would best suit her situation. It hit a lot of people hard but I think Mist is still reeling from the psychological effect the most. Reed was almost a mother to her...and the betrayal was not something she saw coming. Neither did Reed to be honest."

I was biting down on the need to ask for details but something told me that X was not going to share any more than that.

The bastard seemed to have read my mind, "You will have to ask Siem or Mist for the actual details, Kae. I was not...present when the events took place. I only cleaned it up."

That sent a shiver down my spine. "Was it difficult?"

He watches me keenly for a moment, as if assessing my question. "...You mean was it difficult to dispose of another subject or if I had personal ties to Reed that made it difficult?"

"I don't know. Both." I feel Lady putting her head in my lap, wanting a pat and looking for a distraction, I complied.

"...She was built for assassination...and her abilities were based on mine as she was a later subject. But she lacked certain...survival instincts... As for personal...I could overlook any subjective feelings."

I feel like he's skipping over some details here but left it alone.

The microwave dings and he turns around to attend to it. He places a bowl of porridge in front of me and went to go get some milk, honey and a spoon. "You need to eat something. It's been almost twelve hours since your last meal."

I look at the porridge, unsure if I could stomach anything. But, I manage to put the milk and honey onto the rolled oats, stirring the mixture with the spoon before getting the courage to even bother having a bite. I didn't taste it. Instead, I was probably more put off by the novelty of using a m icrowave...food coming from packaging...it's not something I've properly experience in under a decade.

As the silence stretches on, I notice my eyelids getting heavy again and lifting the spoon began to feel like an effort.

"...You changed the medication," I mutter, dropping the spoon back into the almost finished bowl.

"...Your body is becoming resistant to the current drug. I apologise if it makes you angry."

I shake my head, half disagreeing, half shaking off the dizziness that was building. "I trust you, X."

Even though his facial features didn't exactly shift, I felt like he was relieved and happy...and perplexed at feeling happy.

"Is it so weird to feel happiness, X?"

"It is foreign to me. Yes. I do not remember..." he trailed off, I felt like he was unsure to continue. Whether it's because he can't remember or he didn't want to share, I mentally shrug, beats me.

I look back down to the bowl, "I think I need to lie down, again." I stop myself from pushing him. Instead, I get to my feet and head back to bed. Lady helping me every step of the way.

"Kae..." X calls after me. I stop, turning around, surprised to see him right in front of me. "I like it though."

My cheeks suddenly radiate like the sun. "I guess that's...good...?" what am I even saying?

X grabs the sides of my face, tilting my head slightly down as he presses his forehead to mine. "I...wonder if the colours will drown or smother...or fuse into something new..."

Ok.

X is seriously fucking confusing.

And my heart is smacking itself against my ribs. But I feel myself accepting it. Which just confuses me even more. As much as I'm trying to ignore this undercurrent, I know I've felt something for X since the moment I saw him back in those woods. Even when he was the enemy.

"Never the enemy," he whispers. "Never yours."

I almost grin, "I seem to remember that time in the woods differently." How long ago was it now?

"Not even then. Circumstances perhaps make my words doubtful but I promise you, I will never go against you."

"Why?" I find myself saying. What reason could he possibly have to do this? We don't know each other at all. What could I have possibly give back?

"Because a promise is a promise."

I felt like I've heard that somewhere before. A long dead memory fell like dust in my head, slipping away and I felt strangely agitated at the loss...I can't remember it at all.

Chapter Thirty-Seven: Glacial Bear

- -

 /N: so...hi...after sleeping practically 10 hours straight for the last two days...

i managed an update!

- -

Chapter Thirty-Seven: Glacial Bear

If someone's presence could chill a room into glacial silence by just sitting in it; Siem would be the Viking to do it. Which was what I was met with when I walked into the kitchen. He said nothing as I walk on over to the breakfast bar, sitting on the stool next to him, as X handed me the usual water, orange juice and porridge.

The silence is killing me but I'm too scared to open my mouth since the last time I saw him I practically ransacked his secretive meeting room. I stare at the gruel, wishing it would suddenly come alive and swallow me whole but that wish wasn't coming along very well as it just stared back at me.

"How is your health?" Siem asks finally after a billion years in silence.

I couldn't really respond. The truth was, deep down, I have no flipping idea. Most people would be dead. In most circumstances I should be dead. But here I am eating food mixed with painkillers served by X, sitting in the basement of a secret organisation run by a cranky Viking and his deranged sister who I think looks at me like an amoeba that belongs on a petri dish. But I digress. Oh and I can talk to glow in the dark tigers. "I don't really know..." I finally muster. I was going to go with 'fine' but the look he gave me told me to say what I really think.

X instead answers after placing a mug of coffee in front of Siem, "Kae is recovering..."

Siem grunts, "That is good." He picks up the coffee, sipping a bit before looking at me again.

I leap away from him when I feel something touch the side of my face. Looking back, I see it was Siem's fingers.

"The markings have changed," he goes back to drinking his coffee without so much as a blink. "I feel, X. I was only checking. I will not hurt him."

I look over to see X let go of something and realise it was a spoon. My spoon I was using to push around my food. Sitting back down, Siem continues, "I have come here directly to speak. Away from the mess upstairs. Away from Hanna's ears."

"You do not want Hanna around?" I ask without thinking.

"...For the most part, no. She can be...what is the expression...'difficult when excited'."

The would be an understatement.

He must have seen the look on my face as a half-grin crosses his lips. But he loses it just as quickly, "Your recovery progress is...slow compared to previous observations but sufficient...and understandable. It may be because of recent exposure to a Hexer Queen but I will also put it down to overtaxing your body before it has been sufficiently healed. That is a fault on my part. I cannot apologise for my actions but I do apologise for the after affects it has caused."

"...I can hear a 'but'." I mutter, unable to look him in the eye.

An amused sigh escapes Siem's throat. "Indeed."

"You are after a training schedule for him," I feel X rounding the counter to stand beside me.

"Yes," Siem simply replies. "Your condition will continue to deteriorate unless we can build you up. Muscle, stamina...nourishment...have not been well seen to. And no matter what you are or where you come from Kae, I cannot sit by and watch you wither away."

I growl at him, "Because you can't afford to lose the new commodity."

"You are not wrong, Kae." But his voice went quiet, "I also owe you that much."

He got my attention with that last remark, "Huh?"

But his claptrap was as tight as X proves to be.

I'm beginning to see where he got it from.

"There is one other thing I came to speak of..." he switches the subject rather quickly doesn't he?

And I'm waiting in suspense.

"Your family."

I feel blood drain from my face, body and seeping into the floor.

"You do realise that without something to go on, we will not be able to begin the hunt for them."

SO he agreed to an empty promise to start with...and I was stupid enough to believe him. "What do you want?" my voice was so small.

He sighs, his voice grim, "Some way to identify them to put it bluntly."

I look into his eyes, "And what would you want from me?" I rephrase the question.

"Really quite simple little man," Oz's voice echoed from the hallway as he appears, jingling closer. "descriptions...or even better, a photo. Anything visual so that we can lock on them from any camera across the globe."

I frown at the damn pirate as he enters the room. "That all sounds...illegal."

"Mate you are dealing with secret police. None of its 'legal'."

Siem puts his hand up as if to silence him before he could talk, "Seth and Oz can hack into any recording database that uses any of the programs they designed."

"Or any programs that are adapted from them." Oz grins, ignoring Siem's signal.

I look up between them, "We haven't got anything recent like that. Being constantly on the road with the threat of being shot, stabbed or eaten does that to you."

"...Kid has a point."

I continue, thinking more outload at this point, "The only thing we have are family albums from way back before the disaster and they're back in Salford in England...or what's left of it. They're all baby photos though."

Siem went into a troubled silence before finally reaching an answer, "It is something to go on."

"Uh Boss, last time I check, most of Salford...or rather Greater Manchester is a breeder ground for Hexer nests."

"...Indeed troubling."

Not to mention the giant ass crater and forest my younger siblings managed to cook up as well.

I saw a smirk reappear on pirate-man's face, "You don't sound British aye?"

"I'm not. My father was a Czech and my mother was Swiss but we moved around a lot. Cody was born in Canada. I was born in Ireland. Markus and Anne were born in America. We mainly spent our time in England or America but occasionally we went to Switz...erlan...d," my brain decided to throw me back into the haunting dreams of Anne digging in the snow. ..under that tree at that forsaken place. She...something there to keep safe...

We first went to that holiday house right after mum died...and again to visit her about two years ago...

I frown trying to remember. Anne was being secretive about-

My mind casts back to that night. Cody found a camera. He was drunk off the grog he found and decided to take videos of us. Anne disappeared for a few seconds retuning without a word. The pain shot through my skull. I never found out what she did and she refused to tell me. Cody had a hangover and irritated the shit out me with the moaning and groaning about never drinking again, since he downed an entire liquor store and expected to wake the next morning without feeling it. God he's a shithead. And I miss him. The next night he got drunk again and was turning into a weeping drunk because the SD card was missing...and I had to deal with the next hangover before setting the rest of his stash on fire out of spite.

Markus and Anne helped me by bashing pot and pan lids near his ears to distract him as his stash went up in literal smoke. And the satisfaction I felt lasted for weeks.

The SD card was missing...

"Oh," a weight on my shoulder brought me back to reality. Looking over to see X attached to the hand made me blush and the spot burn. But I had to put that hyper awareness to the side for a second. "There may be something near Laax in Switzerland. We were there a few years ago."

Oz 's features darken even more, "We have not information about that area for the last decade. For all we know it could be just as bad or even worse than Salford."

"But it is still something to go on." He then looked over at me. "Very well. When I am able to gather the resources, we can start hunting either place down. Perchance both, if fate allows it."

I stare at him.

"What? Did you think my deal hollow?" A proper smile etches into his feature, "I am a man of my word, Kae. And I do agree with my sister. We cannot afford the wrong people taking advantage of your siblings' abilities."

"And you're the 'right' people?' My voice was venom. I knew that but I couldn't stop myself. I was still...angry...there was so much of it. I haven't been given a chance to put the lid back on it properly. I felt a light squeeze on my shoulder from X but when I look up he was facing Siem.

"I do not advocate that we are. Only that we are not the only ones out there."

"Not to mention there are nastier people out there than this bear with a sore head," Oz juts a thumb in Siem's direction.

"Entirely uncalled for," Siem mutters, finishing off his coffee. As he does, he stands, "I will relay further orders later on. Until then..." I see something pass in his eyes as he took in X and I and I felt the cool air as X removes his hand from my shoulder, "rest as much as you can. I cannot promise you it will be any easier."

Oh like I was so expecting it would be!

With that he left with Oz in tow, leaving me along with X once again.

I sigh out loud and look up at him, "So..."

I gain his attention back at me, making my face flare up again.

"I will be here." He states at me, his hand landing on my head once again.

...He's gotten to the petting stage has he? And I swear he's enjoying making me squirm.

Chapter Thirty-Eight: Illusionary Monsters

A /N: Urrggghhhh I want it to be holidays again. I'm sick of work.

Anywho, update!

Oh and by the by the song:

Illusion by Kozoro

it's free to download if you enjoy it :) just go to https://soundcloud.com /kozoromusic

----

Chapter Thirty-Eight: Illusionary Monsters

For the first time in...I dunno -years, I was able to wake without a crashing wall of pain rattling my body until I feel like I'm chocking on blood. Sure if I touched the yellowing black-purple bruises they hurt like a bitch but that's about it. Realising that X wasn't with me, I look over at the door to the kitchen, thinking that maybe he was out there again.

...But for some reason I could sense that he wasn't. The emptiness was frighteningly hollow within me.

Frowning at this, I get up to have a look. The whoosh door opens as I approach it... The room was dark but a strange moving pattern was forming on the ceiling. I was able to source it to something outside through the window.

Looking at the moving reflection, I see that it's similar to light rebounding off a liquid surface.

Great. In the time I was sleeping I managed to sleep through a flood.

Walking over to get a closer look through the window, half expecting to be under the sea with some fish and/or shark glugging passed the window, I get a bigger shock as the light was too...naturally bright and outside was...as far opposite a sea that I could imagine.

I came face to face with a grassy lawn and a small stream flowing through the middle and sun shining down like I was in fairyland.

...Right.

Ok.

...I was in an underground subway last time I checked.

Underground means no sunlight...right?

....So the new drugs X has fed me are hallucinogenic and I'm having a serious trip right now? Or I'm in a dream again. The thought chilled my insides until it burned.

I look over to the front door and saw it was also whooshy with a touchpad. Giving it a shot, despite expecting the 'access denied' voice to snap back at me, I put my hand to it and it switches green, opening up and letting a faint breeze through.

I could see sky laid out before me. Pale light blue without a single cloud and the sun beating down from overhead. I can feel the heat radiating off my skin. Looking down at the ground, I was standing in soft green grass that just covered my bare feet. It felt too real. I look over to a set of stairs built into the side of a hill I was standing on, leading down to the tiny stream that ran along the grass causeway in front of me.

Walking over to the stone steps, I go down them to the water's edge. Crouching down, I peer at the trickling water that was not much wider than an arm's length across. Smooth grey and black pebbles caused ripples in the water's flow but there wasn't any sound.

I reach out to touch the water.

I frown at the texture. It felt like water slipping between my fingers. It felt cool and wet but it was synthetic.

False. Fake. The words slither in my mind as I drew my fingers away, completely dry. I almost feel a growl gurgling in my throat, surprising myself. I felt a static pulse running over my skin and almost like a glitch in the breeze. It was tiny. Minor. So minuscule that if I wasn't so caught up on the contradictory surroundings, I wouldn't have noticed.

Standing again, I abandoned the silent water and instead followed the direction it flowed. Thinking about it more closely, despite this supposed open space of a wide grassland steppe, I still feel the oppression of cold walls pressing down on me from every angle.

Taking a shuddering breath, I feel myself turn a corner, even though there was no actual corner and suddenly came face to face with a Hexer. Eyes bulging, my body goes rigid as it walks towards me.

Did...-How?

It's mouth wide open, dripping black goo into the grass. Its limbs, awkwardly long were pulled down into a crouch. It was an Alpha. Not as complete as the helmet one that crashed me through a ceiling or four back in Bellasera. It still has flesh along the inside of its arms, stretched and saggy, holding on like torn rags. The chest was in the same state, only I could peak through the skin to see bone being consumed by black crystal. Underneath that was nothing but an empty cavity.

My thoughts constrict in my head, memories flooding, bleeding and pooling in my mind, trying desperately to come up with some sort reason for something like a Hexer is staring at me ready to chow down on me in a split second. All I can do is stare at it as the long spindly fingers reach out towards me. I back up out of its grip, only to hit a solid wall at my back. But there is no wall. Only sky and hills. But I couldn't move any further. The Hexer's slow outreach was torture as I was trapped inside my body, completely unable to move.

My pulse triples with every centimeter, closing the gap between us.

No. No. No-no-no-no-no! After everything. Everything I have been through. When is it going to be enough? Turning my head to the side, my eyes almost closed, ready for the onslaught.

'Don't touch me' The words echo in my head as the fingers reaching towards me begin to glow red to white hot. Just as they almost graze my cheek, it melts away, dripping to the ground as a molten mess of metal.

Metal?

I stare in shock as the metal pools on the grass...not grass...for a second the grass glitches, revealing something like a railing...I was in a subway. I was underground in a subway.

I glare back at the half melted Hexer and the sky behind it as it begins to distort.

This isn't real-

Something suddenly blocks my vision, grabbing me and pulling me back into it.

"Stop now, Kae," X's voice almost liquefies my muscles as the tension suddenly drops from my body. I feel that everything changing...or stopping, like someone turned off a TV screen. The warmth from the sun was replaced by cold dead air that was being ventilated by a series of shafts scattered throughout the underground complex. But the air was still...wrong. Still rotten like the air I was surrounded by since I entered Bolin.

I pull on his hand to let me see the dreary and dark abandoned tunnels I was expecting to see.

In front of me was a half melted metal skeletal...thing that from all the exposed wiring, I could guess would have been some sort of robot.

I suddenly felt tired, the relief was draining to the core. But it was replaced by a bitterness that this fake Hexer exposed about me. I am still hiding in the corner. Still waiting in the dark for either some saviour or death to find me.

X's warmth was very apparent behind me as I realise I was still holding onto his arm when he stopped me. I couldn't help but tighten my grip. Why? Why is there a fucking robot and all this shit down here just to fuck with my head?

"I'm sorry. Seth did not think that the simulation testing would extend this far..." he sounds like he wanted to say something else but he left the sentence hanging and died in the silence. "I went to warn him since the communication line is still shut off down here."

I turn to him, "Why?"

"Why have I cut off any contact?" he looks to the ceiling as if her was trying to collect his thoughts, "Because I did not want any noise."

I exhale, knowing that that's going to be as good an answer from him I'm gonna get. "Where's Lady?"

"Seth has been occupying her with landscape simulations in another tunnel."

"Well, I was until something decided to glitch the system," Seth's voice rebound down the tunnel as he walks towards us, Lady in tow.

'Dreamer stopped fake jungle and fake monkey. Irritation stopped'. Lady padded up to me pressing her forehead to mine, 'Younger human child with raven hair made irritating monkey pull tail.'

"What's this about monkeys and tail-pulling?" I ask out loud.

Seth chuckles as he walks passed me, "A little light exercise for little Lady. Oh wow," he whistles as he stops in front of the melted metal carcass. "Holy shit. Oz ain't gonna like this. But well...at least we know your defenses are all up and running on a more conscious level now...and not when you're high on adrenaline mixed with a concoction of stress and exhaustion with primal survivor instincts. I'll agree with Hanna when she says that ain't a healthy state to be in often."

"It should not have gone into this section in the first place," X states.

"True...but I wonder..." Seth looked to be deep in thought, his eyes switch over to my face for a second before letting out a breath to dismiss it. "Well whatever. Hanna's expertise I guess."

"What is?" I ask.

"Oh nothing. I only downloaded the actions of accumulated data into the system to replicate physical and behaviour patterns of a number of Hexers we come across. The program can be unpredictable...especially with something like you in the equation. Even with the 'attack on sight order' shut off."

"What is that supposed to mean?"

"Easy kid. I'm not saying it as a bad thing...I don't think. My point is that you are an unknown equation on so many levels...and unpredictable."

"Riiiight." Glad we cleared everything up.

"No need to be sassy," Seth smirks before patting me on the shoulder. "The point is, I'm gonna have fun designing your survival courses."

"Uh what?"

"Specially designed for you to train and build up that poor excuse of a physique you've got going on."

"I'll help," X chirps in. He tightens his grip on me. Not harshly but enough to make me uncomfortable aware that we have an audience and my face begins to glow red. I tried pulling on his arm but it wouldn't budge, which just makes me all the more embarrassed. Especially since by the half hidden grin on Seth's face he bloody well knew I was stuck. Asshole

...And they say exercise can kill people. I can tell that this is gonna definitely be the death of me.

Chapter-Thirty Nine: Pool-side

A/N: And good day to you :3

I want to get at least another chapter or two out in the next seven days before work starts up again.

Let's see how that goes...

Chapter Thirty-Nine: Pool-side

At first, the most I was expected to do was walk around the tunnels, looking at the artificial scenery that Oz and Seth cooked up to hide the dark and creepy subway. I walked through savannah and rainforest, tundra and desert. It was all pretty impressive but because I knew that none of it was real and I had seen some of it in real life...it didn't give me the feeling of grandeur that I think they were going for. But that didn't stop me from finding it fascinating, and Lady made up for the both of us, I think.

She was so curious about everything and when I told her that it was all based on real places, I think it was safe to say that she really lost her shit. I had to wonder at where she was before she walked into the rundown café and she only replied with dark emotions...and something that I could only as a place that was completely devoid of colour and light.

They next dropped me into a hidden room that help an Olympic sized swimming pool that looked pretty typical from what I remember a pool should look like; a giant stadium with a body of water in the middle. Pretty standard. The lights were pretty intense as well and I notice on the side was a rapid pool that I knew they were going to expect me to swimming against its goddamn current.

A few of the other people were there from time to time but it appeared to be mostly empty. Aside from the goddamn cat refusing to leave the water for hours on end...she even got to making blowing bubbles in the shallow end with her nose which amused her for days.

Everyone but X, Seth and Oz gave us a wide berth, even leaving the areas completely when we walked towards them. At first it did bother me but Lady soon distracted me and X was never far away. But every day without a word from Siem had me more and more on edge.

I stare at my legs as I dangle from the edge of the pool as they were completely submerged in the water. Lady was busy swimming around in a circle after a giant plastic ball that was slowly filling with water. I had to wonder how long it had been....a week? A month? I had never had to think much about how time was constructed for years. The only way any of us knew if it had been a year or not was because the seasons changed. But now that I have been dragged back into this human contraption we call 'time' I've become painfully aware of every second that ticks by. Every minute lost forever. Every day that I am becoming further and further away from Cody and Anne. Then this constant worry and the nightmares meld together and I forget how much time passes once again only to come back full circle to the fact that I am sitting here on the verge of a breakdown because it feels like I'm doing shit all to fix that.

My gaze moves up to the door that led out of here. It was a simple white door that melded in with the wall and was hard to spot save the for the silver handle shinning at me like a beacon daring me to run and escape. But the next issue was the fact that the only way out of this underground mess involved securely locked doors and I had no way of knowing where I'd end up. I have no knowledge of Bolin. Not to mention X would stop me before I even reach the damn door.

"Yes, I would."

The sudden noise made me jump and turn to see X squatting beside me. "Could you not do that?" I mutter, almost ready to hit him for almost inducing a heart attack for the billionth time. "Another thing. Are you also in my head?" Already have a flippin tiger, why not add X as well. Sounds like a real party.

He cocks his head to the side, evaluating something as he stares directly at my face. "Not...exactly. There is...something blocking like...thick fog." He frowns. "No entry, it hurts. Do not push...must wait for the pull. The pain would be too much. I don't want it to hurt. But sometimes...something pokes through and I feel it. Clear with intent, I can feel...more." He reaches for my face. "Why is it missing?"

"What's missing?" I've become so used to him now that even as his fingers brush my cheek, I don't move even with a pulse of electricity numbing where he touches.

"If I knew, it wouldn't be missing. But...it's very frustrating. Perhaps it will...come with time. But for now, I am...relieved that I can see something at least. Your intent is...frustrating you. I know that much. Words cann ot...soothe that. I am also very bad at communicating in this way. But..." His sentence dies as his fingers touch my hair. He frowns again, looking at something beyond me but then refocuses, his fingers falling away from my face. "It's still too early for you to go anywhere. But...I will do whatever it takes when the time is right. Even if it means betrayal."

Those words were incredibly heavy for some reason and I found it very hard to swallow. "You would seriously go against Siem?"

He nods, moving to a sitting position beside me. "If that becomes something that you desire."

Why? Just why would he go that far? I stare back down at my feet, distorted under the water's surface.

Hearing the door open, I look up to see Seth walking through, "All done for the day?"

I watch him as he walks closer, "For now..."

He smirks, "That's good. Siem's thinking of letting you back up on the surface to get your meals...he thinks it's about time that you slowly get used to being up there as part of the team."

What a brilliant idea Siem! I have just felt the that this was a loving home from the second I landed on this building. The laser guns just gave that extra warm welcome! It just really drives home I'm one of the team.

"I can see the sass just bleeding from your eyes, Kae," he chuckles. "I know it's been...well hell since the moment you've been here. But being locked away any more than this won't help with the tension. And it's not like we're expecting you to sing songs and dance around a camp fire."

"And here I thought that was plan A," I growl.

I can see the grin widening. "Hanna said to either go there tonight and see how it goes or she'll feed you October Orange."

"...Do I dare ask what that is?"

"She said that she has it ready as well as a camera."

Oh that shit. "Is starving an option?"

"Yeah, but I wouldn't."

I stare at him, weighing up my options. Awkward dinner, throwing up with Hanna videoing it or Hanna tying me to a chair and throwing up and Hanna videoing it.

X ran a hand over the back of my head as if to attempt soothing me, "It is not like you will be going in there alone."

Oz had got me with a pair of scissors the other day, so feeling a lack of hair between his touch and the back of my neck was not something I was used to as the chills that went down my spine soon followed. I have not been thankful losing all that hair, even if Oz stated I looked like a muppet that went ass first throw a wind tunnel before being dragged by a cat over dry grass to lure birds that mistook it as a nest...he was very poetic that morning.

"Yeah, X and I are normally treated with a bit of distance usually as well at the dinner table. Gives us a spare table. Maybe with us it will seem a little less...antagonistic," Seth grins.

"Can't wait," I muster, almost tasting the bitterness of what I'm going to have to face.

"There's the spirit! Oz will also be joining us, so it's not like we're pushing you towards the angry mob with poking sticks all on your lonesome."

"Sure as hell feels like it."

"...Siem also told me that I can soften the blow by saying this," he clears his throat and begins imitating a thick uncanny Siem accent, " 'After dinner we will discuss the possibility of searching outside Laax in the next twenty-four hours'. Or so he says, anyway."

I stare at him keenly, "You're serious?"

"No. He's serious. I'm just the fat pigeon he decided to send down cos someone is refusing to lift the intercom silence down here."

I look over at X who just blinks unapologetically back at us.

"Also, I'm going to start amping up the workout regime on you. You will need to start training how to run and," he points to that blasted rapid pool, "using that as well. In the afternoon-" I mentally groan, "Oz has enlisted himself as a trainer. X will also begin teaching you combat basics. Self-defence and mixed martial arts. It's a good source of discipline and if you find yourself in a situation where your mental defence mechanism is on the blink it's good to always have a backup."

Can't I just go back to not doing anything except sleep?

"Anyway, this pigeon delivered the message of the all and powerful king, I'm gonna go find Oz's cookie stash."

"Behind his desk next to his toy dragon," X said without batting an eyelid.

"And thank you all omnipotent X," Seth simply salutes him back before walking out the door. "Seeya tonight, kid."

I'm seriously planning my escape. Tonight. I would rather wander the streets of Bolin, being gunned down for being a Hexer than what they are making me face tonight. Or Spartan training brought to you personally by Oz that Spartan spawn of hell. I'm suspicious he's still pissed that I melted his goddamn robot...but...Siem is going to go look for that SD card. I can't pass that up.

I sigh, another long fucking night.

Chapter Forty: Dinner Date

Chapter Forty: Dinner Date

I glare at the steel doors in front of me, knowing that the moment they open I will be entering the inferno of Hell's kitchen. I have never felt this much anxiety facing a Hexer armada, you'd have to wonder why I'm finding this much more unnerving. Lady forced herself onto the lift, staying nervously quiet as it ascended. I was guiltily happy that she wanted to come as well. At first I thought it would be completely unfair to force her to share this unpleasant experience and she looked like we would have to drain the pool before she'd ever climb out. But she heard the conversation and my mental torment and marched out of the pool and stared me down until I agreed to take her. 'Water fun but not important. Dreamer important. Dreamer will let Lady come or Lady will latch onto Dreamer and Dreamer will have to drag Lady on Dreamer's fake fur,' was her threat. She was ready to bite onto my clothing and make me drag her along, or worse, she'd pick me up and drag me along.

I exhale deeply through my nose, hoping that the lift somehow breaks down in the next two seconds....one second?

Instead the blasted thing dings and the doors open onto the dark hallway I hadn't seen since I first came here with Mist. And that went spectacularly well...

"Kae, you need to step off, mate," Oz pushes.

"No I damn well don't." I can live in here. There's enough room for me to curl up in the corner and mope for the rest of my pathetic and short life, curled up in a ball weeping and feeling sorry for myself. That sounds much better...

X physically pushes me out of the lift with a firm but gentle pressure in the middle of my shoulder blades, "Delaying what may happen will only intensify the experience."

Thank you Yoda X. My feet hit carpet and I wanted to put the brakes on, but X left his hand there to keeping me walking.

"Come on kid, we're with you. It's not like we asked you to sing and dance for 'em," Oz encourages.

That at least will draw some attention away from the 'What the fuck is that freak doing here instead of being destroyed or locked up somewhere where we never have to see of think about it ever again' issue that I'm quite sure has been put in the suggestion box very regularly. Or maybe it might cast a stronger vote towards getting me destroyed like some unwanted mutt.

...I just hit myself with my own words.

"Alrighty, since we didn't do any pre-ordering forms, you are just gonna have to go with what's on offer." He indicates to the serving area near the kitchen n the far right of the room. A small line had already formed in front of us and as I went between Oz at the front and X behind me, the few people in the room went into complete silence. Soon followed by the usual muttered whispers. Those that soon walked into the room to join the line at first would look startled when they notice the giant tiger then frowned when their eyes land on me. They then made a line that gave us a wide berth. I try my best to ignore it and focused on the food we were slowly getting closer to. It was a buffet unit filled to the brim with food. It went from light meals to the mains to salads and the last table was deserts. It composed of a huge pot of soup, bread, roasts, spring rolls, burgers...chips...custard...ice-cream...I think I'm drooling.

"Just grab a plate and get what you want. Simple as that." Oz moves over to a piles of dishes and grabs one for the top and immediately heads for anything meat and pizza related. I go for the fish and chips...it's been almost ten years since I've had properly battered deep sea fish. I also added some salad and fruit. I was surprised that they had star fruit...not something I've seen since I was about five.

I look back over to see X had grabbed mainly vegetables.

'Looks weird but smells good,' Lady contributes, sniffing at the random selection. 'Hunger feeling even though not hungry.'

What does Lady even eat?

She sends a mental image of some sort of deskinned carcass that was brought down on the elevator. She then goes through the motion of her muscles tensing, her teeth itching to sink into the raw muscle-

Ok stop there, Lady.

'Share?'

'No thank you, Lady. Even though it might taste nice to you, I don't eat raw meat.'

'Raw?'

'We cook it on the fire, look at the stove through the serving window. It creates heat and we,' What's the word I'm looking for? '-"burn" things on it.'

She pokes her head through the serving desk that was beside the last part of the self-serving buffet, starling the cooks. 'Strange, but smells good.'

I suppose it's one of the few redeeming qualities a human has.

'Dreamer 'cooks'?' She tasted the word with a strange fire-like texture.

'...Not very well...' Actually I suck. Cody learnt how to catch and skin almost anything from a pig to a horse. We mainly ate a lot of rabbit and venison from the latest area we were roaming through. I on the other hand frequently burnt myself. At best, I could fry an egg.

'Egg is good. Gooey...'

Urgh.... The mental imagery she was giving while liking her chops made my skin crawl.

"Kae, you're blocking the line," Oz's voice made me look up to see him near a fridge full of water, juice and softdrinks.

Oh whoops. I look back to see passed X that no one had entered the serving area. Some people were even leaving the area altogether.

I hold off a mental sigh and walk over to Oz, following him to a table over the back that looked out over the cityscape. Plonking myself down, I suddenly lose my appetite. How long am I going to be the 'Outsider'? Normally this didn't bother me. I was 'Oddball' after all. But I don't have Cody, Anne or even Markus to watch my back.

Anne and Cody...

I look out the window to watch the rain mixing with the busy metropolitan streets down below...I frown at the dream...was this what Anne knew? How much of the future did she see? Why did she say anything? Did she know we would be separated? Why did I have this dream now? Over and over...what will happen once I get that SD card? Will she taunt me with something else?

I bite my lip, trying to surpass the next wave of emotion. She knew I would listen...why didn't she say anything?

Markus is now gone. Can I reverse it somehow? I was tempted to tell Hanna...she knew a lot but...Something deep inside is screaming at me to leave him be. But how can I?

"I didn't realise that fish and chips made one so bloody broody," Oz nudges me with an elbow. I look up so see a lop-sided grin before he takes a swig of whatever softdrink they have here.

"Hello Kae," Seth grins as he sits opposite me. "I saw a dark cloud and immediately knew it was you. Well that and the tiger."

"You fucking brat have been in my stash again," Oz snaps while stabbing a fork into Seth's steak and plonks it onto his.

"That's rude" Seth mutters but doesn't move to take his food back. Instead he begins munching on the chips that were practically swimming in gravy.

"...Kae?"

I look up to see Mist coming over from a group of what I could imagine to be her friends (that were watching from a distance with such blank stares I swear I could clap ad they wouldn't blink) with a wide-eyed look on her face.

Alright, be polite, "Good evening, Mist." Politeness succeeded.

"You've got a haircut."

"Blame Oz."

She smiles shyly at me. "Well it looks good."

Aaaand now it's awkward as fuck.

"Where's Grumps?" Oz asks while reaching for the garlic bread on Seth's plate.

"Rain's on a mission tonight."

I am holding onto that sigh of relief and the tension in my butt cheeks almost-

And in marches Mike- Never mind. Butt cheeks tension level 'Granite' acquired.

He manages hostile eye contact with me before looking away and I'm feeling so much on guard that Lady's ears suddenly flatten as she looks in his general direction.

'Danger?'

I was tempted to say 'yes'. But luckily he didn't have a giant gun anywhere visible. Up his ass more like it.

'...No...it's nothing. I'm just feeling uncomfortable.' I poke a fork into a leaf and munch on it. I could taste that this was grown in controlled conditions. But it was edible. I next go for a chip and it tastes even better than I remembered. Deep fried potato...its making my mouth water even though I'm eating it. And the fish...perfectly flaky and wrapped in batter...I control myself from inhaling it.

I was disrupted from my focus on the food when I felt Mist sitting at the table. But her friends didn't follow, instead I found them sitting near Mike. Who for the most part was pretending to ignore me.

"What?" She mutters as she notices both Oz and Seth staring at her.

"Nothin'," Seth grins and goes back to eating.

And awkwardly silence resumes.

I look over to see X had finished his meal and was looking out into the distance once again.

I have to wonder what he hears when he's like this. Is it so loud that he can't focus on what's right in front of him? It's sort of like what Anne had trouble with in a crowd...I can't imagine what it would be like with an entire city...but...I frown down at my plate. I could 'hear' it as well? I can't hear anything now, except Seth and Oz getting into a strange war of snatching each other's' food from their plates and Mist...I look over at her, seeing that she was torn between being here and sitting with her obviously usual company. Why did she think she needed to be over here? She was transparently uncomfortable.

"How have you been Mist?" I finally ask, wanting some distraction.

"Oh Um...fine. I could ask you the same." She was startled and looks up at me like I caught her at something.

I shrug, putting down my fork, "On the mend I guess." I look over at Lady who went back to lying down on the ground, keenly watching anyone come near us.

"That's good. Your complexion looks better."

I couldn't help wanting to pull up my hood but resisted the urge, I know that action would cause attention on me and I already got enough looks from the tattoo thing on the side of my face. No need to make it more obvious that I was conscious of it. "Thank you..." as something I could at least muster.

X seemed to come back to reality as I feel his gaze switching back into this room. "Have you finished, Kae?"

I nod at him, "I think so."

He takes both my plate and his without a word and walks over to the serving area, putting them down on the serving counter with other stacked dirty dishes. He then walks over and stands in front of me. "Siem should be in his office for the moment."

I didn't need any more inclination to move. The room had acquired a quiet murmur since I sat down and melded into the background but it went back to an immediate dead silence when I stood again.

"Good luck," Oz salutes at me without moving from his seat.

I grunt at him before following X out of the room. Once we were out in the hallway, I couldn't hold off the urge to hide my face any longer and the hood went back up.

I let out a breath the moment we were on the elevator with the big cat finally in and the doors shut and the blasted contraption finally starts moving towards that bastard Viking's office.

Finally.